Praise for the Colorado Wine Mysteries

"*Killer Chardonnay* offers a wonderful blend of suspense and humor. You'll raise your glass to Parker Valentine, the charming sleuth at the center of this twisty and satisfying mystery. A most delightful debut!"

—Cynthia Kuhn, author of the Agatha Award–winning
Lila Maclean Academic Mysteries

"Parker Valentine . . . will steal your heart and pair it with a smooth mystery in this sparkling debut. A wine rack full of suspects won't stop the determined sleuth and vintner from bottling up a killer and saving her dream. *Killer Chardonnay* has legs!"

—Leslie Budewitz, Agatha Award–winning author of
the Spice Shop Mysteries

"*Killer Chardonnay* is an engaging mystery filled with wine knowledge, romance, and a gutsy protagonist. Kate Lansing is a delightful new voice in the mystery genre, and I can't wait to read the next one in this series."

—Nadine Nettmann, author of the Anthony, Agatha, Lefty,
and Mary Higgins Clark award–nominated Sommelier
Mystery series

"Lansing's brisk style and her heroine's efficient approach make her debut a treat." —*Kirkus Reviews*

"Kate Lansing has created a delightful cast of characters coupled with some scrumptious-sounding wines and foods. . . . A killer start to the series!" —RECEIVED

"A solid start to an enjoyable series, especially if you are a fan of the foodie vibe created in this story or a lover of winery mysteries!"   —The Genre Minx

"Likeable characters, engrossing mystery, and excellent storytelling make *Killer Chardonnay* a killer cozy series debut."   —The Book Decoder

"*Killer Chardonnay* is an easy, lighthearted, enjoyable cozy mystery that is just the beginning to what I'm sure is going to be a fantastic series."   —Coffee Books Life

"I absolutely loved this book; the setting of Boulder, Colorado, could not be more perfect. . . . I enjoyed the storyline [and] the side romances, with clues and red herrings thrown in that kept me guessing."
                                    —Cindy's Book Stacks

A Pairing

to Die For

Kate Lansing

BERKLEY PRIME CRIME
New York

BERKLEY PRIME CRIME
Published by Berkley
An imprint of Penguin Random House LLC
penguinrandomhouse.com

ISBN: 9780593100202

First Edition: January 2021

Printed in the United States of America
1 3 5 7 9 10 8 6 4 2

Cover art by Samantha Dion Baker
Cover design by Farjana Yasmin
Book design by Alison Cnockaert

To my parents, the pair who first introduced me to the magic and mystery of books

Chapter One

I should have brought flowers. A pacifying bouquet of lilies, hydrangeas, and daisies. Instead, foolishly, I brought wine, and left myself open to a world of criticism from my boyfriend's judgy family. Because the wine isn't merely some label I picked up at the corner store—pricey enough to impress but not so much to blow my budget—it's my own craftsmanship.

"Colorado wines will never be as flavorful as Napa's," Camilla, the matriarch, says in a superior voice.

She purses her lips in disapproval. With her perfectly styled coiffure and Jackie cardigan, she hails from an era of class and sophistication that apparently doesn't extend to present conversation.

"Everyone is entitled to their own opinion," I say, my cheeks aching from the forced smile on my face.

"My wife is right," Gary chimes in from across the

rustic wooden table, his cable-knit sweater the same shade of burgundy as the pinot we're tasting. "If you had done your research, Napa would have been the smarter choice."

"Perhaps," I say. "But I love Boulder, and the market is just getting going here. It gives me the opportunity to carve a niche for my business." *Which I've already done*, I want to add.

My winery, Vino Valentine, is thriving. I can hardly keep up with demand thanks to a rave review from a popular food-and-wine blogger, monthly VIP parties, and, most recently, supplying varietals to the hip new establishment we're dining at now.

And while I don't own my own vineyard, the grapes I order from growers on the Western Slope of the Rocky Mountains are chock-full of flavor. The higher altitude yields a deeper pigmentation and a more concentrated sugar content, making the fruit—in my humble opinion— ideal for winemaking.

Gary sniffs at his glass surreptitiously and says, his tone veering on mansplaining, "Red wine really ought to be aged in oak."

"Agreed," I say, and add, with relish, "which is why I aged it in oak for six months before moving it to steel."

Gary shoots me a look of utter distrust, clearly one of those people who doesn't believe what he can't see—or rather, taste—and Camilla not so subtly checks the gold-plated watch on her wrist.

I remind myself that I'm doing this for Reid, my boy-friend extraordinaire. I was honored he asked me to come tonight and more than a little curious to meet the family he hasn't spoken to in more than a year. That is, until Camilla pierced me with an icy stare and asked where I got my *cute* dress—the word *cute* sounding like an insult—and Gary's gaze drifted a few degrees south of my face.

And now I'm on my own for this tête-à-tête with his parents since we're dining at Reid's restaurant, Spoons, where he's both the owner and executive chef. He claimed his sous chefs would be able to handle most of the cooking tonight, but then, as soon as we were seated, he dashed back to the kitchen to help with something or other. And his older brothers are conveniently MIA, one having stepped away from the table to take a "very important" business call and the other running late.

I take a large gulp of wine and desperately scan the spacious room for a neutral conversation topic, anything that might turn around this disaster of a dinner.

The chatter of happier tables rises around us, their carefree laughter filling me with envy. Spoons has been packed since it opened last month, and tonight is no exception. The decor is upscale with musical influences—glass lanterns painted with staves, old records that have been fashioned into coasters, trumpets repurposed into sconces, and a stage where local acoustic bands play on Friday nights.

"So are you going to do any hiking while you're in town?" I finally venture.

Colorado is known for outdoor sports—hiking, biking, and climbing in the summer, and skiing, snowboarding, and snowshoeing in the winter. The mountains are the perfect canvas for whatever alfresco adventure you want to try.

Camilla primly adjusts her cardigan. "I'm not sure we'll have time."

"Well, if you change your mind, I'd be happy to go

with you," I say, perking up. "Chautauqua Park is especially beautiful right now with the fall leaves changing color, and you'd get an up-close view of the Flatirons."

The Flatirons are majestic geological formations overlooking Boulder, giant slabs of slanted rock that look like they've been expelled from the mountainous backdrop. Gazing at them always gives me a sense of perspective: that my troubles are small in the grand scheme of things. I could use that reminder now.

Gary tilts his head and sniffs at his wine again, apparently not deeming my offer worth responding to. It's okay, though, because Camilla answers for both of them.

"We don't hike," she snaps, attracting the attention of a neighboring table.

Thoroughly reprimanded, I stare at my place setting: navy napkin with copper flatware nestled on top and a simple white bread plate, my half-eaten roll forgotten.

Hurt, anger, and, worst of all, shame course through my veins and thrum loudly in my ears. My face flushes with heat.

Winemaking is littered with pitfalls—sluggish fermentation, stressed yeast, unbalanced sulfites. Most of the time, if you catch the problem early enough, you can course-correct by adjusting the temperature or adding fresh yeast. If only real life were as easy to correct.

I wanted so badly to help Reid heal whatever is broken in his family, and, fine, I'll admit, *maybe* dazzle them with my wit and charm. But instead, I'm only making things worse.

Luckily, Reid's older brother Tristan chooses that moment to show up. "Sorry I'm late. The last session ran long." Tristan just so happens to be in town for an anesthesiology conference and managed to squeeze in time for this family dinner.

He drapes his suit jacket over the back of his chair and takes a seat next to his father. He could be Reid's twin—they have the same build and thick sandy-blond hair, although Reid inherited his mother's green eyes while Tristan got his father's brown ones. The top few buttons of his shirt are undone, a leather cord necklace peeking out, giving him a suave yet relaxed demeanor.

"Duty calls, son," Gary says, clapping Tristan on the back. I wonder if anyone else would receive that sort of response to being almost an hour late.

I reach my hand across the table. "Parker Valentine. Nice to meet you."

Tristan's smile holds a hint of mischief as he takes my hand. "Where are we in the interrogation?" he asks, pouring himself a generous glass of pinot.

"We weren't interrogating her," Camilla says. "We're simply trying to get to know the girl."

Reid's oldest brother, Ben, returns from his phone call, his client apparently appeased for the moment. He tugs at the tie around his neck, his shoulders so tense they might as well be attached to his ears. He has more wrinkles at the corners of his eyes and thinner hair than his brothers, but he clearly keeps himself in just as good shape.

This family certainly lucked out in the gene department. I'm not sure how I ever thought I could impress them. Or convince them of anything, let alone that Reid is deserving of their support, even if they don't see his profession as being as important as, say, a lawyer or a doctor.

Ben flashes me an encouraging smile and eyes Gary, eyebrow cocked. "Did you swear her in before you started questioning?"

Ben followed in his father's footsteps, working in corporate law at one of the top firms in the country, as both parents proudly told me. When he heard about this little family reunion, he decided to tag along to see his youngest brother in action. Only, he isn't seeing much more than the screen of his phone.

"We were talking about my business," I say, wringing my napkin in my lap. "Which isn't fair since this night should really be about Reid."

As if on cue, Reid appears with a steaming plate of food in each hand and one more balanced on his forearm. Even though we've been dating for nearly four months, his handsome features still take my breath away. Cocksure grin, expertly mussed hair, strong arms lined with silvery scars from oven burns, and eyes that flash with a hint of danger. His chin is covered in scruff from the beard he insists on growing for football season. Not that I'm complaining, mind you. It adds to his intoxicating devil-may-care attitude.

But the best part: he can cook.

Reid deposits plates around the table and my mouth instantly starts watering. The dishes are from the seasonal menu, vetted by yours truly. Butternut squash soup topped with chopped dates and crispy prosciutto. Stuffed pumpkin ravioli in a rich sage and butter sauce. Perfectly grilled flank steak drizzled with roasted salsa verde.

Holy carne asada, Batman.

Reid lingers at my side after relinquishing the last dish, lightly brushing my hair behind my shoulder, the simple touch of his fingers against my skin sending a jolt of electricity snaking down my spine. To the outsider, he may seem like his usual cool self, impossible to rattle, but I know him well enough to recognize the nerves. The extra fidgeting, the furtive glances toward his parents, the inability to stay seated.

"How's everything going?" Reid asks.

"Great," I say a little too loudly, clapping my hands for reinforcement. "Just great."

Camilla and Gary look at me like I'm nuts, which isn't a completely outlandish deduction. I mean, honestly, why did I clap?

"Look at our little bro," Tristan says, gesturing from Reid to our surroundings. "You've come a long way from making mystery hot cocoa."

"And mud pies in the backyard," Ben adds.

Reid sinks into the chair at my side and gently squeezes my knee beneath the table. "Hard to beat Connecticut soil, but I tried."

I feel a rush of gratitude toward Reid. Perhaps we'll be able to salvage this dinner, after all.

But then Oscar Flores, one of Reid's sous chefs, arrives with yet another plate. He sets it in the middle of the table and says with a flourish, "Scallops seared with saffron and lemon, on the house."

Oscar is an old friend of Reid's from culinary school who recently moved back to Boulder to be closer to his family. He has chin-length black hair he keeps tucked behind his ears, rich brown skin, and eyes framed by these long, dark lashes that make him a very eligible bachelor.

He's a fantastic chef in his own right but has this rather pesky habit of talking back in the kitchen and experimenting with tried-and-true recipes. While Reid sees these quirks as an asset—always striving to make his food the best it can be—other chefs aren't as understanding. Which is why Oscar's stuck working as a glorified line cook.

An awkward silence falls over the table, so complete it's almost as if we're absorbing the sounds around us. The tension grows until it's as palpable as tannins in a full-bodied cab.

Eyebrows furrowed, I study each person in turn, trying to figure out what I'm missing.

Gary tightens his grip on his wineglass, his face twisted into a scowl, and Tristan's smile turns almost predatory. The only one seemingly unaffected is Ben, but that could be because his attention is once again on the screen of his phone.

Camilla eyes Oscar from head to toe, not hiding her disdain. "I didn't realize *you* were working here."

Of course Oscar would know the Wallace clan, having been good friends with Reid for the past decade, but the level of undisguised animosity is baffling.

I spare him a pitying glance, selfishly enjoying the momentary relief from the spotlight.

Oscar chuckles nervously and tugs at the neck of his chef's coat. "Reid can't seem to shake me."

"As hard as I keep trying." Reid winks and, in an attempt to diffuse the tension, says, "Let's eat. The scallops are best fresh from the skillet."

Oscar takes one step backward, then another, and when no one protests, makes a hasty retreat. He glances over his shoulder at our table, a strangely hopeful gleam in his eyes, before pushing the door open at the back of the restaurant and disappearing into the kitchen.

The mood slowly returns to normal. And by normal, I mean charged with skepticism.

While Reid doles out the heavenly morsels, I give myself a silent pep talk. If there's one thing I can talk about unabashedly, it's wine.

"The scallops pair best with the Mount Sanitas White," I say, pouring several tasters of my trademark white blend from the second bottle on the table. "It's a lighter blend, especially perfect after a day of hiking. Not that you hike," I add hurriedly to Camilla and Gary. "Just, you know . . ." I trail off and clear my throat.

Camilla and Gary make a show of daintily slicing into their scallops, Tristan maneuvers his silverware with the exacting precision of a doctor, and Ben attacks his plate with gusto.

Following Reid's lead, I take a small bite of scallop and chase it with a sip of wine.

And I blanch. Because something is wrong. Very wrong.

Instead of savory, sweet, and citrus flavors melding together on my tongue, all I get is an overpowering taste of burnt saffron. It's so bitter and intense, my eyes begin to water.

I spit my bite into my napkin.

For a moment, I succumb to panic. Sweat beads on my forehead and stars swirl in my vision. Earlier this year, when my wine didn't taste right, the most renowned critic in the Front Range ended up dead at my tasting bar.

I take a deep yoga breath—in with the good, out with the bad—and ground myself by focusing on the custom-made ceramic tiles on the floor.

Finally, I bring myself to look at Reid. His face is deathly pale and his eyes are horror-struck.

Because it's not just our table whose food isn't right. There's a flurry of activity as protests break out across the entire restaurant.

Chapter Two

The damage is random and inexplicable.

On the outside, the dishes are the pinnacle of fine dining—the meat roasted or seared to perfection, the vegetables boasting impeccable knife cuts, the drizzled sauces and colorful garnishes a thing of beauty. But on the inside, well, not so much.

The problems are varied. Some of the fare is overly salty or spicy, have sauces that are tart or acrid, while others have contradicting herbs sprinkled on top. The one thing they have in common is that the deficiencies have to do with flavor.

Complaints reach our ears. Loud, impatient complaints that make me wince.

"Who's in charge here anyway?" a stout-faced man asks.

"I'm leaving a review right now," announces a foodie, wielding their smartphone like a weapon.

"Overpriced drivel . . ." a woman with decidedly horselike teeth admonishes.

The last thing Reid needs is for them to join forces.

I ignore the sounds of disgust around me and turn to Reid. "Tell me how I can help."

He clenches his jaw, shifting his attention from one proverbial fire to the next. "No offense, Parker, but this isn't really something you can ferment your way out of."

That gives me an idea.

"I can pour free tasters of wine," I suggest. "No one can stay upset when faced with free booze. It's like a universal truth."

Reid snorts but shakes his head. His eyes are surprisingly vulnerable—cautious—when they meet mine. "Keep my family company?"

A pit opens in the bottom of my stomach at his request, and my cheeks flush just thinking of the myriad of ways I'll likely embarrass myself. But faced with his raw desperation, I find myself nodding.

"You can count on me," I say, giving his hand a reassuring squeeze. "Now go work your magic."

Reid holds my gaze for a millisecond longer and then leaps into action.

He's a blur of motion as he dodges between servers, frantically trying to salvage their tips, and outraged customers. He circulates around the dining room, promising corrected dishes and offering complimentary desserts. Stress emanates from him, resulting in a laser focus. Owning a restaurant—creating a community through food—is his dream, and a night like this could destroy everything he's worked for. I know a little bit about having your dream on the line, the toll it can take on your psyche.

At this rate, he'll be slammed for hours.

This fact seems to hit Camilla and me at the same time. We share a look of dread, momentarily united in our apprehension of the other.

I steel myself and ask the table, "More wine, anyone?"

"Please," Tristan answers, waving his empty glass toward me.

Gary crosses his arms over his chest, his lips upturned in a sneer. "So this is what that culinary school education got him."

"This has never happened before," I say, coming to Reid's defense. "There must have been some mistake. Reid will get it sorted."

Gary grumbles something that sounds suspiciously like *entitled*.

He's one to talk. The hair at the nape of my neck rises like hackles. Keeping these people company is completely futile.

Tristan eyes me pointedly over his glass and mimes scooting his chair farther from Gary. Maybe I'm not entirely without an ally. The thought fortifies me.

"Reid's food is amazing," I say. "You should read the reviews. And trust me, critics aren't easily impressed."

"I'm sure," Camilla says, daintily wiping at her lips. "If you'll excuse me, I'm going to visit the powder room."

She leaves and soon, Gary, Ben, and Tristan bend their heads together in conversation. To Tristan's credit, he tries to loop me into their discussion about the state of the economy, but Gary staunchly ignores me, even when I interject my (very insightful) two cents. As if I could possibly understand the intricacies of such things.

Grinding my teeth together, I toss my napkin on the table and excuse myself.

I tug at the beaded necklace around my neck so hard it almost snaps. I let go and grip the fabric of my dress instead. My late aunt Laura gave me this necklace and the last thing I want to do is break it.

What would she do if she were in my situation? I have no idea, because this would never have happened to Aunt Laura. Everyone loved her. She had this ease with people, this accepting aura that was warm and inviting. Until she was unceremoniously killed by a drunk driver two years ago.

I seek asylum in the restroom. It's gorgeous, with elaborate mirrors over mod porcelain sinks, the walls painted a flattering slate. There are musical influences in here, too. Framed magazine covers featuring prominent women musicians hanging between trumpet sconces.

I splash water on my face and dab my cheeks dry with a paper towel, eyeing myself in the mirror. Raven hair cut in an A-line bob, blue-gray eyes, funky-yet-hip tassel earrings, my favorite dress covered with tiny daisies. Whatever it is about me that Camilla and Gary disapprove of, I don't see it.

And that's when it hits me: Camilla isn't in here.

I go back to the main restaurant. She hasn't returned to our table, and Gary, Ben, and Tristan are still immersed in their Boys' Club. There's no way I'm going back there alone.

I follow the sound of Reid's voice to the kitchen, where I fully expect to find him barking orders to Oscar and his other sous chef, Nick, or convincing his pastry chef, Britt, to save the day with her decadent cakes and buttery baklava.

Instead, I find Reid staring down his mother.

I pause before the swinging door, peeking through the thin window. Camilla is standing in the middle of the kitchen, surrounded by state-of-the-art stainless-steel appliances, arms crossed over her chest. She must have ambushed him the moment he stepped back there, not caring how unprofessional that might be.

I mean, they're not even alone. Behind Reid, Nick is busy dicing root vegetables and Britt carefully arranges spiced pears on flaky tartlet crusts, both determinedly ignoring the confrontation unspooling in front of them.

"I don't appreciate being pawned off on some girl," Camilla says.

"Her name is Parker," Reid answers, buttoning his chef's coat over his T-shirt. "And I warned you I was busy."

Hearing my name on Reid's lips makes my cheeks flush. He has enough to worry about without having to come to my rescue.

"I don't understand what you see in her," Camilla says. "She's just a winemaker, for Pete's sake."

My jaw drops in indignation. I knew things weren't going great, but I didn't think they were *that* bad.

"If you knew me at all, it would be obvious," Reid says. He navigates around his mother to the stovetop, where fresh saucepans await his culinary wizardry.

"She's not good enough for you."

My temper flares and I'm tempted to march in there and give her a piece of this *winemaker's* mind, including a few choice words usually reserved for Broncos games or particularly stubborn corks, but Reid's next question roots me in place.

"Why are you even here?"

"What?" Camilla straightens primly, her shoulders back.

Reid removes his preferred knife from his storage roll, a black carrying case for his culinary tools. The knife has a birchwood handle and steel blade that he keeps honed to a precariously sharp edge, and I know it to be one of his most prized possessions. It was given to him as a gift from his mentor and friend, the first chef who gave him a shot straight out of culinary school. He cares for it like it's his baby. Or his cat, as it were.

"Why are you and Dad in town?" Reid asks again, his tone almost conversational as he adds a knob of butter to a pan. "I thought it was to try and make amends, but now I'm not so sure."

Camilla doesn't answer right away, which leads me to believe she's doing some quick thinking. "We came to see you, to dine at your restaurant."

"I don't buy it."

Suddenly, I sense a presence behind me. I spin around and come face-to-face with Oscar.

He gives me this cheeky grin, fully aware he's caught me eavesdropping.

I try for a smile, but it comes across as a grimace. Camilla's harsh words are on repeat through my mind: *just a winemaker, not good enough*. I tell myself not to let her overcritical opinion get to me, but her words still sting.

Tears swim in my eyes and my throat constricts.

"Hey, you okay, Uvas?" Oscar asks.

Oscar has taken to calling me *Uvas*, the Spanish word for "grapes," since he graciously helped me unload a shipment two weeks ago. When growers determine grapes are at their peak ripeness, the fruit is picked overnight and then driven all the way from the Western Slope of the Rocky Mountains, arriving at my winery early the next morning. Which basically means that during harvest, a truckload of grapes can turn up at the drop of a hat and demand immediate attention.

Oscar volunteered—with only minor cajoling from Reid—to help with a delivery of pinot grapes. In return for his labor, he can call me by whatever nickname he wants. Although, if I'm being honest, I kinda dig *Uvas*. It makes me feel like some sort of fermentation superhero.

But at present, I hold my hands to my temples and shake my head, my tassel earrings brushing against the ruffled sleeves of my dress.

He peers into the kitchen over my shoulder and clicks his tongue. "The Wallaces are a nasty piece of work. I don't know how Reid turned out so chill coming from that."

I finally find my voice. It's scratchy and weak and I loathe what Camilla has reduced me to. "She hates me. Camilla doesn't even know me and she hates me."

"Maybe she's more of a margarita chick."

I laugh, which was ultimately his goal, although my head pounds from repressed sobs.

A dimple forms at the corner of his mouth and he rests an elbow nonchalantly against the wall. From the way he holds himself—cool, confident, and a touch mysterious—I can see why servers and hostesses are always vying for his attention.

"Don't worry, Uvas," he says, his eyes kind and earnest. "Reid doesn't put any stock into what she says. He let go of his family a long time ago."

I hadn't even worried about that. That Reid would

actually listen to his mother and start questioning our relationship.

"Yeah, sure," I say, and then change the subject. "So what was the deal with the food tonight?"

"No idea," Oscar says, staring fixedly at the floor. "Nick and I did our usual thing. We were busy, but we were managing." There's a sharpness to his words that sets me on edge.

"Did you change any of the recipes? Add anything during plating, accidentally mislabel the olive oil or something?"

"I know what you're thinking," he says, referencing his penchant for experimenting. "But not this time."

"If you say so . . ." I trail off, watching Oscar carefully.

He shifts on his feet and runs a hand through his hair, an inscrutable expression on his face. There's something he isn't saying, which is odd. My stomach twists, and not from the inedible cuisine.

"I do." He hesitates before opening his mouth to continue, but when the kitchen door swings outward, he freezes.

Camilla is framed in the doorway. Her lips are so thin they're almost invisible and her fingers shake as they touch her coiffure.

I play for sweetness, cocking my head to the side. "I was coming to check on you."

"I'm fine," she says, and steps around us and back to our table.

I turn back to Oscar, but he's already returned to his station in the kitchen, whatever he was going to say forgotten.

* * *

How do you casually mention you overheard a private conversation between two people? What if those two people were your boyfriend and his mother? Oh, and they just happened to be talking about you?

For me, the answer is simple: you don't.

I lean my hip against the cool metal island. From here I have a view of the entire kitchen. Hugging one wall is a deluxe stovetop complete with cast-iron burners, large flat-top griddle, and ovens underneath, and on the opposite wall are sinks and a commercial dishwasher. The prep line features a built-in mahogany cutting board that runs the length of the counter, with custom-built holes for utensils, and shelving overhead holds pristine white plates of various sizes. The dual refrigerators and walk-in freezer are in the far corner, next to Reid's office.

The area is spacious enough that Reid, his two sous chefs, and his pastry chef can work without bumping elbows, but not so spacious that they can't hold a conversation.

The air buzzes with a nervous energy, like the final countdown on one of those stressful cooking competition shows. I roll my neck, riddled with knots, and make a mental note to hit the climbing gym ASAP.

I wish I could handle pressure half as well as Reid's staff. While I'm effectively dodging my one task for this evening, they're busy taking corrective measures.

Oscar busies himself plating. Even though time is of the essence, he moves deliberately, carefully wiping splattered salsa verde from the edge of a plate. After adding a dollop of crème fraîche and a squeeze of lime juice, he moves the plate to the far end of the island, where it awaits delivery.

Reid's other sous chef, Nick Prasad, arranges perfectly cubed butternut squash, sweet potatoes, and parsnips onto a sheet pan and drizzles them with olive oil. Lanky, soft-spoken, and with neatly buzzed hair, Nick is a rule-follower to the core. The most emotion I've seen him express was when he was bickering with Oscar over the correct way to dice cauliflower (for the record, Nick was right).

Reid calls him a technical genius for his impeccable knife skills and knack for memorizing recipes. While Oscar views cooking as an art, Nick views it as a science, cooking with precision over feeling. Together, they make an unbeatable team, although they usually don't see it that way.

Sensing my gaze, Nick glances up, his neck turning blotchy from even that tiny amount of attention. I give him a small smile, but he's already refocused on the sheet pan.

That's more than Britt Hartmann, genius pastry chef and all-around badass, spares me. Britt has a platinum pixie cut, impressively toned arms, and an intimidating demeanor, in large part thanks to her previous job working at a prison. She's moved from her spiced pear tartlets, which are in the oven, to layering freshly whipped cream dotted with specks of vanilla between layers of phyllo.

As for Reid, he's at the stove, adding crushed garlic to the pan of melted butter. It sizzles and snaps and I almost drool for how amazing it smells.

I've spent enough time watching Reid cook to know this is a critical stage. Garlic can go up in smoke faster than, well, this night. Especially during the dinner rush. So, I wait.

I wait while he chops sage with undisguised gusto, adds the green smithereens to the pan of butter and garlic, and rescues ravioli from a pot of boiling water and coats them in the sauce, his motions swift and seamless. In the time it would take me to microwave a Lean Cuisine, Reid has served up a dozen plates of delectable fare.

The servers on duty, Katy and Tony, pause their whispered conversation near the drink station, the only decipherable word of which was *hangry*, to seize the dishes, relief painted on their faces.

It isn't until they've whisked the last plate to the front of the restaurant that Reid turns toward me, dabbing his brow with a towel, a sign that he has a minute to talk. "Look, I'm really sorry about tonight."

"For what?"

"For the way my parents treated you." He drapes the towel over his shoulder, letting out an aggrieved sigh. "I guarantee it was more about me than you. They still don't understand—or agree with—my life choices, which they took out on you."

He pauses and looks at me full-on, his green eyes flashing with emotion. Anger, sadness, remorse.

I'm not sure how to respond. I'm not one of those girls who say things are okay when they aren't. But I'm afraid that if I open my mouth, I'll somehow make the situation worse.

"I wish it were different," Reid continues, turning back to the stovetop. He snags a clean pot from where they hang from hooks beside the range hood. "That I could make them understand, apologize, but it is what it is."

"You told me once that every family has their problems."

"Some worse than others."

The hurt in his voice, how he must feel *still* not having his parents' approval after all he's accomplished, breaks my heart.

"True," I say, pushing myself away from the island and moving to his side. "They're not all bad."

He cocks an eyebrow at me. "Succumbed to Tristan's charms already?"

"Not nearly as much as I have yours."

I wrap my arms around his waist, his muscles taut beneath my embrace, and nuzzle my nose into the nape of his neck. I breathe in his scent, a bouquet of peppermint, citrus, and herbs. He smells more delicious than any aroma coming out of this kitchen, including Britt's spiced pear tartlets.

"Are you sure I can't help with anything?" I whisper, massaging his tense shoulders before I let go.

"Nah, we've got it covered," he says. His focus is entirely on the next course. "Thanks, though."

I realize that's all I'm going to get.

He's got it handled. I need to let it go.

For how amazing our relationship has been going the last couple of months, every once in a while, there are these moments when Reid shuts down. He'll put up a barricade and won't let me in on what's going through his mind, won't let me help. I'm not sure if it's residual independence from his bachelor days or just innate stubbornness, but I know better than to push. Especially when he's in the midst of a decidedly crummy night.

"Okay, well . . ." I trail off with a meaningful look

toward the dining room, dreading returning to the table with his family.

Reid grabs my hand and presses it to his lips. "Why don't you slip out the back? I'll let you know when I'm done here and we'll have a makeup dinner. Just you and me."

Relief surges through my body. "Tell your family it was really—uh—interesting to meet them."

"I'll tell them," he says softly.

I give his hand an extra squeeze before letting myself out through the back door and into the alley behind the restaurant. Freedom never tasted so sweet.

Nestled at the base of the rolling foothills between a boutique and bike shop, Spoons has a prime location on the west end of Pearl Street, the outdoor pedestrian mall that serves as the heart of Boulder.

I turn onto the cobblestone street. The sun has long since set, so old-school lanterns cast a warm glow over the planters of late-season mums and marigolds. Scents of waffle cones, barbecue, and incense perfume the air. It's the place to be. There are people everywhere— frequenting the restaurants and bars, checking out the retail offerings, or simply taking in the atmosphere. Young, old, affluent, down-and-out, there's something for everyone on Pearl Street.

Except, it would seem, for me.

A trio of musicians plays an accordion version of "Bad Romance." I consider joining the throng of onlookers to rinse the foul taste of the evening from my mouth, but the lyrics of the song—*caught in a bad romance*—make me scowl. I meander by the quirky shops selling designer duds, camping gear, and even kites, stopping where a magician is dazzling a crowd by guessing a randomly selected card.

None of it is enough to distract me from my tailspinning thoughts, from the doubt lodged in my throat and the dull ache in my chest.

Instead, I head to the bus stop.

I have another palate cleanser in mind.

Stomp, stomp, stomp.

Grape juice oozes between my toes, not dissimilar from the thoughts seeping through my subconscious.

Just a winemaker. Not good enough.

I stomp my feet into the tub of grapes as I replay the nightmarish evening.

Camilla and Gary belittling my craftsmanship. Gary, Ben, and Tristan excluding me from their conversation. Camilla trying to convince Reid to dump me.

Worst of all, though, was the fact that I didn't have the backbone to stand up to them.

Stomp, stomp, stomp.

Reid didn't invite his mother to malign my character, didn't ask for her opinion. And yet, no matter how much he claims he's separate from his parents, that maternal voice is hard to dispel.

Just ask me and my brother.

Stomp, stomp, stomp.

While I have machinery to help me crush grapes, there's something about the manual process of stomping that produces juice with a more intense, handcrafted flavor. It has to do with control. Knowing exactly when the fermentation process begins, how much juice is released, and how many stems, skins, and seeds are included.

Plus, it doubles as therapy.

I'm adding a grape-stomping activity on the community calendar to give my customers a fun and unique experience, and to demonstrate how wine was made in ancient times. If they can get over the feeling of wading in jelly, I think it'll be a hit.

Still, I should probably plant a few participants—friends and family—to help the event catch on. If Aunt Laura were alive, no doubt she'd be there with her jeans rolled to her knees, a huge grin on her face. But she isn't here. Instead, I'll have to resort to my usual method of recruitment: bribery.

I'll gladly stoop to that level if it means keeping this crazy dream of mine from turning sour.

I admire my winery, the space I'm proud of no matter what anyone says. The back of my shop is more like a warehouse, with soaring vaulted ceilings and concrete flooring. Stainless-steel equipment lines the back of my winery—crusher de-stemmer, state-of-the-art bottling system, and giant wine vats. My cellar is behind a sealed door that keeps the temperature at a crisp fifty-five degrees Fahrenheit. The inventory inside is significantly depleted from a summer of solid business, but it'll be replenished soon enough.

Racked along the back wall are oak barrels containing freshly pressed chardonnay, the sugars, acidity, and yeast working with the oak to create something nuanced and delicious. And taking up the bulk of the floor space are plastic tubs full of different red varietals in early stages of fermentation.

Overall, I'd say I'm about halfway through the harvest, and already my back is aching from working with grapes at various stages and checking and rechecking the Brix, pH, and other compound levels.

And I have to be ready for whenever the next shipment comes in. Which hopefully won't be tomorrow morning, given it must be nearing midnight.

There's a knock at the back door.

Quickly, I towel off my feet and open the door to find Reid. I cross my arms over my chest, my bare legs breaking out in goose bumps from the cool night air.

"Can I come in?" Reid asks.

He's sporting the same sage-green sweater, slim-fitted black jeans, and utility jacket from earlier but seems far more at ease than when I last saw him, scrambling to re-create dishes for every patron in his beloved restaurant.

"That depends," I say, leaning against the door. "What's the password?"

He holds up a bag with the logo for Spoons on it. "Ravioli?"

"Close," I say, cocking my head to the side.

He toes the threshold, his eyes sparkling with humor. "Scallops?"

"Warmer."

He closes the distance between us and leans down to whisper in my ear. "Chocolate truffles."

The feeling of his breath on my neck sends a pleasant shiver down my spine.

"Ding, ding, ding."

I grab the soft fabric of his sweater and tug him inside. Standing on my tiptoes, I brush my lips gently over his in greeting. I make to step away, but Reid spins me into an elegant dip, his arms strong around my waist. He kisses me again, a deep, passionate kiss that could go on forever. His lips are soft against mine, even as the scruff of his beard rubs deliciously against my cheek. A warm tingly feeling spreads through my body.

You'd think in the months since we started dating, I'd have gotten used to kissing Reid. That the butterflies and racing heart I experience in his presence would have lessened. Instead, our chemistry has only intensified.

"I've been thinking about doing that for hours," he says, pulling us both upright, leaving me dizzy.

I'm still somewhat breathless when I speak next, smoothing the front of my dress. "You don't say."

He flashes me that cocksure grin that drives me crazy.

Intoxicating aromas of garlic, lemon, and chocolate waft behind Reid as he puts the food in the fridge next to chilling bottles of wine. He shrugs out of his utility jacket, a bandage standing out on his hand.

"What happened?" I ask, padding to his side. I brush my fingertips over the gauze, my eyebrows furrowed in concern.

"Minor flesh wound."

My face pales as I search his eyes. Were his mother's words so cutting they literally peeled away a layer of his skin?

"I accidentally cut myself," he explains with a shrug. "No big deal."

When I first met Reid, one of the first things I noticed were the thin pale scars lining his forearms, which turned out to be oven burns. I know for a fact he doesn't get injuries as often these days, having learned to keep his cool in the kitchen. Which means, tonight, he was rattled. And rightly so, with both a disapproving parental unit *and* a culinary disaster to contend with.

"Did you get everything sorted at the restaurant?"

"Yeah, thanks to Britt's pear tartlets, although I expect there will be some harsh reviews." He rubs a hand over his face. "Wish I knew what happened."

"You never found out?"

He shakes his head. "Nick and Oscar were as surprised as I was."

The damage was so utterly thorough, there must be some explanation. But Reid's not one to dwell, a trait I've always appreciated about him. If his sous chefs say they don't know what happened, he'll believe them and move on. Better to live in the present with an eye on the future.

An image of Oscar flashes through my mind, the way he didn't quite meet my gaze when I'd prodded him about the food. But Reid trusts him, and surely Oscar wouldn't do anything to jeopardize their friendship.

"And your family?" I ask.

"Left shortly after you did." A dark cloud passes over his features at the mention of his family and a weight seems to rest on his shoulders.

"How long are they in town for again?"

"Through the weekend."

And it's only Wednesday. *Ouch.* I flinch involuntarily.

"I know, right?" Reid stares at the floor, where he notices my bare feet for the first time. He lifts his head, a grin tugging at the corner of his lips. "Stomping grapes?"

"Care to join me?" I ask.

Because, suddenly, I want someone on my side. Correction, not just someone. I want Reid on my side.

It's a testament to how well suited we are that he doesn't make any jokes about toe jam. He merely folds up the bottoms of his jeans and goes to the deep stainless-steel sink to wash his feet. Then he meets me at the tub.

It's made of oak planks and held together with steel hoops, and there's a spigot on one side to drain the juice.

With a four-foot diameter, it's really meant for one person, or for two people who don't mind getting cozy.

Our knees bump against each other as we stomp our way through grapes. My calves burn and my toes prune, and still, we keep going. Until finally, his family, the food fiasco, and the stress of the evening fall away. None of it matters. We're here together, hands clasped and eyes locked.

"This is gonna make one helluva cab," I say.

There's a softness in his eyes, in the way he tucks a strand of hair behind my ear, that makes my heart skip a beat. "I've got just the thing to pair with it."

"What's that?"

In response, he leans down and kisses me again, tantalizing and tender, his fingers gently pressing into my lower back.

"That's great and all," I say, coming up for air. "But what's everyone else going to have?"

He laughs and pulls me closer to him. The warmth of him—his embrace—feels like home, a thought that terrifies me as much as it excites me.

Chapter Three

My phone wakes me up the next morning, a persistent buzzing on my nightstand that finally pulls me from my dreams. Pink rays filter through a crack in the curtains, and outside, all is quiet. Even the songbirds are still asleep.

From her cozy nook at my side, my cat, Zin—short for Zinfandel—looks at the offending smartphone with a huffiness usually reserved for an empty food dish. With gray silky hair, green orblike eyes, and the tip of one ear missing, she's as temperamental as the varietal she's named after, especially when it comes to sleep.

At this particular moment, can't say I blame her. It's too early for someone to be calling. *Unless,* an alarming thought snakes through my mind, *it's an emergency.*

I lunge for my phone, startling Zin, and answer without even checking the caller ID.

"Hello," I say through a yawn, rubbing sleep from my eyes.

There's no greeting, no polite salutation, just four words that send a jolt of electricity coursing through my body: "I need your help."

It's Reid.

I sit up ramrod straight, suddenly wide awake. "What is it? What happened?"

We parted ways only a few hours ago, him back to his place and me to mine, after our impromptu grape-stomping date. He'd told me his day would start early with a trip to the farmers market before heading to Spoons. Which begs the question: What sort of trouble could he have gotten into already?

Then I wince, remembering his family is in town for four more agonizingly long days. He probably wants help facilitating, or keeping them entertained. Which I doubt Gary and Camilla would feel very happy about.

I open my mouth to say as much, but Reid speaks first.

"It's Oscar—" Reid hesitates.

There's a loud clanging in the background on his end of the line and gruff voices. I turn up the volume on my phone.

"Where are you?"

"Jail," he says.

I must have misheard, the background noise muffling his words. "Wait, for a second there I thought you said *jail.*" I chuckle nervously.

"Oscar's gone." Reid sounds bewildered, his voice raspy with sadness and shock. "He was killed last night."

"Wait, our Oscar? As in Oscar Flores?"

"Yes."

All the air seems to whoosh out of my lungs. "You're serious?"

"Deadly."

I hold a hand over my mouth, willing my sluggish brain to catch up with reality. Because Oscar was alive and healthy less than twelve hours ago. He'd stood with me outside the kitchen at Spoons, called me Uvas, kept me from having a full-on meltdown, and offered me relationship advice.

Oscar can't be gone. It makes no sense.

"Sorry, I'm still not following."

"Parker, you're understanding just fine." The steadiness of his tone tethers me to reality.

All at once, I can't be having this conversation in the comfort of my bed. Kicking the covers off, I go into the living room, pacing back and forth. Zin is hot on my heels, thinking it's time for breakfast.

I focus on the details of my surroundings: the geometric print of my arca rug, the russet of my velvet couch, the faded hues of the vintage prints adorning the walls.

My apartment is more of a hallway than a residence, my bedroom opening to a narrow living room with a kitchen at the far end. French doors connect the kitchen to a modest balcony with an unobstructed view of the Flatirons.

The view more than makes up for the cramped quarters. In the mornings, I can watch as the giant slabs of rock are bathed in pink and orange from the sunrise, and in the evenings, observe the angelic rays that are cast when the sun dips below the majestic peaks.

But the view holds no interest for me now.

Instead I take advantage of the runway that is basically my apartment, as I pace from my bedroom to the kitchen, tugging at my raven hair, which is wavy and wild. "Killed as in murdered?"

"Yes."

My knees feel weak and my fingertips tingle with tiny pinpricks. I sink into the couch and focus on my breathing to keep from hyperventilating. Despite my efforts, stars dance in my vision.

Unfortunately, I have some experience with homicide after a renowned critic was murdered in my winery earlier this year. While I may have helped crack the case, it's not something I want to revisit. I still regularly wake up in a cold sweat from nightmares where I discover his lifeless body all over again.

"How?" I croak, my mouth dry. Zin hops into my lap, somehow sensing I need comfort.

"I don't know. Officers keep asking me about some fight they think I had with him, and my chef's knife." Panic enters his voice and I can practically picture him raking a hand through his hair.

Reid rarely goes anywhere without his knives. He carefully straps them in their sleek black case and keeps them in his car or at one of our apartments, like some culinary superhero who's always at the ready to save the day should he encounter any kitchen disasters. This fact, along with the cut on his hand—the so-called minor flesh wound—lodges itself in my brain. I search for reason, like fumbling for a particularly tricky grip at the end of a long climbing session. "But you always take your chef's knife home with you."

"I left it at the restaurant last night."

For him to have left without it means he was far more

distraught than I realized. Or there's something he isn't telling me. An abyss opens in my stomach, and I force myself to swallow the lump in my throat.

"Did you mean to?"

"Of course not," he says, his voice pained. "I just—I just had to get out of there. I wanted to see you."

And the abyss fills with goo.

I sink back into the couch, scratching behind Zin's ears. She kneads my leg, her tiny kitty paws almost acting like a masseuse. A masseuse with very sharp claws. I wince and reposition her on the cushion. A low rumbling purr radiates from her as she watches me steadily, her furry head tilted to the side. It's almost as if she comprehends what's happened.

"I still can't believe Oscar . . ." I trail off, sighing into our connection.

Reid doesn't say anything. He doesn't have to.

It's weird how a silence can communicate more than words.

There's the anticipatory silence before a kiss, which talking would only delay. There's the judgy silence, perfected by Camilla and the rest of the Wallace clan. And then there's this silence, the silence of foreboding, that speaks of something worse yet to come.

Another clang in the background makes me start. That's when I remember where Reid said he's calling from.

My palms grow sweaty and my phone slips. I grip it tighter. "Why are you in jail?"

I brace myself for his answer, but nothing could prepare me for what he finally says.

"They think I did it." His tone is desperate, the raw fear slicing at my heart. "They think I killed my friend."

* * *

When in doubt, call your best friend.

This is true if you need a sympathetic ear after a hard day, you're considering getting bangs, you want to re-hash the latest episode of *Grey's Anatomy*, or, apparently, your boyfriend is wrongfully accused of murder.

Especially if that best friend is a law clerk for the most esteemed judge in Boulder County *and* also happens to be pursuing a career in criminal law.

Sage is as kind as she is brilliant, further proven by her willingness to rush to my aid early on a Thursday morning, which will inevitably make her late for work.

I'm waiting for her on the bottom step of the stairwell that leads to my apartment when she turns into the parking lot. She drives a lime-green Mini Cooper, which somehow perfectly fits her personality. It's tiny, bright, and can handle inclement weather surprisingly well.

I leap to my feet so quickly that I lurch forward, tripping over a crack in the cement. I reach out blindly and cling to the railing, barely saving myself from what was sure to be an embarrassing tumble. I glance around nervously, my knuckles white on the banister.

"Don't worry, no one saw that," Sage says, hopping out of her car.

She shoves her sunglasses on top of her head, her strawberry-blond hair pulled into a high ponytail. Tri-force earrings dangle from her ears, glinting in the sun-light. Her love for everything nerd-canon extends to her wardrobe, which features a mixture of power suits and cosplay. Even dressed professionally, as she is now, she coyly manages to pay homage to her favorite make-believe worlds, like with the Captain Marvel T-shirt peeking out from under her neatly buttoned cardigan.

"Except for you," I point out, raising one eyebrow. I force myself to let go of the railing, steady for the moment.

"Yeah, but I hardly count. I've seen far worse from you, missy."

This is undeniably true. Having been my roommate in college, Sage has seen me at my best (opening day of my winery), my worst (also, ironically, opening day of my winery, post–dead body), and everything in between (let's not mention my hipster phase).

"And I from you." I hold a hand over my heart and give her what is probably my first genuine smile of the day, although it's not long before it transitions back into a tense frown. "My head's in a weird place."

Concern is etched in Sage's face. "Here, this will help. It's your usual." She passes me a to-go mug sporting the logo of my favorite coffee place, the Laughing Rooster. "Skinny latte."

Tears spring to my eyes at the gesture. I wipe the tears away, but not before one slides down my cheek and plops onto the cup's lid.

"Oh, Parker," Sage says, wrapping her arms around me. "Try not to panic. We'll figure this out."

I have my doubts about that, but allow myself to be comforted. I sniff. "It's just such a mess. And poor Oscar."

She gives me one last squeeze before letting go. "Take a sip."

I'm buzzed enough without any caffeine, but I know better than to argue with Sage. The latte is hot and bitter and oddly comforting. I take another, larger gulp.

"Good." Sage nods encouragingly, slurping from her own drink, some sort of fluorescent-blue frozen concoction. "Now, tell me everything."

So I do.

Standing in the shade of my apartment complex, I tell her about the disastrous dinner with Reid's family, from the disgusting food to the impermeable Boys' Club to Camilla's scathing words.

"Oh no, she didn't," Sage says with a huff, indignant on my behalf.

"She did. They all did," I say. Sure, Tristan and Ben may not have piled on the criticism, but they also didn't stand up for me. And sometimes, doing nothing is just as bad as actively participating.

I fiddle with the strings of my hoodie. In my haste to get ready, I grabbed the first clothes I could lay my hands on—beat-up jeans with holes in the knees and a worn CU Buffs sweatshirt.

"What did Reid say?" Sage asks.

"He came to my defense. Turned it back on them and why they were really in town." I shrug and focus on the cup in my hand, the warmth permeating the paper sleeve. "But she's his mother."

"So what?"

Sage has some experience with, as she calls it, mama drama, her mom only contacting her when she needs money, legal advice, or to make someone feel smaller than her.

"So, some people aren't as awesome as you at ignoring unwelcome motherly opinions."

"If they're with you, they should be."

I decide not to pick at that thread and continue with

how I escaped (nay, *fled*) early, and how Reid met up with me later at Vino Valentine. I finish with Reid's phone call this morning, realizing just how little I actually know about his current predicament.

Here's what I do know: Officers showed up at the duplex Reid rents off Pearl Street at four o'clock this morning with a search warrant. They brought him in for questioning about the suspicious death of Oscar Flores, which, before too long, turned into an arrest.

Sage listens silently, her skin growing pale beneath her freckles.

Around us, birds chirp and flit between blue spruce trees, a neighbor greets me on their way to the bus stop, and cars impatiently inch closer to one another on the busy street in front of my apartment, rush hour being in full swing. The normalcy strikes me as cruel and makes me want to crawl out of my skin.

I'm tempted to march to the street corner and shout about the injustices in the world. About lives that end too soon and families left behind heartbroken. About the evil that lurks in all of us and, even more frightening, those who can't control it.

Instead, I take another sip of my latte. Having a massive freak-out won't help anyone.

"Is there any chance Reid could've . . . ?" Sage spares me the rest of the sentence.

I shake my head adamantly. "Absolutely not." I turn to her, imploring her to believe me. "He's a good guy, you know? He would never hurt anyone. Especially not his friend."

"Yeah, I know." Sage dips her chin. "But I had to check."

"That's fair," I say with a sigh. "I'd be lying if I said the thought hadn't crossed my mind." And evaporated immediately. Absently, I touch my lips.

"Okay then." Sage gets to her feet and makes for her car, glancing over her shoulder at me. "You coming?"

I jog to catch up and scramble into the passenger seat. "Where are we going?"

There's a fervor in her eyes usually reserved for new *Star Wars* franchise announcements.

"To get Reid, duh." She shifts into drive and turns onto Broadway. "Let's go make hell."

Chapter Four

The Boulder County Jail is located at the top of a hill that overlooks a public park in East Boulder on the way to the municipal airport. I wonder if the families walking dogs, having picnics, and making use of the biking grounds know they're a few yards away from a compound housing close to five hundred inmates.

The building is intimidating, all concrete and metal. Red accents pop from the otherwise tan exterior on doors, trim, and gates. The landscaping is minimal, primarily composed of gravel, a crowded dirt parking lot, and flagpoles.

I hesitate at the entrance to the facility, my heart pounding so hard I fear it might actually take flight. I wipe my sweaty palms on my jeans. I've been so desperate to do something to help Reid, but now that we're here, I'm riddled with anxiety.

Sage, however, doesn't appear to share my discomfort. She marches through the outer metal door as if she does this on a daily basis. Which, given her career aspirations, is probably a good thing. She's all fire and confidence, from the way she tilts her chin a fraction upward to her thrown-back shoulders. Maybe it's the Captain Marvel T-shirt.

Crossing my arms over my chest, I follow her inside. Nerves accost me, making my actions extra twitchy, and I accidentally step on the back of Sage's shoe.

"Easy there, tiger," she says, pulling at the heel of her Mary Jane flat. "It'll be okay."

I nod, giving her an inch, and we continue through the inner door and into a cramped lobby.

The small space is charged with a weird resigned energy. There are only two rows of plastic chairs, all of which are occupied by people who look as dazed and upset as me. Complimentary lockers for personal belongings line the back wall, and on either side are posters advertising things like the importance of care packages for inmates and instructions for loading minutes onto a calling card.

In the far corner, a receptionist is perched behind a protective caged barricade. I make my way to her, noting her uniform and the badge gleaming on her chest.

Sage gives me the go-ahead at the counter.

Peeling my tongue from the roof of my mouth, I start, "I—uh—want to see an inmate." The last word prickles in my mouth like overly tannic wine.

"Do you have an appointment?" she asks matter-of-factly.

"No."

"You need to schedule a visitation twenty-four hours in advance." She folds her hands over a clipboard.

The reality of the situation hits me afresh and I almost sink to the concrete floor. My boyfriend has been arrested for a crime he didn't commit, and now I can't see him—comfort him—for a bare minimum of twenty-four hours. It's enough to make my eyes sting from repressed tears. Sage rubs my back.

My friend's presence fuels me with courage to try again. "But there must be some mistake. They think—"

The lady officer shakes her head, cutting me off. Not unfriendly, just informative. "You'll have to take that up with the detective handling his or her case." She keeps talking, but my mind snagged on something she said.

Rude as it is midconvo, I fumble for my phone and, finding the contact I'm looking for, press call.

Just as the line starts ringing, the very individual I'm dialing strides through a metal detector down the hallway to my right. My phone is still pressed to my ear, even as the ringing echoes through the nondescript corridor.

Sweet blissful hope surges through me at the sight of Eli Fuller—or, I should say, Detective Fuller. Because, at the moment, he's my best shot at seeing Reid.

Eli digs his phone from his pocket and glances at the screen. He rubs his clean-shaven face before silencing it.

That's right. He had the audacity to ignore my call.

My arm goes slack and my jaw drops in shock.

Eli and I attended high school together, where he was renowned for his antics as the Boulder Cineplex stoner. In the ten years since graduation, he's done an about-face, becoming a clean-cut, rule-abiding detective. Gone are the Birkenstocks, tie-dye, unkempt hair, and blood-shot eyes. In their place are polished leather shoes, a smart navy suit, hair gelled into a suave wave, and analytical brown eyes.

Eli helped me out of a pickle earlier this year when a crazed killer used my winery as the venue for their murdering spree. Since then, I've called him a few times to go climbing, a hobby we share, but he's always declined. Sure, he might have been genuinely busy. Or he might have been avoiding me, like he is now.

I thought we'd be able to move past the awkwardness of my rejecting his romantic advances, but I guess not . . . which hopefully won't dissuade him from assisting my current beau.

"Here goes nothing," I mutter under my breath, stashing my phone in my purse.

"I've got your back," Sage says. She rocks onto the balls of her feet. "And remember, I speak legalese."

With his head bowed, consulting something in his notepad, Eli doesn't notice Sage or me until he's practically on top of us.

I clear my throat and he looks up, startled. We spend a moment pretending he didn't just ignore my call and that I didn't catch him in the act. Suffice it to say, there's a reason neither of us is in theater.

I rest my hand on my hip. "Fancy seeing you here."

Emotions play out on his face as his eyes grow from pained to guarded. "Parker. It's good to see you." His tone betrays the insincerity of his words.

My lips twitch. I'm keenly aware of Sage, at the ready to jump to my defense. But you know what they say about flies and honey. So, I chuckle like someone's told a joke and try for an innocuous tone. "I think there's been some sort of misunderstanding. Reid was brought in early this morning."

Eli flips his notepad closed and tucks it in his jacket pocket, giving us a glimpse of his gun, strapped to his chest by a shoulder harness. "There's been no misunderstanding."

"O-kay," I say, drawing out each syllable of the word. I tap my sneaker-clad foot and wait for him to continue.

I sense the receptionist observing us curiously, no doubt seconds away from calling security. Little does she know, I have an in with the Boulder PD. At least, I hope I do.

Eli exhales. "I'm working the Flores case. We have probable cause that Mr. Wallace is the perpetrator."

And jackpot. I suspected as much given Eli's lack of surprise at seeing me. Here. At the jail. I mean, I know I got entangled in an investigation earlier this year, but that's long over.

"What evidence do you have?" Sage interjects.

Pity flashes across Eli's face, but his voice is stern when he responds, "That's none of your concern."

I feel like I'm a thin-skinned grape being crushed under the harsh foot of the justice system. My breathing hitches and I sway. It takes all my effort to keep myself upright.

"Actually," Sage interjects, her voice steely, "as Reid's legal defense, it is my concern."

Eli raises his eyebrows, skeptical. "I'll have to check with Mr. Wallace. If he agrees to see you, I can grant you fifteen minutes."

I nod mutely, a numbness seeping through my body.

"Only Sage. Sorry, Parker." He gives me another pitying glance, a hint of warmth entering his caramel eyes. "I'll be right back."

He retraces his steps, going back through the metal detector and down the hallway, his shoes squeaking against the polished floor. He disappears through a mystery door, which clangs shut.

I let out an exhale and look at Sage. "Thanks for that."

"This doesn't look good." She ushers me into a recently vacated seat in the lobby and kneels in her pencil skirt so we're at eye level. "Is there anything you want me to tell Reid? Any message I can pass along?"

I think of the night before. Of Reid stomping grapes with me, our knees bumping into each other. His lips on mine as he gracefully dipped me backward in a sweeping embrace. His cocksure grin and the truffles he brought me, my favorite brand of chocolate.

I clamp a hand over my mouth to keep a sob from escaping.

What do you say to someone in this situation? What words could possibly ease the pain of losing a friend *and* the humiliation of being blamed for it?

"Ask him if there's anything I can do. And—" I hesitate, licking my lips. "And tell him I love him."

"You got it."

Sage doesn't know the weight of those three words. Doesn't know it's the first time I'm saying them to Reid. Indirectly, yes, but it still counts. Truth be told, I've felt the capital *L* for Reid for a while now, but my last relationship left me with some undeniable trust issues.

My last boyfriend, Guy, and I were like impersonator champagne. The bubbles and floral aroma might pass for the real thing, but they don't come together quite right.

Unfortunately, it took us years and an ultimatum to figure that out.

After Guy had accepted a political consultant job in D.C., we spent six tense months trying the long-distance thing before he pressured me to play the dutiful girlfriend, abandon my winery plans, and move across the country. I chose myself—my dream—and, while it was ultimately me who broke it off, we both got burned.

Here I thought he'd loved me for my determination, my goals, my brain. Turns out, he loved his vision of me more than the real me.

So, yeah, trust issues.

But it's important Reid knows that I'm here for him, that I believe him, that our relationship is more than the elation of the shiny honeymoon phase. Even if it means waiting to learn how he reacts—if he has a response—through my friend.

I hide my face in my hands.

Eli returns and gestures for Sage to follow him.

I watch Sage and Eli walk away, feeling utterly helpless.

When left unharvested, grapes will shrivel on the vine. The sugars will become too concentrated to use in wine, or in much of anything. But that's not the worst of it. The vine will take this unharvested fruit to mean it doesn't need to produce as many grapes the following year. Which will lead to a steady decline.

I wonder if love is the same way, and what it could mean for me and Reid. I wring my hands in my lap as I wait for Sage. My seat faces a window with a view of the parking lot. A gust of wind kicks up dirt, sending it swirling into the air. A lone tumbleweed rolls past and snags on a fence post.

Eli has since returned. He makes a phone call, pacing far enough away from me that I only hear mumbled words. After he hangs up, he takes one of the coveted chairs at my side, resting his forearms on his knees. He checks his watch at least once a minute, steadfast in his assurance to not give Reid and Sage a millisecond longer than they're allotted.

I try to picture Reid and Sage in one of those cold, dim rooms. I wonder what they're saying. If Sage is using her mental prowess to get Reid out of this, if Reid is drumming his hands on the table, like he's prone to doing when forced to sit too long. What he thought of my message.

I let out an audible exhale. It must not have been my first one, because Eli side-eyes me, his gaze steady.

"Have you been climbing lately?" he asks.

"You know I have," I say quietly. "I've invited you to go."

The thing about climbing is, it's better with a friend. A belayer broadens the range of what you can do and opens up more routes. After randomly bumping into Eli at the gym a few times earlier this summer, I'd harbored hopes we could become regular climbing buddies. But alas, he's always cited some vague excuse for why he can't join me.

"I've been busy."

A vague excuse like that.

"Right." I snort and roll my eyes but let it go. Because, right now, I couldn't care less about Eli's bogus schedule conflicts.

A silence falls between us. An older couple, looking

lost, enters the waiting area, but from the lawyerly figure trailing them, I know they're not lost. I spare them a thought, hoping whomever they're here for is deserving of their devotion.

Eli leans forward, staring at his hands. "Look, I wish there was more I could do."

I cut a sharp glance at him. "Do you, though?"

"Of course." He furrows his eyebrows. "You're the last person I wanted to see here."

I wince. That's harsh.

"You know what I mean. Involved in another one of my cases." He shifts in his seat and runs a hand through his hair, messing up the perfect side part. Frazzled is a completely foreign look on him.

While he's agitated, I make one last play for information. "Why do you think Reid did this?"

I must be the picture of pitiful—red-rimmed eyes, unkempt hair, beat-up jeans—because he actually answers.

He lowers his voice. "This stays between us, and I'm only telling you so you can be on your guard and carefully consider those you associate with."

He doesn't spell it out, but I catch his drift. He's warning me about Reid, challenging my feelings for him. I don't appreciate it.

"The evidence is damning," Eli says. "Mr. Flores was killed with Reid's knife. A witness overheard him and Mr. Flores arguing in the alley behind the establishment called Spoons. They went to check and saw Reid and Oscar fighting, a wrestling match that resulted in the stabbing of Mr. Flores. And then there's Reid's injury."

He waves his hands as if this final fact clinches the deal.

"Reid cut himself in the kitchen. It happens all the time." Even as those last words leave my mouth, I realize they aren't true. In fact, since Reid and I started dating I have never seen him cut himself—not even so much as a nick.

"Could be," Eli says with a shrug. "Or could be it was the result of an altercation with Oscar."

"Reid has an alibi. He was with me at Vino Valentine last night."

"Really?" He gives me a look of sheer disbelief. "You were with him every second? The whole night?"

"Well, no," I admit.

Eli looks so smug he might as well be twirling a handlebar mustache between two fingers. "The coroner places the murder happening sometime between ten and two o'clock."

I'm not sure exactly what time Reid got to Vino Valentine, having been occupied in my therapeutic stomping, but it'd been late, probably close to midnight, well after Spoons closed.

But Reid is often at the restaurant late—whether for extra cleaning, taking stock of ingredients, or prepping for the next day. I just wish I knew what kept him last night.

"What about a motive?" I ask. "Reid and Oscar are friends, have been for ages."

"The psychology of a murderer is not always easy to understand."

"Reid isn't a murderer." I grind my teeth.

Eli is on the verge of saying something else but stops. "I've told you too much already. We have probable cause. He could be a danger to himself or others."

With that, frowning, he turns his attention to the screen of his phone.

I want to retort that the only danger will be me if my boyfriend isn't released soon. But it would be pointless.

Instead, I get to my feet in a huff and move closer to the receptionist, stuffing my hands in the pocket of my hoodie.

Stupid detectives and their stupid protocol.

I sense motion on the other side of the metal detector and gaze down the hallway in time to see Sage emerge from a room that must be used for visitations. And behind her, flanked by officers, is Reid.

Reid almost appears the same. Roguish good looks enhanced by his beard and lean muscles. Sandy-blond hair with coppery undertones the color of port. Skin tanned from hiking and perusing the outdoor farmers market. The same except, of course, for the orange jumpsuit, handcuffs, and laceless slippers.

Sage says something to him and he nods, his gaze fixed on the floor before him. Even though he's standing tall, there's a tension in his shoulders and his jaw is clenched.

I stare at him, directing my mental focus to send him a message via whatever version of the Force really exists: *look this way.*

And then he does.

Our eyes meet and his demeanor transforms. Relief washes over his face and his shoulders relax. He drinks in my face like a dehydrated runner at the top of Mount Sanitas drinks water. I do the same with his.

His lips twitch and he forces a cocky smile on his face. I can tell it's for show, his way of saying he's okay.

I shake my head, letting him know I don't buy it.

He shrugs, like, *It was worth a shot.*

He starts to mouth something but an officer grabs him by the upper arm and pulls him in the opposite direction. Reid gives me one last look before turning the corner and disappearing into the folds of the prison.

I'm still staring down the hallway when Sage waves her hands in front of my face. "Earth to Parker."

"Sorry, just . . ."

"Engaging in a visual lip-lock. I get it."

I blink at her, my tone turning defensive as I respond, "Making the most of the only contact I can have with my boyfriend."

"Let's fix that, shall we?" Sage links her arm through mine and guides me to the receptionist.

I allow her to tug me along, still reeling from seeing Reid manhandled in handcuffs, the bright orange of his jumpsuit seared into my mind.

"Excuse me," Sage says through the wire mesh. "We'd like to schedule a visitation for tomorrow."

"Fill this out." The officer slides a clipboard, sheet of paper, and pen through the small opening in the barrier. "As long as you're on the inmate's list, it shouldn't be a problem."

Sage accepts the form on my behalf, which is probably for the best given the way the font swims before my eyes, and begins jotting down answers to the questions—my name, birth date, even my address.

While Sage writes, I search her face for an indication as to how the visit went. You know, a sign that this nightmare will be over stat or, at the very least, that my boy-friend responded to my declaration of love.

I can't read her expression.

We return the application and, a minute later, I'm officially entered into the system and given a slot for the following day. There's a flutter of nerves and anticipation in my chest, and the fleetest stirring of hope.

Eli drifts to our side.

Sage straightens and raises her chin, leveraging every inch of her petite frame. She strikes the very definition of a power pose as she addresses Eli. "I'd like to petition to have my client's arraignment hearing as soon as possible."

Eli chuckles. "You'll have to take that up with the DA. Mr. Wallace's first appearance has already been set for tomorrow morning."

"Can't it be any sooner? This afternoon?"

"Doubtful," he says, sliding his fingers through his belt loop. "This is all pretty standard. Since he was booked this morning, it'll be the following day." Eli shifts his attention from Sage to me. "Reid will be okay for one night."

"If you say so." I want to believe Eli. Really, I do. But in the back of my mind, there's this niggling voice telling me it could be more than one night. That there's a chance Reid *won't* be okay.

Sage gives Eli a curt nod, narrowing her eyes. "I expect you'll let me know if there's any news."

I'd hate to be opposite Sage in a courtroom. She's exuding an air of assertiveness that no doubt some would interpret as catty. As for me? I couldn't be prouder.

Eli's lips tighten into a thin line, but he responds, "You bet."

"Great," Sage says. "Let's go, Parker."

"I'll walk you guys out," Eli says.

Sage shoots him a look that would turn all the grapes at the back of my winery into raisins.

He backpedals, gesturing vaguely toward the receptionist. "Actually, I've gotta check on something."

I give Eli a little wave before following Sage, who's already a few paces ahead of me.

She marches through the doors of the jail and across the parking lot at such a grueling pace I have to jog to catch up. It's not until we reach her car that she says something.

"I'm not going to lie to you, it doesn't look good." She slumps into the driver's seat of her Mini Cooper.

"I know." I massage my temples, replaying all the facts Eli gave me. "How is he?"

"Surprisingly calm given the situation and not nearly as cooperative as he should be."

"What do you mean?"

"There are holes in his timeline from last night." She fiddles with her car keys. "And I basically had to coerce every bit of information out of him."

"What holes?" I ask. "I can tell you where he was."

"You sure about that?"

"Yes," I say, hating the uncertainty in my voice. "He was at the restaurant, then Vino Valentine, and then his place."

Sage pierces me with her blue eyes, musing. "Either way, I got what I needed."

She starts the car, turning up the AC, the sun having

baked the dark seats. I buckle my seat belt, wondering what exactly Sage isn't saying.

I can barely bring myself to ask the next question. "Did Reid—uh—say anything?"

"He wanted me to tell you three things," she starts, twisting in her seat so she can face me. "The first is if you'd be willing to check on William."

William is Reid's cat. He's a sweet tuxedo kitty named after the war hero from *Braveheart*, as Reid would proudly proclaim. It's high time William and Zin spent some time together. I nod. So far, so good.

"The second is to call his mother and let her know the situation." She adds hurriedly, "So, yeah, good luck with that."

I wince. That's going to be one painful phone call.

Sage continues, "Third, shut down Spoons. Temporarily."

The planner in me immediately constructs a to-do list. This request will involve a stop by the restaurant and likely enlisting the help of Britt or Nick, but I'll do anything I can to help Reid.

I wait for Sage to continue. To tell me my boyfriend loves me with the passion of the ages—of poets, artists, and vintners.

But she shifts her car into reverse and backs out of the parking lot.

"Wait, that's it?"

"Well, he also said not to worry about him, but I figure there's a fat chance of that happening."

She's right. I'm basically a bundle of nerves and caffeine, a recipe for anxiety.

"But, yep, that's all she wrote. Or he wrote." She shakes

her head, her ponytail swinging back and forth. "Whatever."

I tell myself not to panic. Reid clearly has other things on his mind. Besides, I'm a strong, independent woman; I don't need a man's validation. Still, my cheeks flush in embarrassment. Why did I choose today to drop the L-word again?

I take a deep yoga breath and focus on what's important. "Can you get him out of this?"

Sage pulls the car to a stop at an intersection, the ticking of her blinker the only sound. Even though there are no cars in either direction, she doesn't proceed down the hilly road.

"I'm going to try my hardest, but I don't know," she says, her knuckles white on the steering wheel, her demeanor a far cry from the confidence she was radiating minutes ago. "At least you have a visitation scheduled for tomorrow in case the arraignment doesn't sway in his favor."

She eyes me warily, like I might burst into tears again. Can't say I blame her.

However, far from provoking sadness, the sight of Reid incarcerated reinforced my steadfast belief in his innocence, and it effectively pissed me off.

New businesses have enough hurdles without a misplaced murder accusation. The harsh reality is this: with Reid out of commission combined with the backlash this debacle will incite, Spoons may not survive.

Not to mention our relationship. Am I really going to let Eli, the authorities, or some faceless judge ruin our chance at a long-lasting romance? I think not.

And that's not all. Our partnership—pairing food and wine—was just getting off the ground. Sure, Vino

Valentine might weather this storm, but working with Reid has been a dream, and I'm not ready for it to end.

Then there's Oscar.

My chest clenches. I'll never get to hear Oscar call me *Uvas* again. Never get to marvel at the flavors he coaxes out of simple ingredients. Never get to relish his playful banter.

Oscar didn't deserve to die. Especially not by his friend's sword—er, knife.

With all of these thoughts swirling through my mind, I vow to uncover what really happened last night.

Chapter Five

There are a few things I imagined telling Camilla the next time I chatted with her. One, that Reid and I are stronger than ever and definitely *not* breaking up. Two, that winemaking is freaking hard and the fact that Vino Valentine is flourishing speaks volumes more about my craft than any of her or Gary's veiled criticisms. Three, that many popular lifestyle brands endorse hiking as a means to achieve mindfulness.

That her son has been arrested for murder never made the list. Never even entered my mind as being in the realm of possibility. Which is probably why I've failed to find the words.

I couldn't find the words on the ride back to my apartment. Or during the long, hot shower I treated myself to after Sage left for work. Or while I transformed my appearance into that of a professional entrepreneur.

I applied lip gloss, dabbed jasmine perfume on the insides of my wrists, and ran my fingers through my hair until the raven locks got an intentionally mussed look. Then I changed into slate-gray slacks and a sapphire sweater that brings out the blue in my eyes. Lastly, I clasped my beaded necklace around my neck—a fine white-gold chain dotted with miniature crystal grapes—willing my aunt's gift to give me strength today.

Not only was Aunt Laura the cool aunt everybody wished they had, always there for my brother, Liam, and me, sneaking us sweets when we were younger and shooters when we were older, but she was also my staunchest supporter.

She was the first person I told about my plans to open Vino Valentine and, far from talking me out of it like my mom would have done (and eventually did try to do), she invested in it. Her belief in me gave me the confidence to follow through with my dream. However crazy it may have seemed.

Even though she's been gone for more than two years, there are times I keenly feel her presence.

And what she would tell me now is this: *stop avoiding the inevitable*.

She would be right; I've put off this task long enough.

I plant myself on my couch with my phone in my lap, chewing on my lower lip. Should I engage in small talk, ask how their trip is going so far, or just rip off the Band-Aid? Should I start with *hi* or *hello*?

You'd think I'd never used a telephone before.

Zin hops onto the couch beside me and kneads at her favorite afghan blanket, a sunbeam stretching across the russet surface and onto the geometric-print rug. I scratch behind her ears and she purrs, rubbing her kitty cheek against my fingers. One of the great things about pets is that they love you no matter what outlandish things may be going on in your life.

With that thought in mind, I call the St Julien Hotel and ask for the Wallaces' room.

"Yes," a poised voice answers.

Suave broad that I am, I immediately drop my phone and scramble to pick it up. "Hi, Camilla?"

There's a long sigh into the phone. "And who might this be?"

"It's Parker. Parker Valentine. Reid's girlfriend."

"Yes. Hello." Her disappointment is tangible, and it's only going to get worse.

"I—uh—well, I don't quite know how to say this, so I'm just going to spit it out." I give a nervous chuckle and continue, "Reid's been arrested. For the murder of his sous chef Oscar Flores." On a roll now, the words pour out. "Only, there's been some sort of mistake. There's no way he could have done it, no matter how much evidence the detective thinks he has. Anyway, Reid wanted me to call you and let you know. So . . ." I trail off, taking a much-needed breath.

"Oh," Camilla says.

There's a long pause, so long I must have missed something. "Sorry, I think you cut out for a minute there."

"No, I'm here." She pauses again. "That is . . . unfortunate."

"That's an understatement," I bite back, my voice growing defensive.

"Is that all?" Camilla asks.

"I guess so." Anger churns in my stomach at Camilla's complete disregard for her son's welfare. Not to mention her rude dismissal of me.

Then I recall the weirdness I observed between the Wallaces and Oscar. There was a history there, something that was left unsaid.

"Actually, Camilla," I say before she can hang up. "Could I stop by and talk to you all later on today?"

"Whatever for?"

Is she really that clueless? Does she dislike me *that* much? Or is there another reason for her evasiveness?

"For Oscar," I say evenly, clenching my free hand into a fist. "And for Reid. In order to be of any assistance, I need to learn as much as I can about that night. Anything you guys remember could come in handy."

I don't add another tidbit I'm hoping to find out, which is this: if any of them had motive to kill Oscar. Camilla, for one, certainly seems coldhearted enough.

Another lengthy sigh. Seriously, if there were Olympic medals awarded for excessive sighing, she'd win the gold.

"We have dinner reservations at the Flagstaff House for seven o'clock. Stop by before then."

Because their son's arrest is such an inconvenience. I roll my eyes and say through gritted teeth, "See you then."

I hang up and let my head fall between my knees. Concerned, Zin meows and paws at my arm.

I give her a small smile to let her know I'm okay and scratch behind her ears. "How do you feel about a houseguest?"

She purrs and curls up for her morning nap. I'm going to take that as her assent.

I let myself into Reid's apartment with the spare key he had made for me.

Reid gave it to me over a late-summer picnic lunch at Chautauqua—one of those rare days we both had off. He'd pressed the piece of metal into my palm like it was no big deal. But I knew better. I knew he'd never taken that step in a relationship before, had never been in one long enough.

A giddy smile had spread over my face. "What's this for?"

"In case you need it," he'd said simply, intertwining his fingers through mine.

I highly doubt this is what he'd had in mind.

His duplex smells like him—peppermint, citrus, and a mix of herbs. It's intoxicating; savory, refreshing, and, above all, comforting.

While I'm going to wait to bring William to my apartment, wanting to be there to ensure he and Zin get along as well as their human counterparts do, that doesn't mean he should have to wait for food. Because if he's anything like Zin, he's probably already panicking over the dwindling amount of kibble in his dish. And I have more than an hour until the opening bell at Vino Valentine.

"William," I say, and then add kiss noises. I go to the closet where his food is kept and shake the kibble bag, a gesture that would usually send Zin screeching to my side.

I repeat my call for William, scooping food into his bowl. Still nothing.

I seek him out in Reid's bedroom. The space is all masculine. Dim lighting from a black floor lamp, leather accents, king bed strewn with a navy comforter, unmade, as he was forced to leave it.

The rest of his room is tidy. Clothes tucked away in the closet, notecards neatly stacked on his nightstand in case inspiration for recipes strikes in the middle of the night, and a tasteful speaker perched on the windowsill. A photograph of Reid's alt-rock band, Spatula—he's the drummer—hangs on the wall. It's in black and white, showcasing the members in action, their attention focused solely on their instruments. I smile at the photo, recognizing my brother's handiwork.

It was thanks to Spatula, and my brother subbing for their bassist once, that I eventually met Reid. They'd become fast friends. Reid tagged along with Liam to my winery's grand opening and wasn't scared away after the most renowned critic in the Front Range wound up dead after tasting my craftsmanship. The rest, as they say, is history. Although hopefully not *history* history.

I click my tongue and go to make Reid's bed, knowing he would appreciate the gesture. When I pull the comforter tight, I notice a small mound in the middle of the bed. Nestled between the sheets and cover is William. He lifts his furry black head and peers at me with wary blue eyes.

"Hey there, buddy," I say, letting him sniff my finger. Once I've gained his trust, I scratch under his chin.

Usually William is strutting about with his tail in the air, tracking the squirrels out the window or batting his catnip ball across the kitchen floor. Cats have a sixth sense for when something is amiss, and poor William is clearly freaked out.

"How would you like to come stay with me tonight?"

He doesn't respond, which, given how often I talk to cats, is probably a good sign for my sanity.

"I'll be back later. I promise."

I tuck William back in and make for the front door. It's time I was on my way.

I'm letting myself out when something on the ledge,

just inside the door, catches my eye. Underneath Reid's keys and sunglasses is a slip of paper with a name and phone number on it.

Susie 303-555-8756

I frown, staring at the offending Post-it.

I pride myself on my logic. On not obsessing over things until I know the full story. But no matter what I tell myself, my brain is already in overdrive wondering who exactly this Susie is and why her number is in my boyfriend's apartment.

I remind myself that Reid has never given me a reason to distrust him. In fact, secrecy isn't his style. He's direct, forgoing drama to get straight to the point. It's something I've always loved—damn that word—about him.

Still, seemingly of their own accord, my fingers enter the digits into my phone and press call.

While the line rings, I sift through plausible reasons I can give for dialing this random number and seeking out information.

I come up blank.

It doesn't matter anyway, because my call goes to voice mail. The bubbly voice of Susie instructs me to leave a message, signing off with a flirtatious giggle.

And that giggle? It rattles in my ears as I lock up, making my jaw clench and my stomach churn. I may shut the door slightly harder than necessary.

Pearl Street is bustling with professionals on their way to work, exercise gurus on the hunt for protein-packed smoothies, and college students roosting at cafés.

A bulk of the shops and restaurants are still dark inside (a testament to just how early my morning started). The same holds true for Spoons.

On either side of a solid wooden door with ladles for handles, rays of sun pour through storefront windows. Chairs with their legs in the air rest on the tops of tables, and every surface has been polished to a sheen. The stage where musicians play is clear. It's weird to see the space this way—calm, quiet, empty.

My kitten heels click against cobblestone as I traipse farther down Pearl Street, past the neighboring luxe beauty supply store, to where there's a street that cuts to the alleyway.

The back of Spoons is not nearly as welcoming as the front. There's a large metal door that leads to the kitchen, and bins for trash, recycling, and compost. The alley is barely wide enough for delivery trucks to back into and unload goods, a practice that happens twice a week. Weeds poke through cracks in the cement, dried and brown in deference to the changing season.

This is where Eli said someone witnessed Reid and Oscar fighting. Where Oscar's body was eventually discovered.

The hair raises at the nape of my neck and my palms grow clammy.

I take a step forward, scanning the area.

The only sign of there having been a crime scene is a single strip of yellow CAUTION tape snagged on a nearby telephone pole. The tape flaps in the breeze, making a snapping sound as it hits the side of the restaurant.

A brownish stain the length of my shadow stretches across the ground. Unbidden, an image of Oscar enters my mind. Him lying in this very spot, the life slowly bleeding out of him. His handsome face turning ashen, his eyes dull and glassy.

I suppress a shudder.

Who had Oscar really been fighting with? What could the argument have been about? And why would someone assume it was Reid?

Tucking my purse under my arm, I comb the area. It's doubtful that Eli or his crew would leave something behind, but there's always the chance I might find a clue they overlooked.

But there's nothing. They must have done a clean sweep.

I peek inside each of the bins. The trash can is full of black bags deftly knotted at the top; I defer further investigation for now. I open the lid to the recycling to find it full of clear plastic containers and empty wine bottles sporting the Vino Valentine logo—crisscrossing grapevines punctuated by the sun. The compost bin yields nothing, apart from the unpleasant stench of spoiled produce.

As I slam the last lid shut, something on the ground glints in the sunlight. I kneel down for a closer look. Wedged between the wheel of the compost bin and the cement is a pearly white button.

I know better than to directly touch anything. After digging in my purse for a tissue, I pick up the button and hold it up to the light, studying it. There's a smudge of brownish-red on the outer edge, but otherwise it's your standard-fare button.

Of course, there's a chance it could have been here for ages, maybe popped off after someone overindulged during a night on the town. But there's also the chance it came off during the skirmish last night, especially given the blood-colored splotch.

I stash the button in my purse, just in case. I'm fastening the brass clasp when I hear a voice behind me.

"Can I help you?"

Nick Prasad eyes me warily. He freezes in place, a few paces away, his chef's coat tucked under one arm. His appearance is as pristine as you'd expect, given his rule-abiding personality. Buzz cut, clean-shaven (although that could be because he can't get more than peach fuzz to grow), straight pearly whites, and slacks with a pressed crease along the side.

Nick squints and, recognition dawning, says flatly, "Oh, it's you."

"Ah," I say sweetly. "The way every girl dreams of being greeted."

"I only meant . . ."

But whatever he meant is interrupted by Britt's arrival.

She's lugging a tote with apples peeking out of the top. No doubt the bag is heavy, but she makes it look like it weighs nothing, her arms strong from kneading pastry dough. Her pixie cut is styled into platinum spikes and a tattoo snakes down the side of her neck, a cursive script I've never been able to read.

I squirm under her gaze, her gray eyes seeming to take in more than everyone else's. "Is Reid with you?" she asks. "I've gotta talk to him about the menu. The pears were no good, I think we're better off going with an apple pastry tonight, and I've got something new I've been wanting to try."

I glance from Britt to Nick, inwardly wincing. Oscar's murder, Reid's arrest—they don't know about any of it. How would they? *Unless one of them was there.*

"You haven't heard?" I probe.

"Heard what?" Britt asks.

Something tells me to withhold specifics until I have a chance to chat with each of them independently. I cross my arms over my chest, deciding to keep it vague. "Reid is taking a little involuntary time off."

"Maybe he caught what Katy has," Nick suggests, forehead creased in concern.

If only Reid were suffering from a virus. "Katy Gonzales?"

Katy is one of those servers who never writes any orders down. The first time she waited on me, I played it safe and kept my order straightforward. Since then, I've gotten more . . . creative. No matter how hard I've tried to stump her, she always gets my order right. Through this weird game of restaurant-chess, we've become something akin to friends. She also happened to be working last night.

I recall the way Katy and the other server, Tony Robson, had their heads together, their hushed whispers as they watched their tables, their tips dwindling as the minutes ticked by. I'd be inclined to call in sick after a shift like that, too.

Nick nods, fiddling with the key he'd just dug out of his pocket. "She sent a group text an hour ago, said she was out sick." He walks around me and unlocks the door to the kitchen.

"How much time is Reid taking?" Britt asks, still holding her hefty tote. "What are we supposed to do?"

"Those are totally fair questions and ones I have every intention of answering." *Once I figure out how*, I think.

To buy myself time, I pivot on my kitten heels so I'm facing Nick straight on. "But first, Nick, mind if I have a word with you?"

Nick drops his arm from the handle of the door, his neck growing blotchy. "I guess."

"Come find me when you have those answers," Britt says, giving me a pointed look. She nudges past Nick and me and goes into the kitchen.

"What's up?" Nick asks as the door clicks shut.

I carefully consider my words, not wanting to give anything away. "Have you seen Reid's chef's knife?"

"No, but I haven't clocked in yet."

"Did you notice it last night?"

"You mean apart from when Reid was using it?"

"Yes," I say, biting my tongue to keep from adding an *obviously*.

He scratches the side of his nose. "He left it out on the island counter. Knowing what it means to him, I moved it to the magnetic block."

I feel like my limbs have been doused in ice at the revelation. I try to play it cool. "I thought it was, like, sacrilegious to handle another chef's knife without their permission."

"I was doing him a solid. He must've forgotten it after the mess with the food and his family being there and all." His neck flushes an even deeper shade of red. "I figured it was better on the magnetic block than out in the open."

"Fair enough," I say, holding up both hands in mock surrender. "How late were you here?"

"Around midnight," he answers.

"Are you usually here that late?" I ask. I mean, I know the restaurant business demands long hours, but that is conveniently in the time frame when Oscar was supposedly killed.

"Sure, when I'm in charge of inventory," he says. He shifts on his feet, shielding his eyes from the sun.

He's getting impatient, which means I need to get a move on with my questions.

"Did you see anyone when you were leaving?"

He shakes his head. "Look, did something happen I should know about?"

I ignore his question, leaning my back against the kitchen door. "How are things between you and Oscar?"

"Fine, I guess."

"Really?" I challenge, raising one eyebrow. "Because from what Reid has said, you two don't always see eye to eye."

He doesn't answer immediately and I find myself waiting, somehow knowing he'll eventually cave. Overhead, a flock of geese fly by, their honking punctuating the morning silence. A car creeps by on the street at the end of the alley, no doubt seeking a coveted parking spot.

Finally, he shrugs. "We're not best friends or anything, but we get along okay." His tone is placid and completely unbelievable.

"I'm just trying to figure out how deep the resentment goes."

"We disagree sometimes, but what coworkers don't?"

Now we're getting somewhere. I stand up straighter. "Did you guys have a disagreement last night?"

He opens and closes his mouth. "I don't see what this has to do with anything."

I change tactics. "Do you know what happened to the food?"

"Oscar probably experimented with the recipes," he snaps. Even the tips of his ears are flushed red. "He does that a lot."

"I take it you don't like it when he experiments?"

"It makes for inconsistencies between plates. And what makes him think his palate is better than Reid's?" He rubs one hand over his buzzed head, clearly having kept his frustration pent up for a long time. "Have you ever had anyone change a recipe you painstakingly tested until it was perfect?"

"There are no recipes in winemaking. Everything can change depending on the grape harvest, the sugar concentration, the speed of fermentation." I tick each point off on my fingers, thinking of the harvest in progress at my shop. "I would think the same would be true of cooking. It's an art, open to interpretation."

"You sound like Oscar," Nick says with a pitying smile. "Cooking is a science, requiring precision."

"Maybe," I concede. "But Oscar said he didn't change anything in the recipes last night. He was adamant about it."

I remember the way Oscar's eyes had darted about, how he'd been on the verge of saying something when Camilla disrupted our conversation. If only I could go back in time and make him spill what he knew.

"Too bad Oscar isn't here to defend himself," Nick hisses, then clamps his jaw shut.

My breath comes up short at the harshness in his voice.

"For a good reason," I choke out. "Oscar was murdered last night."

I watch as these words land. Watch as comprehension sinks in.

Blood drains from Nick's face and his grip on his coat slackens. He leans against the wall, bringing his hands to his face, his chest rising and falling erratically.

Is his shock genuine, like he wants me to believe? Or carefully rehearsed?

Either way, I need to keep an eye on Nick. Because right now, he has the greatest motive for killing Oscar. They didn't see eye to eye on pretty much anything in the kitchen, and Nick has kept his frustration bottled up for so long, who knows what he's capable of?

I leave him alone in the alley.

Britt is hard at work in the kitchen. She's layering phyllo dough with butter and a mixture of cinnamon, sugar, and finely chopped pecans. Draped across the kitchen island, the delicate sheets of pastry are so thin they're almost transparent.

"Hate to break it to you, but the restaurant will be closed today," I say, hanging my purse on a spare hook. "And tomorrow, barring some sort of miracle." Call me naive, but I refuse to believe Reid's incarceration will last beyond that.

Britt continues brushing melted butter on the sheet of dough, her hand impressively steady. "It'd be a shame for these ingredients to go to waste."

"What are you making?"

"A spin on baklava, topped with honeyed apples."

My mouth instantly starts watering. Not dissimilar

from a kid in the midst of a long road trip hopefully que-
rying *Are we there yet?* I ask, "When will it be ready?"

"Not for a few hours. I've still gotta work through
that bag." She nods toward her tote, resting next to the
farmhouse sink.

The rest of the kitchen is pristine, all shiny stainless
steel. Without the clanging of pots and pans and sizzling
from the stovetop, the only sound is the hum of appliances. It's oddly comforting.

Britt carefully moves a sheet of phyllo dough using a
rolling pin, tucking it snugly in the pan. Then she brushes
on melted butter and adds a generous portion of the spice-
and-nut mixture on top. The scents wafting from the dish
are heavenly.

"So where is Reid really?" she asks, a stud piercing
twinkling from her nose.

"Arrested." I meet her gaze, the drool-inducing dough
momentarily forgotten. "For Oscar's murder."

"Oscar's what?" she asks, twitching and almost up-
turning the spice mixture.

"Oscar was killed last night," I explain somberly. "In
the alley."

She wipes her brow with her forearm, leaving a trace
of cinnamon there. "Shit."

"You can say that again," I grumble.

"Shit."

I give her a sad smile and she returns to her work, her
fingers deft as they smooth out nonexistent wrinkles
from the most recent layer of phyllo. Emotions dance
over her face—bewilderment, sadness, and uncertainty.
I just dumped a lot on her.

"Reid didn't do it," I say.

"I know," she says. "He doesn't have it in him."

"He's in jail." I take a shaky breath, swallowing the lump in my throat. "Will he be okay?"

Britt is probably the only person I trust to answer this question. In a former life, she worked as a prison line cook in a dinky town in Kansas. Not the most glamorous gig, but with it she paid her way through the pastry arts program at culinary school. After my visit to the local penitentiary this morning, I have even more respect for her.

Britt nods once. "He'll be all right in county."

Relief seeps through my body like that first sip of wine after a long day. I exhale a shaky breath, one I didn't realize I'd been holding.

Britt continues, shaking her head, buttering and sprinkling another layer of phyllo, "But federal prison is another story. I don't know many who would be okay in there, and they're *not right* if they are."

The relief I was just feeling curdles in my stomach. "I have to get him out of there."

She barks a laugh, the light glinting off her platinum hair. "What, like pull a *Shawshank*?"

"More like find the real culprit," I say. "Do you know why anyone would want to kill Oscar?"

"Kill? No. Strangle?" Britt considers this, her lips pursed. "I think Nick would have taken a swing at Oscar if he thought he stood any chance of coming out on top."

I glance toward the door to the alley, where presumably Nick is still processing Oscar's death. I feel a pang of pity for my harsh delivery and vow to check on him soon.

"What makes you say that?" I ask.

"Well, take last night for example, they were at each other's throats."

During the Dinner That Shall Not Be Named. Coincidence? I think not. "What happened?"

"The usual—Nick went off on Oscar for not measuring accurately, and Oscar told Nick to mind his own prep work. I'd had just about enough of their bickering."

There's a pressure in my chest, like Zin is perched right over my heart. Business owners have enough at stake without worrying about squabbles between employees. I wonder if Reid knew how close his sous chefs were to an all-out brawl.

I think back to last night, how Reid left me to fend for myself with his parents, allegedly because of some disaster that required his attention. "That's why Reid rushed back to the kitchen."

"He told us ahead of time not to bug him unless the kitchen was on fire, but by that point, it practically was. He came back and within minutes, order had been restored."

"Not fast enough to save the food, though," I say, musing. "Anything else you noticed?"

She covers the sheet pan and places it in one of the refrigerators. Wiping her hands on a towel tucked into her apron, she says, "Do you know why I became a pastry chef?"

I shake my head, resting my elbows on the island, the metal cool against my skin.

"Because I'm largely left to my own devices." She walks to the sink and starts rinsing apples. "I get to work alone, without having to worry about what's going on around me."

"Right," I say, my cheeks flushing. She as good as told me to bugger off.

I hesitate before asking my next question, swishing the words in my mouth like I would wine during a tasting. "Did you and Oscar get along?"

Britt doesn't answer right away, her focus on polishing the reddish-orange apples until they shine.

"You may as well ask your real question: Did I kill Oscar?"

"Well, did you?" I ask, taking in her toned arms. Britt is certainly strong enough to have overtaken Oscar.

"No," she says simply.

I push away from the island, where I've been idling for too long. "Can you and Nick handle canceling reservations? And letting the rest of the staff know the restaurant is closed until further notice?"

"Sure thing," she says.

I grab my purse and, fiddling with the strap, add, "And if you could, please be subtle."

"Don't worry," Britt says, her gray eyes boring into mine. "I know how to keep my mouth shut."

Her last statement does little to ease my anxiety.

Chapter
Six

The scent of my winery greets me like an old friend. The woody aroma of oak barrels, a hint of sweetness from the grapes, and a touch of acidity from the alcohol. The fresh-paint smell has faded over the last of couple of months, settling into a comforting bouquet that, like a good red wine, is only getting better with age.

Sunlight pours through the storefront floor-to-ceiling windows, dousing the space in a cheerful glow. The oak-barrel tables are surrounded by simple espresso folding chairs and topped with vases of sunflowers and pillar candles—unscented so as not to interfere with the delicate aromas of the wines. Photographs of vineyards from around the world adorn the walls, and wine-bottle lanterns add a touch of whimsy to the decor.

Vino Valentine is located in a modern shopping center in the industrial part of North Boulder. The exterior is clean, white cement and charcoal awnings, with pots full of crimson and golden mums dotting the sidewalk.

Even before the craft breweries and art studios moved in, I saw potential in this location. It's off the beaten track, but not so much as to deter tourists from visiting. There's a hip café next door and, across the street, a nursery with acres of shrubs and gourds galore that lead to the base of the foothills.

I flip the sign on the door from CLOSED to OPEN at precisely eleven o'clock, the clinking glasses welcoming patrons who will start arriving any minute. I bustle around my winery, polishing glasses, organizing the bottles behind the bar from lightest to heaviest, and setting out baskets of palate-cleansing crackers.

It's hard to believe I have a full day ahead of me after the events of the morning. I catch myself yawning as my assistant traipses through the door.

"Not yawning already," Felix says, his voice as deep and velvety as a Syrah.

Felix has jet-black hair, angular eyes, and an infinitely better fashion sense than me. Take today, for example—he's paired skinny jeans and a cardigan with round tortoiseshell glasses and faux fur–lined moccasins. And his palate is even more impressive—and exotic—than his style.

He's worked here for two months now and, while he's done a stupendous job overall, there is one slight hitch: he's a self-proclaimed nomad. Felix told me point blank during his interview that he doesn't stay in the same place for long. He must be close to my age and already he's lived in major cities across the U.S., plus Reykjavik, Prague, and even a short stint in Tokyo. Which is great for conversation but not so great for longevity.

"Rough morning," I say by way of an explanation.

"Want me to do a coffee run?"

"Only if you *don't* want to catch me snoozing in the wine cellar this afternoon," I say, not entirely kidding.

He flashes me a smile. "Be right back." The bell over the door jingles at his departure.

Felix returns five minutes later carrying two to-go mugs and a paper bag. He offers me a blueberry scone and, still peckish after watching Britt make dessert, I readily accept.

"So, what happened this morning?" he asks, biting into a chocolate croissant.

Nibbling on my scone, I give him an abbreviated version.

He watches, slack-jawed, and then shakes his head. "This one time, in Amsterdam, a dude claimed he was on the run for killing the guy who messed with his sister."

Another perk about Felix—he's not easily rattled. There's nary a thing he hasn't seen or heard. "Was he for real?" I ask.

"Never did find out, but he made one helluva paella." He shrugs, polishing off the rest of his croissant. "That's the hostel life—you share your life story over communal dinner then never see each other again."

There's a part of me that envies Felix's ability to move from place to place without looking back, skipping through life like a smooth stone over water. "Not gonna lie, that doesn't sound half-bad right now."

"Don't worry," Felix says, calm as can be. "Everything will work out."

That's easy for him to say; he didn't see Reid handcuffed and unceremoniously yanked down the hall of the jail.

I rub my arms, suddenly chilled. "I hope so."

Felix tosses the pastry bag into the trash bin and washes his hands in the sink. "How's the fall harvest coming along?"

"I stomped cab grapes last night and got them moved to a vat to start fermentation."

"Ah." He gives me a mock pout. "I wanted to help stomp grapes."

"Desperate times," I say vaguely. No need to share how badly I needed to stomp for therapeutic reasons. "You can lead the community event."

"Just as long as I get to experience grape juice squishing between my toes sometime this fall."

"Duly noted." And suddenly all I can think about is Reid. His willingness to dive into a jammy barrel with me, how the world melted away with him by my side. My throat constricts and there's a tightening in my chest. I'm one breath away from succumbing to a massive panic attack.

Luckily, the bell over the door jingles, pulling me back from the proverbial void.

A group of ladies cluster together as they enter the tasting room. They're dressed in head-to-toe royal purple: pantsuits, blouses, and embellished hats. They clutch their handbags (also purple) to their chests as they give the space a once-over before selecting a large table, front and center.

"I'm gonna guess Ralphie's Riesling," I say.

Felix takes his time appraising the group. "They look spicy. Campy Cab, for sure."

"Loser gets coffee tomorrow."

"Deal," Felix says, collecting tasting menus and past-ing a winning smile on his face. "I've got the front. Looks like you have company."

And he's right, I do.

My older brother slouches onto a stool at the tasting bar, setting his ever-present camera bag on the hard maple countertop. Liam's wearing faded jeans, a plain white T-shirt, and work boots, which tells me he's en route to his job, landscaping for the city.

With our matching raven hair, olive skin, and blue-gray eyes, we're obviously related. But appearances aside, we're as different as Côtes du Rhône and Welch's grape juice (I'll let you decide who's who).

While I've always been inherently driven, Liam's primary life goal has been to have a good time, responsibilities be damned. But I've got to give him credit. Recently, he's changed his ways. He moved out of Mom and Dad's basement and into his own place, has had his longest employment stint to date, and, after years of hobby hopping, finally discovered his true passion: photography.

And he's talented. *Really* talented. The pictures on Vino Valentine's website are thanks to his artistic eye, as is the second-place award he nabbed in a local contest.

"Hey, li'l sis," Liam says. "How's it hanging?"

Tears threaten to pour out of my eyes. I stave them off with a smile. "You know about Reid, don't you?"

"A little birdie told me."

"Does this little birdie happen to have red hair, an enviable closet, and the best legal brain on either side of the Mississippi?"

"Sage texted me, not so much requesting as demanding I check on you."

A flicker of amusement lights in my eyes. Liam has had a mega crush on Sage practically forever. And even though she's newly single, for some reason, he hasn't made his move.

He gives a nonchalant shrug. "Reid's gotten into worse jams than this before. He'll be fine."

No doubt Reid and Liam have had exploits in their day, things I'd rather not hear about as Reid's current girlfriend. Still, that's quite the claim.

I cock my head to the side. "I find that hard to believe."

"Fine, fine," he says, throwing his hands up in mock defense. "Nobody expects the Spanish Inquisition!"

And despite the situation, I laugh at my brother's Monty Python impersonation. That is the power of Liam.

I hold up the bottle of cherry wine I know to be Liam's favorite despite his ardent denials of preferring what he refers to as *the pink one*. He shakes his head, which is probably wise given he'll be operating machinery on-site.

From across the floor of my winery, Felix is still charming the table of purple-clad dames. Their table erupts in laughter at something my witty assistant said.

I return my attention to my brother. "So, you're still working the friend angle with Sage, huh?" I scrub down the countertop with a cloth, cleaning up the crumbs from my scone.

"I don't know what you're talking about."

"Yeah, you do," I say, flashing him a knowing smirk. "You should really just ask her out before it's too late."

"I hardly think you're in a position to be giving anyone love advice."

I wince, the innocent ribbing cutting deep. "That was harsh."

"Sorry," Liam says, shifting in his seat sheepishly. "To make it up to you, I'll give you a little warning. Mom's having Sai Iyers and his wife over for dinner tonight." Mom is a lead chemical engineer at NIST Laboratories and Sai Iyers is head of the analytics team there. Although for all intents and purposes, he's who my mom dreams I'll someday work for after I give up on this whole winery endeavor. "Start brainstorming ways to get out of it now because I already heard your name mentioned in that weird hopeful voice of hers."

Generally speaking, things with my parents have been improving. While they don't fully understand my passion for winemaking, they at least want me to be happy, which is more than can be said for Reid's family. Although this dinner invite feels like backsliding, like my mom still hasn't accepted my profession.

"I won't have to try very hard," I grumble, thinking of my rendezvous with the Wallaces. "Have you met Reid's family?"

He holds a hand over his chest. "Sadly, our relationship never progressed to the meet-the-parents stage."

I roll my eyes, a smile playing at the corners of my lips. "What about Oscar?"

"Sure, he was a nice guy. Unreal foosball player." He furrows his eyebrows and coughs to clear his throat. "I was sorry to hear what happened to him."

"Me too. Know anyone who would want to hurt him?"

"Why?" He draws out the question. "Thinking of conducting your own investigation?"

"Something like that."

Liam exhales deeply, leaning his head back. "The guy moved back for his family. The ladies seemed to dig him. Reid trusted him. That's all I've got."

The information wedges itself in my brain. I tuck it away to analyze later. "What excuse are you going to use tonight?" I ask curiously.

"None," he says. "Unlike you, dear sister, I never turn down free food, especially before night class."

"Always looking out for yourself," I say, but inside, I'm beaming. "What's the course?"

"Modernism in Film."

Felix returns behind the tasting bar, a satisfied grin in place. "Four glasses of the Campy Cab. You owe me a coffee." He stacks the menus next to the discard vase and gives Liam a fist bump, the two having met on prior occasions. He continues, "Think I'll go big. Caramel macchiato. No, wait, pumpkin."

Honestly, it's almost like I have two brothers. I heave an exaggerated sigh.

" 'Tis the season, I suppose." I pour glasses of the maroon wine, scents of tobacco and cherries rising from the crystal bowls, and arrange the glasses carefully on a tray. Hopefully the ladies will be impressed enough to purchase a few bottles.

"I'll let you get back to work," Liam says, getting to his feet. "See you tomorrow morning."

"What's tomorrow morning?" I ask as Felix whisks the tray away.

"Reid's arraignment."

Wordlessly, I go around the tasting bar and give Liam a hug. He lifts me off the ground and I swat at him to set me back down, my vision blurry from tears.

"Thanks," I say, sniffling.

"Yeah, yeah," he says, grabbing his camera bag. "Now get back to work, slacker."

The nature of winemaking involves looking forward—creating vintages that need to age for months, or even years, before tasting. It gets one thinking about permanence.

My roots, like those of grapevines, run deep. My family, my business, and my cat are all in Boulder. It's where I've always felt I belong.

Still, who's to say where I'll be next year? What will become of Reid and me? If Vino Valentine will still be a thing?

The truth is: life holds too many unknowns. The only thing we can do is put one foot in front of the other and focus on what we *can* control. Which is exactly what I intend to do.

With Felix manning the storefront, I sneak into the back to work on the harvest.

While the tasting room is warm and welcoming, the back is pure business, stainless steel as far as the eye can see. Along one wall, giant vats reach all the way to the arched ceiling, and opposite those are the crusher de-stemmer, state-of-the-art bottling system, and grape-sorting table. Oak barrels with steel rims dramatically line the back wall, some of the barrels containing a brand-new chardonnay, and others, aging reds.

Giant plastic bins full of red grape varietals early in the fermentation process stand center stage. These grapes have been crushed into a goop called must, which, along with the juices, includes skins, stems, and seeds. At this point, they require attention multiple times a day to ensure that the cap—the grapes floating at the top—doesn't dry out and halt the chemical breakdowns.

It's the latter I focus on now. I grab my punch-down tool from where it's hanging on a rack in the corner, a long pole with a round disk at the end that I've spent far too much time with.

I maneuver the hefty lid off a tub housing pinot noir grapes. Sweet and fruity aromas waft from the surface, with just a hint of tartness. I love the way my winery smells during harvest. Like a farmers market, jam factory, and potential.

Stepping on a stool for extra leverage, I wield the long metal pole. Using the end with the circular disk, I push the cap toward the bottom of the bin, giving a little extra squeeze to coax even more juice from the grapes, and then urge the liquid underneath to the surface.

I repeat these steps—punch down, squeeze, and mix—moving my stool as needed.

To think, it was just two weeks ago when these grapes arrived on my doorstep. They were tiny, only the size of my thumbnail, and a deep shade of purple. Reid, Oscar, and Felix helped me unload the crates.

The sky was tinged with pink and the air crisp as we made trip after trip, moving the crates to the grape-sorting table to remove sticks and stones, and then to the crusher de-stemmer, and finally dumping the must into this bin. It was hard work and we didn't hesitate to voice our complaints, stretching our backs and rubbing sore muscles. All, that is, except for Oscar.

I'd wondered about it afterward and eventually mustered the nerve to ask. Turns out, Oscar was no stranger to hard labor. He'd worked construction jobs throughout high school and culinary school, and even for a short stint afterward when chefs were reluctant to hire someone rumored to have a hard time following directions. Oscar spoke with pride about the work, of what it had allowed him to accomplish, had even referenced picking up a few extra hours on the side to supplement his income. Though I'm not sure why he would have needed to.

The door leading to the storefront opens and I snap back to the present.

Expecting Felix, I shout, not taking my eyes off my task, "You can put some of this in your shoes if you want to feel jelly between your toes."

Imagine my surprise when it's my mother who answers, "Maybe some other time."

I accidentally slop must down my sweater. *Smooth, Parker.*

"What are you doing here?" I ask, hopping down from the stool. I grab a cloth and mop up my shirt, but it's no use; I'm going to have to change.

My mom's frizzy hair bounds out in all directions and her cat-eye glasses are perched at the end of her nose. "Can't a mother sporadically stop by to have a heart-to-heart with her daughter?"

"I guess." My apprehension remains. Because my mom never *stops by* and we don't do *heart-to-hearts*.

When Liam warned me I'd be getting an invite to dinner, I expected a phone call or, if my mom was feeling especially hip, a text message. She's a busy lady with her job, and frankly, I think her equations and experiments make more sense to her than I ever have.

She clutches her periodic table tote to her side. "Liam told me about Reid."

"Oh, right."

I turn my back on my mother so she won't see the heartbreak written on my face. I hang up my punch-down tool, focusing on my smarting palms. Harvest is only half over and already calluses are forming. Just not fast enough.

"How are you?"

"I'm . . ." I trail off, unsure how to respond since I don't even know the answer. "Fine."

She purses her lips. "Sure you are."

I hold a hand to my forehead and then remember it's covered in grape juice, which basically sums up my current emotional state. I clean my face with the same cloth I used on my sweater.

"I'm in shock," I say. "And I have no idea how to help him."

She dips her chin. "Sometimes people have to fight their own battles."

My mom has this annoying tendency of being right. All the time. But I refuse to budge on this; the stakes are too high.

I shake my head, a few strands of hair escaping my headband. "Some battles are too big to face alone."

She nods but doesn't say anything else.

Restless, I pad over to the shelving unit where I store my lab kit.

Yes, winemaking is largely an art, but it's aided by a decent amount of science. And, ever the model student, I've always felt like the more information I have, the better. Which is why, at this point, I take daily measurements.

I bring my lab kit to the bin of pinot and go about my routine, testing the Brix—the amount of residual sugar in the fruit—titratable acidity, and pH, finding them within the limits of what I'd expect.

"What are you doing?" my mom asks, appearing at my shoulder.

"Determining the chemical makeup of the grapes."

"Really?"

"Of course," I say, glancing at her, slightly puzzled. "It helps me determine if fermentation is progressing as it should, or if I need to course-correct."

She pushes her glasses up her nose. "Huh."

I continue, testing the SO2 level and cross-checking this with the volume. Seeing it's a touch lower than I like, I add a couple drops of sulfur dioxide. "To prevent spoilage," I explain. "And to keep the wine tasting fresh."

Mom looks mildly interested, the crow's-feet around her eyes becoming more prominent as she crinkles her forehead.

I clamp the lid on the bin and wipe my hands together.

"That's it?" she asks.

"For now. I'll do another punch down later."

She nods, fiddling with the straps of her tote. "Do you want to come to dinner tonight? The Iyerses are coming over and I'm making enchiladas."

My mom isn't much of a cook. There's really only one dish she knows how to make, and that's chicken enchiladas. They're spicy, savory, and, for me, the ultimate comfort food, but even those saucy rolls of perfection aren't enough to entice me to partake in her career-matchmaking scheme.

"Thanks," I say, and take a sip of water. "But I already have plans to see Reid's family."

"I'll save you a plate in case you change your mind." She gives me a quick hug and then leaves.

As most interactions go with my mom, I'm left feeling the worse for wear. A feat I didn't think was possible. Now, in addition to shock and sadness, guilt gnaws at my stomach.

I wish I was a better daughter, one who could make her proud.

But I have other things to worry about. Things that are in my control. Like finding out why my boyfriend's family was so twitchy around the man he supposedly murdered.

Chapter Seven

There's a fountain outside the St Julien Hotel, only instead of water, it overflows with flowers. Gorgeous blooms that even in autumn encompass a wide range of colors—yellow sunflowers, maroon mums, and fuchsia coneflowers.

The hotel rises in the background, a striking combination of old-school class and new age sleek, with sandstone siding, black-framed tinted windows, and flags welcoming guests from every corner of the globe.

And then there's the valet parking. Not that I own a car.

I used to drive a tan Toyota Camry, my car being inextricably linked to freedom. But after Aunt Laura's accident, nightmarish visions kept flashing before my eyes every time I got behind the wheel. Cars screeching into mine, shattered glass raining down on me in the intersection, and my aunt's bloody face slowly transforming into my own. My chest would grow tight and my palms sweaty, and before too long my nerves couldn't take any more.

Luckily, all of this coincided with the rise of ride-sharing. That, along with public transit, made it easier to find alternative modes of transportation rather than dig into my psyche.

So, yeah, I don't have a car.

Instead, I wave at the valet attendant and enter the posh hotel. The first thing that hits me is the scent. It smells like money—clean, luxurious, and perfumed with some exotic flower. The next thing is the hardwood. Giant pillars, pristine floors, and gorgeous countertops, all made of warm shades of wood.

The lobby oozes comfort with tables and cushiony chairs scattered throughout, dimmed modern lights, and a dual-sided fireplace.

A good-natured concierge stops me, a polite smile on her face. "Can I help you?"

Given that I'm dressed in mismatched slacks and a T-shirt that reads *Got wine?*—the only spare shirt I had at my shop—I appreciate her kindness.

I rest my forearm on the edge of her podium. "I'm here to see the Wallaces. They're expecting me."

She taps a few strokes on her keyboard, her finger-nails expertly painted with tiny pumpkins, and then makes a phone call.

"Good afternoon, Mrs. Wallace, there's a young lady here to see you by the name of—" She holds a hand over the receiver and gestures at me with her hand.

"Parker," I supply.

She relays my name and there's lots of *mmhmm*ing as

she listens to whatever's being said on the other end of the line, her eyes flitting curiously to me.

My palms grow sweaty as I consider the possibility that the Wallaces might refuse to see me, might turn me away, or pretend they don't know me. Which would be the epitome of embarrassing.

Finally, the concierge hangs up and says, "Suite 408. Grab the elevator, just over there—" She nods in the direction of an archway. "When you get to the fourth floor, take a right and keep walking straight on till morning."

"Thanks," I say with a small smile.

I follow her directions into an elevator, studying my reflection in the paneled mirror. I came straight from closing up at Vino Valentine. In a desperate attempt to freshen up, I give my T-shirt a French tuck and finger-comb my hair. It's the best I can do.

The elevator chimes and opens.

For the dread building in my body, you'd think I was doing a death march through Stephen King's version of the Stanley Hotel and not walking down a posh hallway on my way to see my boyfriend's vacationing family.

I reach suite 408 and knock loudly, half hoping they've already left for their dinner in the time it took me to reach the fourth floor. No such luck.

Camilla answers, looking as poised as ever. Cash-mere cardigan, pearls, and snake-embossed heels. With pristine posture, she gives me a once-over, her lips curling malevolently as she takes in the lettering of my T-shirt.

I insulate myself against her icy stare, willing my skin to grow thicker. "Uh—hi, Mrs. Wallace. I mean, Camilla," I say, stumbling over the words. "Mind if I come in?"

"I suppose, but we have to leave soon."

She regally opens the door to their suite. And that clunk you hear? That's my jaw hitting the floor.

Their suite has a full sitting area with a sofa and two lounge chairs surrounding a wrought iron coffee table. Off to one side is the master bedroom with a four-poster king bed, and through a sliding glass door is a private balcony with a breathtaking view of the grassy foothills and slanted Flatirons.

It's that odd time in Colorado when the sun has disappeared behind the mountains but hasn't officially set yet. The sky is still crisp blue, the only sign of impending darkness a yellowish tint to the clouds.

"Hey, Parker," Ben says from where he's parked on the sofa. He's in a suit similar to the one from last night, only now paired with a cream shirt the color of butter.

His father sits beside him, absorbed in the talking heads on whatever news show they're watching on TV. Gary gives me the barest nod of acknowledgment. His face is red and the top button of his shirt is undone, a tumbler of amber liquid in his hand.

"I didn't know you were coming to dinner tonight," Ben says, absently swiping at the screen of his phone. Honestly, it's more like an extension of his hand than a mobile device.

Camila and I speak at the same time—

"She's not."

"I'm not."

Tristan saunters in from the balcony, leaning coolly against the doorframe. He looks like a movie star. Tousled hair, sunglasses, V-neck showcasing a leather necklace with some sort of bronze pendant.

I read once that nerves associated with public speak-

ing stem from the primal part of our brain that feels
threatened when eyes are on us, as if sensing we're being
hunted by a predator. I feel that way now. Like I'm in a
den of wolves.

I swallow and force myself to continue, "I wanted to
talk with you. All of you. About Reid."

"I need another drink," Gary says. He goes to the wet
bar and pours himself a finger of whiskey from a bottle
that probably costs more than my monthly rent.

"What about Reid?" Camilla asks, crossing her arms
over her chest.

"Well, to start, have you tried visiting him?"

"I've been more focused on things that matter." She
primly squares her shoulders. "Like hiring a lawyer."

"Oh," I say, cocking my head to the side. I shouldn't
be surprised that Camilla's answer is basically to throw
money at the situation. Still, the more people on Reid's
side, the better. "My friend is happy to help as long as
you need. She's really good, I promise."

Camilla purses her lips. "I'm sure your friend is fine
for some people, but Reid needs the best. The legal
counsel I've secured will sort out this colossal misunderstanding. Hopefully before our family name is
dragged through the mud."

Of course Camilla is more worried about how this will
affect their reputation—their precious family name—
than about their son. Although, as I home in on her, I
notice flyaway strands from her chignon and extra con-
cealer dabbed around her eyes. Perhaps Reid's arrest is
affecting her more than she's letting on.

"I can't even imagine what people will think if they
find out," Camilla says, arms crossed over her chest.

"They're going to blame us, obviously," Gary grumbles at his wife. "Always blame the parents. Even though I warned Reid about Oscar years ago."

"Warned him how?" I ask. I rest my hands on my hips and lift my chin, trying to mimic Sage's power pose from earlier. Pretty sure it comes across as awkward and stiff. At least I fit in with this crowd.

"That Oscar is nothing but a freeloader," he hisses. "A leech. He roomed with Reid, slept on the couch, while *we*, hardworking Americans, paid for the roof over our son's head." Gary straightens to his full height, his deep voice taking on an alarming tone. "Then there were all the free meals."

The entire room is silent at this proclamation and I catch Ben and Tristan exchanging a worried look, obviously embarrassed by their father's blatant racism, as they should be.

I furrow my eyebrows, unable to stop myself from grinding my teeth. From what I knew of Oscar, he was definitely not a freeloader. "There's no such thing as a free lunch," I mutter under my breath, referencing the first rule of economics.

Gary looks me straight in the eye for maybe the first time. "Oscar tried to prove otherwise."

Well, this explains the tension I noticed between the Wallaces and Oscar. Could it have been something from his past, some misunderstanding from culinary school, that got him killed?

Gary takes a sip from his tumbler and, incidentally, I wonder how many he's had. "He was doing it again."

"That's enough," Camilla cuts in.

"Doing what again?" I prod.

"Taking advantage of my son," he says, his knuckles white around his glass.

"No more." Camilla's hands are visibly shaking. "I can't take any more. It's time to get ready for dinner." With that, she storms into their en suite, slamming the door behind her.

I blink rapidly, unsure how to proceed.

"Well, that's one way to make an exit," Tristan says, pushing his sunglasses on top of his head and slouching into one of the lounge chairs.

"I'd better go fix this." Gary follows after his wife. Their not-so-dulcet voices seep through the door, but their words are too muddled to understand.

And then there were three: Ben, Tristan, and me.

If there's one thing I've learned while owning a business, it's how to force a smile. For the annoying customer who asks question after question about my winemaking process and then doesn't buy a single bottle. For the loud customer who, unprompted, lets everyone know their opinions on everything. And for the slob, who can't seem to eat a palate-cleansing cracker without leaving a Hansel and Gretel–like trail through my winery.

I invoke just such a smile now.

"I didn't know there would be a show before dinner," I say, trying for a joke.

Tristan chuckles but then rubs his temples, turning to his brother. "What are the odds we can get out of going tonight?"

"Zero," Ben says. "Check that, below zero."

"It seems horribly inappropriate," Tristan says. He props his sandal-clad feet on the coffee table. "Our brother is in jail, for chrissake."

The sun basks Tristan in a glow, and suddenly my

heart clenches at how similar he looks to Reid. And Ben, too, really. Sandy-blond hair with amber undertones, somewhat large ears sticking out, and lean builds. Even their mannerisms are the same. From the way they hold themselves to the dimples that form when they smile. It makes me miss Reid even more.

"Can't say I'm surprised," Ben says. He turns up the volume on the TV to block out Camilla's and Gary's voices. Or perhaps it's to veil our conversation.

"Surprised that Reid was arrested?" I ask, perching on the edge of the other lounge chair.

"Well, yeah, given—"

"Now, Ben, there's no need to scare the lady here with our family drama," Tristan says. He acts nonchalant, hands clasped behind his head, but there's a warning in his voice. "Our baby brother has actually managed to secure a girlfriend, let's not ruin it for him."

Properly chastised, Ben mimes locking his lips.

"Wait, you can't leave me hanging like that," I urge, my curiosity heightened. "For what it's worth, I'm in it for the long haul."

Ben spins his phone between two fingers, glancing meaningfully at Tristan. "If that's the case, she deserves to know what she's getting herself into."

"*She* most certainly does," I say before Tristan can impose another gag order. "What exactly am I getting myself into?"

"Strictly speaking, I'm not convinced he's innocent."

It's as if Ben's brutal honesty sucks all the air from the room. The newscasters on the TV rage about a recent political fiasco, their voices fading to a dull buzz in my ears. I stare at the floor, my tongue plastered to the roof of my mouth.

Tristan slides his feet from the table to the plush carpeted floor in one swift motion. "I refuse to believe Reid is capable of murder. If you insist on entertaining the notion that he is, I'm leaving."

They glare at each other and the moment stretches until the tension is palpable. I lean back in my seat, wishing I could be absorbed in the striped upholstery.

"Fine," Tristan says. "I'm outta here."

The door clicks shut behind him. I raise one eyebrow and turn back to Ben, slightly apprehensive at being left alone with the eldest Wallace sibling.

While Sage is a brilliant lawyer, she's never really fit the stereotype. The same can't be said for Ben. He's clean-cut, cold, and calculating, even when it's just the two of us.

I try to camouflage my unease. "So, what exactly makes you believe Reid could be guilty?"

Ben rubs his chin, a gold wedding band glinting on his ring finger. I know from Reid that Ben is married to a woman named Liza, and that they have a two-year-old son, Linus. The last time Reid went home was to meet his then-infant nephew. He'd brought a tiny chef's hat, apron onesie, and whisk-shaped rattle for the little tyke. These innocuous gifts led to Camilla effectively blowing a gasket.

Words were launched like missiles, accusations made about how Reid shouldn't encourage Linus. How the child hadn't ruined his potential yet, still had a chance to make something of himself.

Reid left in a fury and decided that if his family wanted to be a part of his life, they could come to him. And here they are. Though now it strikes me as odd that Liza and Linus didn't come along for this family reunion.

"The thing is," Ben starts, "ever since I heard about Reid and Oscar, this one story keeps coming back to me." He balances his phone on the remote control, more for something to do with his hands than for any practical purpose.

I sense that if I stay silent, he'll continue, and my intuition is proven right a minute later.

"Reid and Tristan used to be best friends. Being closest in age, it made sense." He says this flatly, without even a hint of emotion. "Then one day, everything changed.

"The basement at my parents' house is a dark place. Cavernous, dimly lit, full of dust and cobwebs and appliances prone to loud clanking sounds. We rarely went down there, and when we did, we never went alone."

My blood turns cold and my stomach flips, much like the creeping anticipation on a roller coaster moments before the plummet.

Ben continues, "One day over summer break, Tristan and Reid went down there, looking for a Nerf gun or some other form of childish entertainment."

He hesitates, his face half obscured by slanted shadows. "Are you sure you want to hear this?"

There's no unknowing some things so I pause.

Do I really want to hear this story? From Ben, of all people? Wouldn't it be better to ask Reid?

Only, Reid isn't in a position to tell me. And I have a hunch this is important. If not directly to the case, then to understanding the man I've come to love.

"Yes," I say.

Ben nods once. "Reid apparently came upstairs first and thought it would be funny to lock Tristan down there. He wedged a chair under the doorknob and left him in the basement, through Tristan's escalating pleas, his shouts, his sobs. By our nanny's account, Tristan was down there for two hours before she finally found him. While Tristan was scared to the point of wetting himself, Reid had grown bored and went to play a video game.

"After that, Tristan and Reid were never as close."

As he finishes the tale, my forearms are covered in goose bumps and I feel nauseated, like I've had wine on an empty stomach. I wipe my clammy palms on my knees.

Reid always made it sound like he was in the right in this ongoing battle with his family. Which goes to show there's always more to a story.

Tristan's adamant defense of his brother is admirable and slightly surprising. It makes me wonder if he's protecting Reid or his own masculinity. That's certainly not an anecdote I would want circulated.

I hear my own voice as if from afar. "That doesn't sound like Reid."

Even now, I'm instinctively protecting him. Love has either emboldened me or blinded me.

"I've known him longer than you," Ben answers.

"Touché," I say, giving him a faux-sweet smile. "What do you think is more important, knowing where someone came from or knowing who they are today?"

"You can't have one without the other." He chuckles and scratches the back of his head, amused. "Reid's always had a way with the ladies."

I sit up straighter. "This has nothing to do with me and Reid."

"Right," he says, obviously not buying it. "For what it's worth, I've never met one of his girlfriends." The pitying look he gives me makes me feel vulnerable and naive.

I fold my arms over my chest. "Gee, thanks."

Ben's phone buzzes and he checks the screen. "I have to take this. It's a client."

"Very important, no doubt."

"There's no other kind."

Ben turns his back to me and answers his phone with a professional greeting.

I see myself out, a mess of uncertainty riddling my psyche.

Although I want nothing more than to hightail it home and immerse myself in Zin—the cat and the wine—I want to talk to Tristan first.

I find him relaxing at a wrought iron patio table just outside the hotel lobby. He seems to take up as much space as possible with his legs stretched out before him and both arms draped over the back of his chair.

It's as if his abrupt departure upstairs never happened.

He grins at me when I plop down next to him. "Had enough of the Addams Family?"

I snort. "Let the record show, those are your words, not mine."

Inside the hotel, a wedding party is assembling outside the main ballroom. A bride dressed in head-to-toe tulle clasps a cascading bouquet of calla lilies. Her four bridesmaids hover around her in matching bubble-gum pink dresses, alternately shaking out her train and veil. What an odd tradition our society partakes in.

Not that I'm opposed to the whole *till death do us part* bit, merely the pressure and formality surrounding it.

Tristan turns to me, his sunglasses back on despite the impending dusk. "You're lasting longer than I thought."

"I don't scare easily."

He appraises me—hair caught in a headband, bare arms, and beaded necklace around my neck. I resist the urge to look away.

"No, I don't think you do."

The embellished wooden doors to the ballroom open, letting a serenade of strings escape. The friendly concierge from earlier directs the bridesmaids through the entrance, a task that loosely resembles herding cats. Speaking of cats . . . Reid's kitty is in dire need of rescuing. Best get a move on this conversation.

"How's your conference going?" I ask, remembering the real reason Tristan is in town.

He shrugs. "Eh, too much pomp for my taste."

I give him a bemused smile.

"I know what you're thinking: bloody hypocrite."

He's right; that's pretty much exactly what I was thinking.

"Thing is, if the pomp and schmoozing doesn't benefit me, it's just not worth it."

I shift in my seat to face him. "And it doesn't?"

"I've climbed as high as I care to in the medical field." He says this like it's no big deal, but it makes me wonder if Reid isn't the only Wallace unhappy under the weight of parental expectations.

"What made you decide to become an anesthesiologist?"

"Everyone's happy to see me," he says, brightening. "I bring relief from pain."

"I've never thought of it that way," I concede. "It's

nice you're so protective of Reid." *Especially after the basement debacle*, I hold back, not wanting to make him feel uncomfortable.

"He's my kid brother, what else would you expect?"

The bride disappears into the ballroom, her arm looped through her father's. I watch her march toward her partner, wistfully, until the doors shut, closing off the ceremony to rubberneckers like me.

I change the topic, hoping my abruptness takes him by surprise. "Why were you on edge with Oscar last night?"

"Look, it's not really my thing to talk crap about someone behind their back."

"I respect that," I say. "But how else are we going to find out what really happened?"

Tristan pushes his sunglasses on top of his head, giving me full access to his striking brown eyes, almost gold in this light. And the color isn't the only way they're different from Reid's. Whereas his always hold a spark of passion and impulsivity, Tristan's are intelligent and a touch playful.

He leans forward and rests his elbows on the grooved patio table, searching my face. "You really don't think Reid did it, do you?"

"No, I don't." I cross my arms over my chest. "And I'm getting sick of explaining why to everyone."

"Preaching to the choir," he says, raising his hands in mock defense. "He's lucky to have you, you know."

"Thanks."

"How did you two meet?" he asks. "I take it, it wasn't Tinder."

"Reid came to my winery's opening." I smile at the memory.

Back then, he was nothing more than my brother's new mystery friend. Very hot mystery friend, but off-limits, all the same. My, how things change.

Tristan cups his chin with his hand and gazes at me like I'm another species—an insect, perhaps—that he's trying to make sense of. His attention is unnerving.

"I'd like to see your winery. Vino Valentine, right?"

"That's right." I shift in my chair, the cushion moving with me.

"Tristan, let's go," Camilla says, suddenly behind us. "We don't want to be late."

My body recoils as if she were scratching her nails down a chalkboard.

"Enjoy your dinner," I say. "Flagstaff is really beautiful this time of night."

Flagstaff is the mountain overlooking Boulder, adjacent to the Flatirons, and perched at the top is its name-sake restaurant. The Flagstaff House is notable for its mountain cuisine—bison, elk, and other Colorado specialties—and Camilla mentioned they had reservations there.

"Thank you," Camilla says curtly, her fingers resting on the tabletop. Before she turns away, she adds, in a softer tone than I thought possible, "Let me know if you hear from my son."

"Of course."

The Wallaces depart together, but there's enough distance between each of them that they might as well be walking alone.

Chapter Eight

Back at my apartment, I urge William out of his kitty carrier.

He's a gorgeous cat, sleek black except for a triangle of white on his chest, and wise blue eyes.

I unpack his belongings—his favorite squishy guitar toy, catnip ball, food dish, and water bowl. I set them up close to Zin's, but not so close that she'll sneakily scarf down all his food. Or at least, hopefully she won't.

My feline companion sniffs at William curiously, swishing her tail uncertainly.

William allows her assessment, his ears twitching.

They circle each other, dancing on their paws, and then, in a majorly anticlimactic moment, proceed to go about their own business.

William pads to the corner and commences giving himself a bath, starting with his hind leg.

As for Zin, she basically does the kitty equivalent of shrugging before traipsing to her food dish.

Cats seen to, I luxuriate in a steamy shower, finally washing the must of the day off. I towel-dry my hair and pull on my coziest sweats, hoodie, and socks.

My stomach rumbles and I find myself wishing for a plate of my mom's enchiladas. Instead, I settle for lemon-garlic linguine topped with fresh-grated Parmesan. One perk of dating a chef is that my fridge is usually stocked with delicious leftovers or overflow ingredients from the market.

Thus begins what's sure to be a long night of trying, and failing, to not think of Reid.

Of him in a cold cell. Alone. Of the slip of paper I found in his apartment with another woman's name and phone number on it.

I open the French doors to my balcony a crack, letting in the cool night air and songs of crickets. The soothing sounds and earthy scents ground me. The stillness serves as a barrier to the melancholy threatening to consume me.

Before I shut the door, I pluck a couple leaves of catnip from the plant I keep out there. I'll need to move it inside before the first frost, which could be any day now, given the chill in the air.

I dispense the greenery to each cat, William currently skulking behind a curtain, and Zin on the sofa.

We nibble together—the cats on their leaves and me on my noodles. I pause intermittently to take a sip of hard-earned wine, a red blend from a competing winery whose owners are also good friends of mine. The food and wine successfully fortify me.

Zin mews for another leaf of catnip. I scoop her into

my arms and butt heads with her. "Little glutton," I coo at her.

She gazes at me in complete adoration, a steady purr emanating from her as I scratch behind her ears. Maybe the real love of a lifetime is that between a girl and her cat.

I case her onto her favorite afghan blanket on the sofa and scratch behind her ears. She curls herself in a ball and is soon fast asleep.

I have a feeling sleep is not in my immediate future.

Instead, I dig in my purse for the button I found at the crime scene, still safely wrapped in a Kleenex. Holding the bundle carefully in one hand, I pull back the tissue until I can see the button, careful not to touch it directly in case it's a legit clue.

In this lighting, the cream color looks more golden, too yellow to belong to the stark white chef's coats Reid and his employees wear. There's a tiny bit of thread attached, as if it was unceremoniously pulled from its garment.

I wonder if it belonged to whoever got in a fight with Oscar, or simply to a random tourist lost on Pearl Street.

Either way, I tuck it safely in a Ziploc bag and stash it in the junk drawer, making a mental note to share my discovery with Eli. Then I settle in next to Zin and open my laptop.

The childhood story about Reid is like an earworm writhing through my mind, playing over and over. It makes me wonder: Do I really know him as well as I think I do? And if I don't know the man I've given my heart to, what about someone like Oscar? Who knows what sort of woes might be hidden in his past?

I find myself navigating social media and scrolling through Oscar's feed.

He hadn't been very active in recent days, likely having been too busy with work, family, or the sheer effort of adulting.

I delve deeper into his past, where a photo from nearly a decade ago catches my eye. It's of him and Reid, their arms thrown around each other's shoulders and carefree grins on their faces. Their free hands are extended, holding matching plates of some fancy dish—French, by the look of the sauce. From the dozens of comments, I gather they'd just been named first and second in their class at the Culinary Institute of America.

I switch to Spoons's profile. Social media can be harsh, trolls and misinformation in abundance. But, as it turns out, the media has been kinder to Reid than it was to me. Whereas the masses blamed me and my chardonnay for the death of a renowned critic faster than you can say Gewürztraminer, complete with its own damning hashtag, Reid is being hailed as a genius chef who was in the wrong place at the wrong time. A double standard, perhaps, or maybe stabbing is more acceptable than poison in our industry.

Opening a new tab, I type *Oscar Flores* into a search window. Articles with today's date float to the top. I click on one by a local publication called the *Boulder Camera*.

The article doesn't say much more than what I already know. Oscar was found dead in the early hours of the morning under suspicious circumstances. A suspect was in custody based on witness testimony. The law enforcement agency was making the case a priority. Which, based on my knowledge of such things, means they want this case wrapped up and the perpetrator behind bars right quick.

And then I find the break I need—the smallest detail that probably wouldn't mean anything to anyone but me: the witness is an accordionist who performed on Pearl Street earlier that evening.

Details come back to me. The scents—waffle cones, incense, barbecue—and then the sounds. There was an accordion trio playing "Bad Romance" on Pearl Street the night of the Dinner That Shall Not Be Named. I'd passed it, had even contemplated stopping and listening, before opting for grape stomping instead.

Opening yet another fresh tab, I search for accordion bands in the area. From there, I scroll through the results until I see a photo accompanying a link that looks promising. The Squeeze Keys are a group formed of three guys who came together because of their mutual appreciation for the worldly instrument.

The best part: their schedule is on their website. And conveniently, they'll be playing at Union Station in Denver Saturday afternoon, which is only two days away.

Hopefully this mess will be over by then, but if not, at least I have a lead.

You can tell a lot simply by looking at a glass of wine. The color, consistency, legs. All of this hints at the alcohol concentration, aging (if there was any), flavors, and presence of tannins.

People are the same way.

Whether we like it or not, the way we dress and carry ourselves says something about our person, our confidence, and our credibility.

Which is probably why I'm putting way too much effort into deciding what to wear this morning.

I don't know why I'm bothering. It's not like the judge is going to notice my pencil skirt and blouse and say, *Oh, that ensemble is so fabulous—that maroon tweed, that embellished lace!—obviously this has all been a huge mistake and your boyfriend is completely innocent!*

And yet, I can't help but try on outfit after outfit until I find the perfect one.

Checking my reflection in the mirror, I tuck in the front of my blouse and smooth out the wool of my pencil skirt. My usual beaded necklace is strung around my neck and my locks are straightened to frame my face.

I do a cat-check before I leave. Zin stares longingly through the panes in the French doors where a songbird hops from foot to foot on the balcony. And William, much like his human counterpart would be doing at this hour, is prowling in the kitchen.

After topping off their food and making sure their toys are placed for maximum entertainment, I wish them a harried good-bye. "Wish me luck. Or Reid, really. And I really need to stop talking to cats."

Reid's arraignment is being held at a courthouse inside Boulder County Jail. Which means I need to get an Uber. To the jail. It's as awkward a ride as it sounds.

The driver who accepts my request is a scrawny guy named Earnest who eyes me curiously in the rearview mirror as we make our way to East Boulder and turn down Airport Road. We pass the park, where dogs are playing fetch and bikers are showing off their moves, and make our final ascent up a hill with a breathtaking view of the mountains.

Earnest slows after we enter the parking lot, uncertain where to drop me off.

"The main entrance is on the north side."

"Been here before?" he asks, following my directions.

"No, but I figured it was time I turned myself in." I wait half a beat, my eyes meeting his briefly in the mirror before I add, "I'm kidding."

He chuckles halfheartedly and seems all too relieved when I finally get out of his Impala, practically peeling away in the dirt parking lot.

Sage is waiting for me outside the entrance to the jail. She's wearing slate-gray slacks, an emerald-green shirt, and lightning bolt earrings. Her hair is swept back into a low ponytail and she's clutching a no-nonsense leather briefcase.

"I thought Camilla kicked you to the curb," I say by way of a greeting.

"She tried," Sage responds huffily. "But Reid refused to meet with her fancy-schmancy lawyer, insisting on sticking with yours truly." There's an unmistakable hint of pride in her voice. "Did you get any sleep?"

"A little," I say. Although, honestly, I'd be surprised if I managed to get more than a couple of hours with my brain mulling everything over and two cats vying for space in my bed.

Sage sees through my lie. "Don't worry, these usually go fast."

I shift to the side to let an older gentleman pass us, gravel crunching beneath my feet. The compound is just as intimidating as it was yesterday. The concrete is cold and the bright-red accents come across as harsh.

Sage's phone buzzes, offering a welcome distraction. She checks the screen and looks up in surprise. "Wow, he's on time for once."

"Who?"

"Liam." She stashes her phone in her pocket and cranes her neck, scanning the full parking lot.

I can't help the grin that spreads across my face. "So, you two have been texting a lot," I say, baiting her for information.

She brushes a stray lock of strawberry-blond hair from her face. "You think so?"

"More than he texts with his own sister."

She frowns, as if this hadn't occurred to her. "Well, we've been worried about you, Miss Never-Asks-for-Help."

"Hey, I've gotten better," I say defensively. It's true; while I used to see myself as an island, fully capable of doing everything solo, I've recently tried to take my self-reliance down a notch. "I asked you for help."

She bats her eyelashes at me. "And aren't you glad you did?"

"Indubitably." I hold a hand over my heart. "I bow before your brilliance and beauty."

"Not before I regale you about your wit, charm, and general badassery."

"Aw, talking about me?" Liam asks, sauntering up. "Don't stop on my account."

He's wearing checkerboard Vans, slim jeans that accentuate his gangly limbs, and a TARDIS T-shirt, which tells me he has the day off work. He adjusts his camera bag, slung over one shoulder.

A tinge of red appears on Sage's cheeks.

"You wish," I quip, going in for a side hug. He crushes me with his arm, surprisingly strong from all the landscaping. "Thanks for coming."

"Wouldn't miss it," Liam says. "Gotta have something to hold over Reid. The last time he got in trouble was a bar fight in Telluride, and that was ages ago."

"Can you please refrain from mentioning that inside?" Sage asks. "No reason to cast any more suspicion on my client." Her voice swells as she says *my client*.

"Sure thing." Liam salutes her and then focuses on me. "You doing okay, Parker?"

Early on, Liam cast himself in the role of my protector. In elementary school, when I was bullied for requesting extra math assignments (served me right, I know), through high school, when the class jerk spread a nasty rumor about me (which put me off hotdogs for life). And now in adulthood.

"Fine," I answer, crossing my arms over my chest. "You should really be more worried about how Reid is doing."

"He's okay," Sage says. "There's a good chance we'll get him off the hook."

"And if we don't?" I ask, my stomach twisting itself into knots that rival those I use for climbing.

"Then we hope bail is set low enough that he can sleep in his own bed tonight." She glances at the screen of her phone. "Let's get inside. It's showtime."

My only experience with courtroom drama is from *Law & Order* reruns, and they apparently leave out some details.

The courtroom consists of three sections, each separated by a glass partition.

The first is for the general public, and is almost as small as the lobby, with three measly benches. Liam and

I wedge ourselves among parents, siblings, friends, and significant others of inmates. I rubberneck my fellow onlookers, trying not to seem too obvious.

I hardly expected Reid's family to show up, but it still stings that they couldn't make time for the son they supposedly came into town to visit.

I continue my cursory scan, surprised to see Eli Fuller in the back row, his gaze stubbornly fixed ahead of him. And I'm even more surprised to see Britt Hartmann a few seats to his right. What Reid's pastry chef is doing here, I don't know. She catches my eye and I hurriedly face forward.

Sage is in the central area, where the proceedings will take place, relegated to the perimeter with the other defense lawyers until their respective case numbers are called. She doesn't seem the least bit nervous, no doubt thanks to her experience clerking for the esteemed Judge Manuel Acosta, or The Manual, as he's affectionately known to us for his encyclopedic knowledge of everything related to the law profession. He expects the best from his protégés and, in return, is their staunchest supporter. Which is maybe why he's cool with Sage doing this pro bono—to give her a taste of her career aspiration: criminal law.

Public prosecutors lounge at a long table piled high with manila folders, chattering pleasantly while they wait for the session to start. The judge's bench towers above us lowly commoners, vacant except for a bailiff hastily organizing papers. The bench itself is gorgeous, mahogany sporting a placard engraved with Boulder County judicial district information, and perched off to the side is the recorder, sipping from a Big Gulp with a bored expression on her face. Officers flank every entrance.

There's movement across the way as a dozen inmates are led into the third glass-encased area.

I dig my fingers into the armrest to keep grounded as I scan each face for Reid. He comes in last, followed by a deputy who chuckles at something Reid's just said.

The sight of him sends a jolt of electricity through my body. Leave it to Reid to somehow pull off an orange jumpsuit. The cut enhances the strong angles of his cheekbones; the orange, the copper undertones in his hair; and the thin fabric, his lean muscles.

My breath hitches as I wonder when the next time I'll be able to hug him—to even touch him—will be.

Reid gazes hungrily through the glass partitions, scouring the courtroom and then the visitors' area. When his eyes finally meet mine, they lock on and, I kid you not, he winks.

At least he still has his good humor.

"Knew he'd be happy to see me," Liam whispers at my side.

"Uh-huh," I say, the entirety of my focus on Reid.

Even though he exudes his usual air of nonchalance, there are dark circles under his eyes and a bruise blossoming around the gauze covering his original cut. I have a hunch he slept less than I did last night, that he couldn't afford to.

"All rise," the bailiff says. "Honorable Judge Rhya Jones presiding."

I get to my feet as the judge, a steely-eyed woman with her hair pulled into a severe knot, enters the courtroom, her black gown cinched with a golden pin. She settles at her podium and shuffles through the papers the bailiff worked so hard to organize.

"Please be seated," Judge Rhya Jones says in a commanding voice. With a pointed look at an inmate who stubbornly remained on his derriere, she adds, "For those of you who actually stood." She's clearly not one to be trifled with.

I sit back down, tucking my pencil skirt beneath my legs.

"Let's start with case number"—the judge rattles off a stream of nonsensical digits—"Reid Michael Wallace."

The judge peers toward where Reid is standing with his cuffed hands clasped in front of him. "Hi, Reid," she says.

"Your Honor," Reid answers, nodding respectfully.

She shifts her attention to the attendants in the courtroom. "Will the counselors please announce their names for the record?"

Sage springs to her feet and makes her way to the podium. She lowers the microphone and states, "Sage Bennet on behalf of Mr. Wallace."

The judge continues and soon I'm so lost in the legalese she might as well be speaking a foreign language. The words that stand out chill me to my core: "First-degree murder of Oscar Hernandez Flores."

Sage stands ramrod straight, her hands gripping the sides of the podium as she listens intently. There's a tiny crease between her eyebrows that speaks to her mounting concern. It's the same look she had going into the final Avengers film.

The judge comes to a brusque close. "How will the defendant plead?"

"Not guilty," Sage says, her voice strong.

Reid doesn't blink, doesn't seem to breathe. His shoulders are back, though he must be crushed by the weight of all that's transpired.

Judge Rhya Jones looks down her nose at Reid. "Further proceedings will be set for the thirteenth of September," she says.

I feel a stab to my heart. That's three days from now, an entire weekend away. I stare at Reid, my vision growing blurry around the edges.

At my side, Liam takes my hand and squeezes it.

The judge continues, "Bail will be set to four hundred thousand U.S. dollars."

A wave of dizziness overwhelms me as the reality of what I just heard sinks in. Liam's hand is the only thing keeping me level, like an anchor to a balloon threatening to escape.

Reid starts, "Your Honor—"

"Young man, I would advise you to let your attorney speak for you," she interjects. "Given the circumstances, be grateful I set bail at all." And with that, the hearing is over. The judge shuffles through papers, already moving on to the next case.

I slump forward, my elbows on my knees, fighting the sobs threatening to rack my body. I bite my lower lip, hard enough that it brings me back to the present.

Keep yourself together, I tell myself, *for Reid.*

So, I take a shuddering breath and lift my chin, just in time to watch Reid escorted from the courtroom.

I don't like what I see in his downcast eyes. His hunched posture.

Defeat.

Chapter Nine

Though it grates on my psyche to admit it, there's only one person I can think of who might be able to help Reid.

I stumble outside the jail to make my call, leaning against one of the red metal pillars framing the entrance. My hand shakes as I bring the phone to my ear.

Camilla answers on the first ring.

I don't have the energy for pleasantries, so I cut to the chase, telling her about Reid's arraignment and the astronomically high bail set by the judge.

"Reid needs you," I say, my voice full of anguish. "Please."

"He made it very clear he doesn't need me or my money."

"At the moment, he could use both." The door to the jail opens behind me, but I ignore it, covering my other ear with my free hand.

A gust of wind sends dirt and dried leaves skittering across the parking lot, the dry air reeking of exhaust from a nearby construction site. It's enough to make my already-uneasy stomach clench.

I hold my breath as Camilla chats with someone on her side of the line, a muffled conversation I can't make out.

When she returns, her tone is huffy. "I'm afraid that won't be possible."

My hope evaporates like the angel's share of wine— lost to the wind. "Why not?"

"Because when Reid cut ties with our family, he cut ties with our bank account as well," she says curtly. "He can't decide he wants to be a part of this family when it suits his needs."

"But he's your son," I argue. "You have to do something."

"I tried to do something and Reid dismissed me without so much as a thank-you," she hisses. "He got himself into this mess, he can get himself out of it."

Bile coats my throat as I all but gnash my teeth in frustration. "But he didn't. You don't understand."

"I understand more than you know, young lady," she says.

I freeze, an iciness spreading through my limbs. "Wait, what does *that* mean?"

"I must be going."

Before I can utter a protest, the line goes dead. Camilla hung up on me. And just when things were getting interesting.

I stare at my phone, my mind reeling through possibilities. My head hurts from all the different jigsaw pieces, none of which seem to fit together.

"Sounds like that went well," a voice says behind me.

I spin around to find Britt watching me. In the sunlight, her spiky platinum hair is so bright I have to shield my eyes. Her skin is tanned and tough like leather, and she's wearing cargo pants with more pockets than I have utensils.

"Yeah, about as good as Reid's hearing went," I say sarcastically.

"The judge was tough," she says, giving me a wry smile. "From her perspective, she's protecting citizens by keeping a potential murderer off the street."

If possible, my spirits plummet even further. "Is that supposed to make me feel better?"

"No," she says. "But you don't strike me as someone who'd prefer niceties instead of perspective."

I can only blink at that.

Her face impossible to read, she takes a step toward me. She's so close I can almost make out the cursive of the tattoo winding up her neck, the lower letters hidden by her black tank top.

"Guess this means Spoons will be closed this weekend," she says.

I exaggerate a wince. "That's gonna hurt the bottom line."

"And then some. I'll alert the forces."

"Thanks, Britt," I say. "You were able to get ahold of everyone yesterday?"

"All except for Katy. I left voice mails but never heard back."

A jolt of anxiety slithers up my spine. Nick mentioned Katy was sick yesterday. I wonder if she's really at home fighting off a bout of the flu, or if she has some other reason for lying low. Either way, it's time I paid Katy a visit. "I'll let her know. Hey, why did you come?"

She shifts uncomfortably and, for a second, I'm not sure if she'll respond. "Solidarity. Because I know what Reid's up against."

"Oh."

Britt shrugs, entirely unconcerned.

The awkwardness of the moment stretches on and I can sense her desperation to escape. But I have one more question first: "What does your tattoo say?"

"'Time is undefeated.'"

"Who said that? Gandhi?"

"Rocky Balboa," she says, sliding aviator shades in place. "Tell Reid I said to hang in there."

I chuckle and then rub my neck, thinking about the pain threshold required to have a tattoo etched into that sensitive patch of skin.

Sage helps me check in for my visitation with Reid.

I honestly don't know what I would do without her. Not see my boyfriend, for one. Wallow in a massive vat of self-pity, for another, and probably consume far too many pints of Ben & Jerry's.

Instead, Sage stands next to me in the dinky jail lobby, all of the seats currently occupied, while I wait for the receptionist to call my name.

Liam is outside snapping pictures with his Canon Rebel T7i—something about forced captivity juxtaposed with Colorado open space—although I have a hunch he's lingering for moral support. I appreciate the gesture.

I can't stop fidgeting, adjusting the frills of my blouse and straightening the chain of my beaded necklace. When an officer finally calls my name, I practically leap out of my suede ankle boots.

"Be right back," I say to Sage, my voice sounding weird and distant.

"Remember," she mock-chides. "Only *virtual* lip-locks allowed."

"I'll try to contain myself."

More names are called and five other visitors line up to step through the metal detector.

Our designated officer/guide has the open and fresh face of an idealist. A few years my junior, his uniform is still shiny and new.

He lists rules as we follow him through institutional hallways that smell like bleach. I try to keep track of the many things we're not allowed to do, but by the time he pauses outside a red metal door, I've already forgotten the first thing he said.

The visitation room is sparse. The walls are bare and the only furnishings are cold metal tables and matching chairs. I realize, with a jolt, this is probably to keep inmates from trying anything that might harm visitors, or themselves.

Before I've fully oriented myself, Reid enters the room, escorted by an officer. He's still in handcuffs, an orange jumpsuit, and slippers. Because even shoelaces could conceivably be a weapon in a cellblock.

Reid and I settle into chairs across from each other, while other visitors and inmates do the same. I'm tempted to reach across the table and take his hand, but touch of any kind is strictly forbidden.

So, instead, I settle for a lighthearted greeting. "William says hello."

Relief washes over Reid's face and he cracks a smile. "Is he at your place? Is Zin okay with it?"

"Zin has been very accommodating, although I suspect she was waiting until I left to pilfer his food."

"Don't worry, he can handle himself around the la-dies," he says, chuckling, referencing yet another thing William has in common with his human counterpart. "How's the harvest?"

"Good." I raise one eyebrow at him. "You know this doesn't count as an excuse to skip out on punch downs."

"Damn." He snaps his fingers. "Why else would I be in here?" Then he breaks out the dimples. The blessed dimples, visible even through his beard. "Any more shipments come in yet?"

"Thankfully, no. The last thing I need right now is for a truckload of grapes to show up unannounced." I lick my lips, my carefree facade slipping. "I can't believe this is all happening."

He rubs his face with both hands, the handcuffs clinking. Shock and sadness are etched in his features, in his downcast eyes and creased forehead.

He lets out a shuddering exhale as he says, "Tell me about it."

I lean forward. "Are you okay in here?"

"The food leaves something to be desired." An ironic grin spreads across his face. "If I'm on my best behavior, eventually I may be able to help out in the kitchen."

My heart plummets to somewhere around my navel. "You're not going to be in here forever. We'll get you out." My voice wavers, peeling away at my fake bravado.

He just shakes his head.

"Seriously, things just don't line up. I was talking to your family and—"

Reid interrupts me, his voice eerily quiet. "You talked to my family?"

"Well, yeah, you asked me to call your mom," I say. "And I tried to get them to post bail."

He drops his head into his hands, his fingers mussing his hair even more. His jaw is set when he lifts his chin. "I don't need or want their help."

"But—"

"Parker, stop," he says. "I mean it. I don't want anything from them."

"Fine, then tell me where you went between leaving the restaurant and coming to Vino Valentine." I feel feverish with excitement, like the flush after a few sips of celebratory champagne. "If we just confirm where you were the rest of the night, maybe this will all go away."

He shakes his head, sadness dampening the movement. "The detective, Sage, they already know my alibi. It doesn't account for enough time, doesn't even matter."

It matters to me! I want to shout. Steam practically spouts from my ears.

I keep my tone even as I say, "I'd like to hear it."

"Why? So you can go on some wild sleuthing goose chase?" He shifts in his seat and readjusts his hands, the metal of the handcuffs biting into his raw wrists. "I won't let you put yourself in danger. Not for me."

The softness in his voice takes me aback. I'm hyperaware of our precious seconds together, ticking by as I struggle to find words.

"I have to do this for you," I finally choke out.

We stare at each other, his eyes flashing like lightning in a storm, and mine full of stubbornness and pride.

His gaze falls to the tabletop, his mouth twisted into an uncharacteristic frown. "Somehow, I knew you'd say that."

"What else would I do?"

"Leave it to the law enforcement agents and focus on the harvest, your business—"

"Which wouldn't be where it is without you," I snap, earning a warning look from an officer. I wave an apology and continue in a whisper, "What about Spoons, your dream?"

"Maybe not all dreams are meant to come true," Reid says with a shrug.

"I refuse to believe that."

We settle back in our chairs and I imagine what the officers guarding the visitation room must see—just another couple, a boyfriend behind bars and his devoted girlfriend staring doe-eyed at him. When in reality, we're patsies caught in the cross fire of a killer's agenda.

And it stings. It really stings.

Reid maneuvers his hands to the center of the table. I do the same. They're mere centimeters from each other; one movement and we would be touching. The noncontact, the sheer closeness, sends electricity from my fingertips all the way to the tips of my toes.

Our surroundings melt away—the cold metal of the chairs, the hushed whispers of conversations of other visits, the officers monitoring our every move. For a moment, it's as if we're enclosed in our own private bubble.

Reid watches our hands, mesmerized. "At least promise me you'll be careful."

"I promise," I say, keenly aware of our nontouching and sorely tempted to twitch my finger. "So, tell me more about that night."

"There's not much to tell. I saw my family off, worked in the kitchen until we were caught back up, and then packed up and left."

"What did you pack up? Where did you go?"

And with my entirely reasonable questions, the bubble pops.

Reid moves his hands to his lap and I can practically see the cogs churning in his brain, trying to discern which scrap of information to give me.

Maybe he's still upset that I went to his parents for money without his permission, or maybe this is another play to keep me safe, because in the end, he doles out as little as possible: "I didn't do this, Parker."

"I know." I nod at the gauze on his forearm. "How's your cut?"

"It's nothing."

"Just like your alibi is nothing?" My patience unravels at the seams, my composure falling away like forgotten grapes from a vine. "Like your response to when I told you I loved you."

And do you know what Reid says to that? Nothing.

Because the same severe guard who escorted Reid in approaches our table. A weight settles over my chest even before he opens his mouth to speak the dreaded words that are coming too soon, too fast: "Time's up."

I can barely stand the look on Reid's face—torn, pained, like there are a million things he wishes he could say. But if wishes were horses, beggars would ride, millennials would never have to engage in phone conversations, and Oscar would still be alive.

Reid is forced to his feet and tugged away from me. The silence between us grows into an abyss as the door slams shut behind him.

One thing becomes abundantly clear: I'm in way over my head, romantically and otherwise.

Chapter Ten

I've always loved the way Reid eats. That might sound strange, but it's true.

When Reid eats, he loses himself in flavors and textures, commenting on various ingredients and cooking styles, lamenting the artistry of unique combinations and techniques. With him, food is more than nourishment, it's an experience.

I reflect on this as I sit in a booth across from Liam and Sage. We're at the Twenty Ninth Street mall at a trendy diner called Snooze, complete with retro vinyl, wingback chairs, and pendant lamps. The menu features classic brunch staples—pancakes, eggs, hash browns—along with a few modern dishes that are all the rage, like the avocado toast in front of me.

Emotions swirl through me like snowflakes in a blizzard. The events of the morning crowd my mind, vying for attention, each one a stab at my carefully constructed veneer.

The judge's allegation, *First-degree murder of Oscar Hernandez Flores.*

Camilla's callous assertion, *He got himself into this mess, he can get himself out of it.*

And Reid's defeated remark, *Maybe not all dreams are meant to come true.*

I've barely said a word since returning from my visit with Reid, which is probably why Sage and Liam dragged me here. They took one look at my face and ushered me from the jail and all that it contains.

"Okay, spill," Sage says, setting her silverware down with a *clink.* Her giant stack of blueberry pancakes is already half-demolished.

"It's nothing," I say.

To avoid having to talk, I take a bite of avocado toast, topped with a soft-boiled egg, dill, and a splash of fresh-squeezed lemon juice. I might as well be chewing saw-dust, to no fault of the food. I chase it with a sip of coffee, cradling the mug.

Sage and Liam exchange a pointed glance. Maybe the two of them together isn't such a good idea. Think of all the trouble they could cause me if they teamed up.

"I just . . . can't."

Liam lets out an aggravated sigh. "Am I gonna have to kick Reid's ass when he gets out of there?"

"No," I say quickly, knowing Liam would 100 percent follow through if he thought I was being mistreated. "That won't be necessary."

"Then you've got to give us something," Sage says. "What happened in there?"

"Reid's keeping me at a distance because he's trying to protect me."

I rub my temples, replaying our conversation. All of the things he said and, more important, didn't say.

That's when I remember something. "Sage, where did Reid go before coming to Vino Valentine that night? What's the rest of his alibi?"

Sage opens and closes her mouth, bunching her napkin in her fingers. "I can't tell you."

"Very funny." I fake-laugh but then blanch at the resolve in her eyes. "You're serious?"

"Client confidentiality," Sage says with a tiny shrug.

She leaves the table before she accidentally lets anything slip, Liam not so subtly studying her retreating figure.

I don't know what to make of Sage's silence except that, client privilege or not, she wouldn't hang me out to dry. I have to believe that whatever Reid was up to, it has nothing to do with me or our relationship. But then, why does he have the name and number of some random chick in his apartment? A chick who has a bubbly voice and annoyingly flirtatious laugh.

"Do you know a Susie?" I ask Liam.

He shifts his focus to me. "Several, in fact."

"Are any of them close with Reid?"

A shadow passes over his features and he narrows his eyes. "I'm not sure. Why?"

"No reason." I take another bite of toast, my appetite still nonexistent. "So, how are things with Sage?"

"Eh," Liam says, snapping a pic of his half-consumed breakfast burrito.

He's of the belief that perfectly curated foodie photos

are on their way out of style and reality is on the rise. I'm apprehensive, to say the least.

He continues, slouching deeper in the booth, "I'm afraid I'm stuck in the friend zone."

"But you two seem to really be connecting."

"Sure, we text and hang out more, just not over candlelit dinners." He takes another shot, this time including my plate in the frame as well.

I cock my head to the side and take a sip of coffee. "Well, have you asked her to a candlelit dinner?"

He lazily scratches the top of his head, his dark hair sticking out in all directions. "Not exactly."

"I'll take that as a hard no." I click my tongue. "You should ask her. Before it's too late."

"Before what's too late?" Sage asks. She slides back into our booth and spears a bite of pancakes with her fork.

"Nothing," Liam and I say in unison.

"Okay, moving on." She points her fork at me. "I have news."

I practically bounce in my seat, fully expecting news related to the investigation. Instead, Sage surprises me. "I have a date tonight."

Liam chokes on his orange juice, coughing into his napkin.

"Really?" I ask, overenunciating the word.

Sage ended things with her longtime boyfriend, short-time fiancé earlier this summer. It was a big deal and left her uncertain about what she wants in life and love. To my knowledge, she hasn't been out with anyone since, apart from my brother, which was apparently just as friends.

"Who's the lucky guy?" I ask, since Liam is still sputtering.

"His name's Arthur. He works for a local firm we have a lot of dealings with. The Manual introduced us."

"A lawyer?" Liam asks, his voice raspy.

"Yes." She crinkles her nose. "It'll be fine, right?"

She looks from me to Liam, her freckles practically jittering in agitation. Her panic is enough to compel Liam and me to set aside our own concerns.

"Definitely," Liam says, flashing her a supportive smile. My heart breaks at how hard that one word must have been for him to utter.

"Absolutely." I raise my mug to hers in a mock toast. "I'll come over later and help you get ready."

While I'm always happy to help a friend in need, I have ulterior motives. I want to pick Sage's brain and find out if my brother stands a chance with her or if she's really serious about this new guy. Either way, it's nice to get my mind off murder.

Pumpkin macchiato in hand, I open the door of Vino Valentine, the bell jingling overhead.

When I asked Felix to open the shop for me, he readily agreed, with a friendly reminder that I owed him coffee.

He's manning the tasting bar now, where a young couple is perched, swirling and sipping like pros. Felix is talking them through my winemaking process in that deep, gravelly voice of his, making it sound much more glamorous than it is.

Today his hip yet eclectic fashion has him in a chambray shirt, tweed slacks, and a thick tortoiseshell bracelet that matches his glasses. His black hair is styled into a fauxhawk and, if I'm not mistaken, he applied mascara to the lashes around his eyes.

Felix finishes listing the varietals that compose my Mount Sanitas White before meeting me at the other end of the bar.

"Special delivery," I say, depositing his to-go mug on the maple countertop.

He sniffs at the steam rising through the tiny opening in the lid. "I detect sweet notes, a bitter earthiness, and a bouquet of autumnal spices."

I snort, shaking my head. "You've been spending too much time here." I stash my purse beneath the cash register. "How are things?"

"Uneventful." He takes a large gulp of his macchiato. "How was your morning?"

Not sure how to sum it up, I go with the simplest answer: "Eventful."

He furrows his eyebrows together, gesturing with his mug. "Your favorite customer is here."

A genuine smile spreads across my face. Perched at an oak-barrel table near the storefront windows is an older lady named Gladys. Clad in all velvet and proudly displaying a head of silver hair, she's an intimidating broad. Until you get to know her, that is. Then she's a marshmallow.

After she attended my first VIP party, she quickly turned into one of my biggest fans, usually bringing one of her many friends or grown godchildren with her to my winery. Today, though, she's alone. She's gazing at the rolling foothills out the window, where the wind is whipping the trees and grass against the slope, making the shimmering glades into a pattern resembling large fish scales.

Gladys is sipping a taster of the Snowy Day Syrah, which I know to be her favorite. I bring the bottle with me and top off her glass. "Staying out of trouble?"

"Not if I can help it." Her eyes twinkle as much as the sparkly brooch on her chest.

"That's what I like to hear."

"Do you have anything new to taste?" she asks, leaning forward in anticipation. "A new blend, perhaps?"

Nerves course through me at her eagerness. My dream of opening a winery may have come true, but keeping it alive is a horse of a different varietal. My hard-earned customers expect—and deserve—something new. Something unexpected, with incredible depth of flavor, and dangerously drinkable.

Only, there's this underlying fear: What if I can't deliver?

When I'm doing manual work like punch downs, I can squash my self-doubt by focusing on the process. But blends require repetition and finesse. Altering the proportions of each varietal that compose the blend by even a fraction of a percent changes the outcome. And with infinite possibilities, it's hard to stay out of my own head.

I swallow the lump in my throat. "You'll be the first to know when there is." I tap my fingers against the neck of the bottle and redirect, my favorite brand of denial. "Stay tuned for a grape-stomping activity in the next month. Then you can put your own stamp on the next harvest."

She wiggles in her seat. "I've always wanted to try that."

"You'll be a natural," I say, slowly backing away from her table. "I'll send you the details as soon as I've got them. Enjoy your wine."

I return to the tasting bar, where Felix is pouring a

taster of the Mile High Merlot for the young couple, discussing the aging techniques used (lightly smoked in an American oak barrel for twelve months prior to bottling).

"Can you cover the front?" I ask, returning the Snowy Day Syrah to its place on the long wooden tray behind the counter. "I've got work to do."

"Sure thing, boss," Felix says.

"You're a lifesaver."

The bell over the door jingles again and a group of business-casual individuals stroll in—coworkers, if their awkward interactions are any indication. They're likely here for some sort of team-bonding activity. Leaves scatter across the hardwood floor from a gust of wind, strong enough to hold the door open.

"Go be brilliant," Felix says. "I've got this." He plasters a winning smile on his face and greets the new arrivals, gracefully bypassing the leaves and clicking the door shut.

He'll have them eating—er, sipping—out of the palm of his hand in no time.

As for me, I slip into the back.

Fun fact: most red wines stem from the same species of grape called *Vitis vinifera*. So, no matter how different the evolutionary path might have been, a red blend is ultimately a return to a similar root. I keep this in mind as I dole out samples of different vintages into vials.

The Malbec, cabernet sauvignon, cabernet franc, and merlot from last year's harvest have finally each achieved just the right individual flavors for blending, a practice typically done after independent fermentation in order to better balance the final product.

Propelled by Gladys's inquiry, I set up a station on the stainless-steel counter. Empty beakers, fresh pipettes, and blank labels are at the ready. With my hair secured by a tie-dye headband and my hands gloved, all I need are safety goggles to complete the transformation from vintner into mad scientist.

The wind beats against the outside of my winery, sending a chill through the cavernous space. The stainless steel and vaulted ceilings sufficiently keep this area a few degrees cooler than the tasting room, which is preferable for fermentation, but not so much for idling.

My fingers dance over each of the vials, the shades ranging from a nearly translucent coral to an inky purple, and the viscosity from watery to jamlike.

The key to blends, like relationships, is balance. Combining wines already good on their own in such a way that the whole becomes greater than the sum of the parts. Easier said than done.

I gather a bit of merlot into a pipette and squeeze it into a beaker, carefully noting the exact amount of milliliters on the label. The sweet simplicity of merlot makes it the perfect starting canvas. Next, I add cabernet franc, a varietal renowned for intense peppery flavors and tobacco aromas.

Then I pause.

Should I go with old reliable, cabernet sauvignon, or something spicier, like a Malbec? And how much of each dare I try? The last thing I want to do is add so much of one that it overshadows the nuanced flavors of the others.

This is why you're testing, Parker, I remind myself. *It doesn't have to be perfect.*

Still, my brain seems to be incapable of making a decision. Or of thinking about anything except Reid and how maybe wine blends are like romantic pairings. A relationship either grows stronger during times of stress and change, or breaks down completely.

When the door to the storefront opens, I welcome the interruption. That is, until I realize it's my mom, who, for the second time this week, has dropped by unannounced.

"Okay, seriously, someone didn't die, did they?" I ask. *Someone else,* I'm tempted to amend.

"Of course not," she says. She's in a block-print tunic, leggings, and loafers. "I just wanted to bring you something."

She digs through her tote. It's a truth universally acknowledged that items are almost impossible to locate in a woman's bag. "To help with your winemaking."

Well, color me intrigued, and slightly stupefied.

"How were the Iyerses?" I ask, removing my latex gloves. Honestly, what I'm really wondering is if there are more enchiladas up for grabs.

She continues sifting through her belongings. "Oh, fine, dear. They asked about you and your business." She purses her lips as she says this.

Yet another reminder that if my mom had her way, I'd be working with her at NIST as an underling analyst for Sai instead of an entrepreneur hocking an alcoholic beverage, hallowed as it may be. Too bad I've always had a mind of my own.

"Ah, here it is," my mom says, passing me what looks like a red thermometer.

"Uh, cool?"

"That's my favorite pH tester," she explains. "I was reading that precision is important for fermentation, and this is the most precise in the field."

Her words catch me off guard. "I—uh—wow," I say, readjusting my headband. Finally, I remember my manners. "Thank you."

She shrugs like it's no big deal. But this right here— my mom and I having a real conversation about my vocation—is something I've craved for longer than I care to admit.

I consider her again. Frizzy raven hair laced with silver, trademark cat-eye glasses, and short pear-shaped frame. It's my mom, all right.

My attention snags on something she just said. "Did you say you were reading about fermentation?"

"Yes," she says. "What you said yesterday got me thinking, winemaking is a little bit like chemistry, isn't it?"

"I suppose it is." I crack a smile, dipping my chin. "Do you want to stick around while I take measurements today? You can even take a turn at punch downs if you play your cards right." I tap my biceps.

She eyes the bins of grapes surreptitiously and then checks her watch, the numbers of which are in radians. "I'd better be going."

My spirit depletes faster than a bottle of wine at a book club. Clutching my new pH tester, my voice reaches a false pitch as I respond, "Right. Maybe another time."

She nods, her frizzy hair as flustered as she is. "Any news on Reid?"

"He had his arraignment this morning. Long story

short, it didn't go well." I navigate around my mom and place my new pH tester on the shelving unit where I store my lab kit, next to the crusher de-stemmer.

I turn back around and find her watching me, the lines around her eyes drawn in pity.

Let me tell you, the only thing worse than your mom saying something you don't want to hear is when she's intentionally biting her tongue.

"I'll let you get back to work," she eventually says. She squeezes my hand as she passes, showing herself out through the door that leads into the back alley.

I sniff loudly, my nose suddenly runny, turning my attention back to my blending station. A sense of helplessness settles over me.

Oscar would have loved this task. The experimenting and tweaking to come up with something truly special, the finesse and patience required. He'd thrived under pressure and embraced challenges, and even rushed to the aid of others facing hardships. He was passionate and good, and it's not fair that he's gone.

But I can't think any more about Oscar. Or Reid, for that matter. Because thinking isn't *doing*.

And I finally know what to do.

Chapter
Eleven

I've only been to Katy's place once, when Reid needed to deliver her tips, which she'd somehow forgotten despite her otherwise near-perfect memory.

Katy lives in a quaint cottage bordering Chautauqua Park. With wildflowers out front, their blooms giving one last hurrah for the season, and the sloping Flatirons for a backdrop, it's picturesque. Which probably makes up for the cost of leasing such a rustic space.

After begging Felix to manage the shop so I could take a lunch break, I find myself outside Katy's door.

The trailhead that winds up and up and into the park is bustling with hikers, even with the gales of wind swaying the trees. The expansive sky is such a crisp blue I can't help but wonder if it's real. I've spent many a day exploring these trails, breathing in the thin air that smells of pine needles and tree sap. The locale puts me at ease.

The covered porch is a study of shadows—that of the rocking chair, the hummingbird feeders, and my own. A lamp shines through the eyelet holes of her curtains, which means there's a good chance Katy is home.

I knock on her door and wait, arms crossed over my chest.

There's no answer.

I knock again, louder this time, the floorboards creaking beneath my feet.

Katy's sharp voice carries through the log siding. "I have a 'No Soliciting' sign."

"It's Parker," I answer.

The curtain flutters and, a moment later, the dead bolt unlocks.

I hardly recognize the woman who greets me. Usually Katy is bubbly, wearing a number of funky accessories, her hair done up with barrettes and intricate braids, her nails expertly manicured. Right now, she looks wilted, like bygone spring blossoms.

Her black hair is knotted in a messy bun on top of her head. Her eyes are red and she sniffles loudly. Maybe she really is sick. Then I notice what she's wearing—a baggy Culinary Institute of America hoodie.

I recognize the design, having "borrowed" Reid's, and there's only one other person I know of who graduated from that program in New York City: Oscar.

"What are you doing here?" Katy asks, leaning against the doorframe, her curvy figure effectively blocking the way.

"You haven't returned any of Britt's calls."

"What's it to you?"

"I heard you were sick and wanted to check on you." My eyebrows furrow in concern.

She crosses her arms over her chest and stares at the threshold, the point where the creaky floorboards meet smooth hardwood. "I'm fine."

"Are you sure?" I ask. "Because you don't seem fine."

"You hardly even know me."

I'm ready to wax something philosophical about how we don't really know anyone. How even those who we're closest to have secrets, including yours truly (if pressed, I'll deny ever crushing on Archie Andrews). But Katy doesn't seem in the mood for life musings. Instead, I go for flattery.

"Maybe not well, but I like to think we're friendly," I say, smiling sweetly. "And you're by far my favorite server."

Katy doesn't budge, her chin jutting out. "Just because I gave you extra bacon-wrapped dates the first time you came into the restaurant."

"And I savored every bite." My stomach rumbles at the memory. What I wouldn't give for a few of those heavenly morsels now. To lessen the blow of my unexpected drop-by, obviously.

I continue, "It's not only that, though. You leave extra tips for the busboy, who totally needs it, and you have an impeccable memory. You never write any orders down and yet you always—*always*—get them right. And I know you're an artist."

"You pay attention," Katy says.

"I can't afford not to," I say with a shrug. "Reid and I are partners."

"In more ways than one, apparently." Katy opens the door wider and waves me inside.

She pads over to a table, where she sinks into a chair and picks up a paintbrush, not bothering anymore with pleasantries.

The cottage is small—even smaller than my apartment, which is saying something—and every bit of space is covered with artwork. Watercolors, oil paintings, and charcoal sketches. They vary from vibrant to melancholy, some capturing the mountainous landscape behind her cottage, others something only she can see.

From the bedecked futon and folded clothes lining the shelves of her entertainment center, I suspect the living room doubles as her bedroom. The kitchen is barely large enough for a compact drop-leaf table, and there are only the most rudimentary of appliances.

Unsure where to perch, I take the chair opposite Katy at the table, watching curiously as she dabs a paintbrush into a mason jar of water and then presses it into the indigo shade of her watercolor palette. Vivid colors leap from the paper, spring-green vines dotted with scarlet flowers that weave with what looks like a dark mask.

"How is your art?" I ask.

Katy's cheeks are angled like a model's and strewn with faint freckles and, at the moment, tears. One rolls down her cheek and plops onto her canvas, blurring the edges of the mask. Without missing a beat, she swirls the teardrop with the indigo paint, dabs the brush with a sponge, then melds it into the picture.

"It's not so much about the art itself as how it makes you feel when you create it," she says, and, with a quick glance at me, continues, "I'm working toward my masters in art therapy."

"Oh," I say, impressed. "That's really cool."

"I just wanna teach people how to process their emotions—grief, anger, fear—through a healthy medium like paint. It's helped me." She sniffs loudly and seems to fold within herself, arched back and shoulders hitched toward her ears. "So, are you going to tell Reid I'm playing hooky?"

"That's the least of his concerns right now." I cock my head to the side and study her motions, smooth and purposeful. "What's it going to be?"

"A gift for Oscar's family. For Día de Muertos."

"I didn't think Day of the Dead was for another month."

"It's not. But practice what you preach, right?" She focuses intently on her strokes, another tear clinging to her eyelashes. "What do you mean, Reid's not in a position to worry?"

I click my tongue. "I was hoping you wouldn't ask."

"Well, I'm asking." She rinses her paintbrush in the mason jar, letting it rest there. "Because it would royally blow to lose a boyfriend and a job in the same week."

Even though I'd begun suspecting, the confirmation takes me by surprise. I fold my hands in front of me. "I didn't know."

"Know what?"

"That you and Oscar were involved."

The revelation of Oscar and Katy's relationship unfolds like the flavors of a really good cab finally allowed to breathe.

I sift through my memories.

Of the night Reid and I brought Katy her "forgotten" tips. Her embarrassment, and the flash of disappointment on her face, makes sense now. She'd hoped Oscar would volunteer for that task.

And Oscar, with his head down at the stovetop at Spoons, meticulously seasoning a sauce, his fingers tattooed with the first letter of each family member's name. Katy sidling to his side and razzing him for the length of his ponytail, a smile on her face.

Sure, Oscar flirted with Katy, but he flirted with everyone. What I missed was the way his eyes lit up when she came back into the kitchen, and how she sought him out whenever she needed a dish prepared on the fly.

Sometimes there's no making sense of matters of the heart, but, now that I think of it, these two fit. Oscar, who is—was—spontaneous, creative, and loyal. And Katy, fun, artistic, and kind.

Another tear trickles down Katy's cheek and onto the canvas. "We didn't want anyone at the restaurant to know, until we figured out how Reid felt about that sort of thing."

"He wouldn't have minded," I say gently. "He isn't really a stickler for rules like that."

Truth is, I'd been the one to hesitate about our embarking on a relationship while we were conducting business. Reid was all for it, once he realized he wanted to give the whole commitment thing a shot.

Ever since, he's been a surprisingly attentive boyfriend. I mean, he even used his one phone call from jail to contact me. That's a good sign, right? Even if he didn't say he loved me. The thought feels like a wound splitting open afresh.

Katy lets out a long exhale. "Doesn't matter anymore, does it?"

I don't know how to answer that question, so instead I ask another. "How long were you two together?"

"A month."

Which is, coincidentally, how long Spoons has been open.

"The therapist in me knows I'm probably mourning the loss of a potential future more than the man I hadn't known for very long. But that doesn't make it hurt any less."

I reach for her free hand and squeeze it. "I'm hurting, too." At the loss of Oscar, at Reid being blamed. So many things.

"This needs to dry before I add another layer." She gestures at her watercolor painting and gets to her feet, stretching her fingers like I do after rock climbing. "Can I get you something?"

She goes into her tiny kitchen, which is packed with more art supplies than food, and adds water to a teapot.

"Tea would be great. Whatever you're having."

She busies herself with mugs and a Celestial Seasonings box. The teapot whistles and a minute later, she carries over two steaming cups of tea. Mint, by the refreshing and soothing aromas.

"When did you see Oscar last?" I ask over my mug, swirls of steam rising like ghosts from the surface.

Katy pulls a knee to her chest, gripping her own mug with white knuckles. "The night he—" She pauses, blowing on her tea. "We had plans to hang out after work, but he insisted I go ahead without him. He said he'd catch up with me later."

There's a longer pause this time as she takes a sip. I

mirror her action to put her at ease, even though the liquid is scalding.

Eventually, she picks up the thread of her story again. "I tried to wait up for him but accidentally fell asleep—it's been tough juggling classes and work and art. When I woke up and realized he never showed, hadn't even texted, I freaked. Then Oscar's sister called and told me."

Her hand shakes so badly water splashes over the side of her mug and threatens to ruin her painting. I help ease her mug back to the tabletop.

"It's my fault," she chokes out. "If I'd waited for him, stayed awake . . ."

"No," I interrupt. "It's not your fault. It's no one's fault except who did this."

She nods but doesn't seem convinced.

"What was Oscar doing at the restaurant that late?" I ask, my thoughts snagging on that particular detail.

"He said he had to talk with an old friend."

"Did he mention a name?"

"No, he said exactly that: *an old friend.*"

"Are you sure?" I press, because something about that phrasing feels off. If Oscar was meeting with someone he was close to, like Reid, he would have just used his name.

"How often have I forgotten your order?"

"Never," I answer. "As hard as I've tried to stump you."

It's true. All those times I tested her, ordering dishes without cheese, or with extra sauce or a different side, she'd never missed a beat.

The barest hint of a smile crosses her lips.

"Was Reid with him?" I ask. Even though I know Reid had nothing to do with Oscar's death, I'd feel better knowing where he was before he showed up on my doorstep.

"Reid took off when I did."

"And what time was that?"

If she catches the weird clip in my tone, she doesn't let on. "Oh, probably ten-ish. He was carrying a take-out bag and another reusable grocery bag."

I frown, a wave of self-doubt slithering up my spine. He only had the carryout bag when he came to Vino Valentine. I shake my head; his actions and whereabouts are a puzzle for another time.

I change tactics. "What about Nick? Had he and Oscar been bickering more than usual?"

A cloud passes over her face. "Not any more than usual. I know I'm supposed to be on Oscar's side, but those two have always acted like middle schoolers. Passive-aggressive BS."

"Any chance it could have gone past passive?"

She eyes me for a minute, considering. "Maybe. Nick doesn't seem like the type to break the law, but it was no secret he was jealous of Oscar."

I frowned; that'd never been my impression. "Jealous? I always thought they didn't get along because of their different cooking philosophies."

"Well, sure, there was that," she says. "And also Reid's preferential treatment. Nick resented that Reid favored Oscar."

Now *this* takes me by surprise. "What does he expect?" I ask, leaning forward. "They've been friends for a decade."

"I know, it's just the way Nick saw it. Thought it was unfair, that he'd never get his shot with Oscar hogging the spotlight."

I chew on my bottom lip, musing over this piece of information. That gives Nick even more of a motive.

"Anything else you can tell me about Oscar?" I ask. "Had he been acting weird, stressed about anything?"

She opens her mouth to answer but then freezes, rubbing the back of her neck. Eventually, she shakes her head.

"What is it?" I press.

"It doesn't have to do with anything."

"How can you be sure?"

She shrugs in a *whatever* sort of way. "He's been really worried about his mom. She has chronic migraines and can't get the meds she needs to manage the pain. Like I said, it's not relevant."

From the way she avoids my gaze, I sense there's more to the story, but I've imposed enough for one afternoon.

"One last question and then I'll get out of your hair," I say. "What were you and Tony talking about in the kitchen that night?"

Tony Robson is the other server at Spoons, who I suspect works more for the free meal he gets with every shift than a paycheck. He's a little pudgy around the middle and is warm and welcoming with a booming laugh that rattles the cutlery. I remember the hushed whispers between him and Katy following the food mishap, how they'd had their heads bent together privately. I'd assumed they were having a moment of shared exasperation, but maybe it was something else.

Katy carries our mugs into the kitchen, setting them in a sink littered with paintbrushes. "When?"

"While Reid was prepping new plates."

"How we'd be lucky if we got any tips and—" She

hesitates, turning back to me, holding my gaze. "The rest is really for Tony to tell. It's not my place."

My shoulders slump. If only I had Tony's contact info. "Call me if you think of anything else," I say, jotting my cell number on the paper towel she uses for paint blotting. "Or if you just need someone to talk to."

Chapter Twelve

My preferred climbing gym features challenging climbing routes along each wall and a cavelike area devoted to bouldering. In an attached room, shallow grooves are etched at eye level to strengthen fingertips, and a low-oxygen chamber mimics even higher altitude than our mile-high city already boasts.

Murals of popular local mountainscapes line the walls—Garden of the Gods, Rocky Mountain National Park, Black Canyon. Some of which I've been to, many of which I hope to summit someday.

I bounce across the cushioned floor mat to the bouldering wall, strapping my chalk bag around my waist and figuring I'll start with bouldering. My arms are tired from the evening round of punch downs, but the rest of my muscles are tense. After closing up shop, I donned leggings and a tank top and came here. To loosen up and seek clarity, the exercise being as much for my mind as my body.

I have the area to myself, so I select a purple route that starts with a move that stretches me to my full five-foot-three-inch height. There are no ropes, no harnesses, no spotters in bouldering. It's about getting from one point to the next by strategically moving your limbs in different ways and leveraging every muscle. There's no *right* way to make a move; there's only getting there.

My brain churns through puzzle pieces that don't quite fit—Nick's jealousy, the old friend Oscar was supposedly going to meet, and the eyewitness testimony. Suffice it to say, clarity evades me.

I'm halfway down the wall when I sense someone join me in the bouldering cave. Dangling from one arm, I dip my free fingers into my chalk bag, peeking under my arm at the newcomer.

Dark hair slicked to the side, toned muscles, Led Zeppelin T-shirt. I immediately recognize the distinguished figure and brace myself for a charged interaction with the detective heading Oscar's case.

When Eli notices me, his step falters. There's a brief hesitation, a half step backward, like he might retreat.

Oh, I am *not* going to stand for that.

Instead of the graceful dismount I envisioned, I proceed to fall flat on my bum. My pride smarts as much as my backside. At least it did the trick.

Eli moves to my side and helps me up, his hand warm in mine. He lets go as soon as I gain my balance.

"Fancy seeing you here," he says, throwing my line from the jail back at me.

I raise one eyebrow. "Especially since I thought you were too busy to go climbing."

"An unexpected slot opened up in my calendar." He has a smooth smile on his face, but there's no warmth in his caramel eyes.

"I see." I dig the toe of my climbing shoe into the floor mat. I love my climbing shoes, how they make my feet both dainty and powerful at the same time. "Care for a game? Add On, Take Away, Memory?" I prattle off all the climbing games I know.

He scratches the back of his head, maybe considering, or maybe trying to think of an excuse.

I thought we were friends, reacquainted nearly a decade after those awkward high school years where we were playing at whom we would eventually become. Thought we'd connected over what it meant to be judged on assumption instead of who we really are.

Guess I was wrong.

"I'll pass," he says.

Despite the frustration seeping through my veins, I give him a playful smirk. "I get it, you don't think you can keep up."

I move to a different part of the bouldering wall, feeling his eyes on my back as I hoist myself up and start a challenging orange route.

"I can keep up fine," he finally says, a spark of competition entering his eyes. "I just don't think it's a good idea. Under the circumstances." There's an iciness in his tone, a warning.

I lunge for a grip and use my fingertips to pull the rest of my body along until my foot can reach the next hold. "You mean because you wrongfully accused my boyfriend of murder?"

A girl who'd just entered the cave with us turns on her heel and, understandably, makes for the climbing wall on the opposite side of the gym.

Eli's attention never wavers from me. "How can you be so certain Mr. Wallace isn't guilty?"

"You can call him Reid, you know." I pant as I finish the route, hopping backward onto the mat in a slightly more redeeming move than my last dismount. "And it's because I know him. The evidence doesn't line up. Speaking of which, I have something that might interest you."

"That remains to be seen."

I'm seeing a new side of Eli, the hard-detective side, and I'm not sure I like it. I rest my hands on my hips, opting to play nice with him.

"I found a button outside Spoons yesterday, in the back alley where it all went down. Something you and your band must have missed."

"I highly doubt that. We thoroughly combed that area. Whatever you found was likely dropped there after we left and has nothing to do with the case."

"Are you willing to stake your reputation on that?"

One thing I know about Eli—he values his reputation. When we were in high school together, he was the school stoner, getting high being his one and only hobby, a means, as I later learned, of coping with a less-than-stellar home situation. It took him a long time for the world to see him as something more. There's no way he would jeopardize his current good standing.

"We'll take a look," he acquiesces.

"That's all I ask." I give him a sweet smile.

Eli opens and closes his carabiner, studying me. I

fidget under his scrutiny, shifting on my feet, adjusting my chalk bag.

"I don't see how you can trust him so completely."

"It's like climbing," I say, gesturing around us. "You have to trust your equipment, and your belaying partner, to not let you fall."

"If I recall correctly, you had a climbing tumble earlier this year due to faulty equipment."

The faulty equipment he's referencing was courtesy of someone I'd mistakenly put my faith in, and the damage she inflicted on my tie-in loop. While her attempted sabotage left me unscathed, her betrayal still smarts, and is no doubt a contributing factor to my ongoing trust issues.

Goose bumps form on my arms at the memory, but I refuse to let Eli know he's rattled me. "Luckily I was belaying with someone skilled enough to catch me." I nudge his shoulder as I walk by.

I'm tempted to look back, but I force myself to keep walking, my eyes locked on the ground.

"Why did I agree to this?" Sage asks, studying herself in her full-length mirror.

"Because you have to get back on the bike, or horse, or whatever," I say with a twirl of my finger.

I'm lounging on her bed, nestled among a sea of cushy pillows, a dewy glass of crisp sauvignon blanc clutched in one hand.

Sage's bedroom pays homage to her many interests. Cosplay outfits hang in her closet, my personal favorite being her Éowyn ensemble—battle armor over a dress, because girls can defeat Ringwraiths, too. Law tomes mingle with fantasy novels in her bookcase. And there's a small flat-screen TV in the corner, so she can watch reruns of her favorite shows while working through the piles of work she always has.

After bumping into Eli at the climbing gym, I was more than happy to come over and help Sage get ready for her date, not eager to spend the evening dwelling on Eli's remarks. Even now, my jaw clenches at his haughty tone: *If I recall correctly, you had a climbing tumble earlier this year due to faulty equipment.*

Stubborn, self-righteous, and a few other choice obscenities reel through my mind.

I take sip of wine, a practice that involves the sense of smell as much as the taste buds. Just as my nose detects floral notes and honeysuckle, citrusy grapefruit bursts forth on my tongue. It soothes my frustration.

Sage turns to me and asks for my opinion on her current outfit. I shake my head. "Needs more pizzazz. More you. More fantastical elements."

She perches on the quilt at the end of her bed. "But shouldn't I wait to spring my crazy on him until the second date?"

"First off, your crazy is awesome." I wait a beat, letting that point sink in. "Secondly, if he can't handle your awesomeness, then he's not worth your time."

Sage waves at my glass and I pass it to her. She takes a large gulp—not bothering with the savoring bit, though I can't blame her—and hands it back.

Then she returns to her closet. Her strawberry-blond hair is pinned back with bobby pins sporting Wonder Woman logos, and she twirls an elfin ring around her thumb. Before too long, she snags a hanger and holds it up, one eyebrow raised.

I nod so enthusiastically my tie-dye headband slips down my forehead. "Tonight absolutely calls for the big guns."

Honestly, I've never been that into fandom, having a hard time keeping up with the hot new books, movies, and shows. But having a best friend like Sage means I pick up on a thing or two. Like that Dungeons & Dragons is basically a video game minus the CGI and controller. Or how *Star Wars* can bring generations together just as well as the best-set dinner table.

She models her final outfit—a funky AT-AT shirt, breezy peasant skirt, and cropped denim jacket. She twirls and I *ooh* and *aah* accordingly.

We relocate to the living room of Sage's studio apartment, adjacent to casement windows that overlook Walnut Street. Below, passersby traipse along the sidewalk. The wind has died down and the sun is almost completely camouflaged by mountain peaks. All in all, it's an ideal evening for a date.

I decide it's now or never for Liam. "Do you mind if I ask you something?"

"Has that ever stopped you?"

"Are you interested in my brother as more than just friends, or is it purely friendly affection?"

Her motions slow as if she's moving through molasses. "I feel weird talking about this before a date."

"A first date," I clarify, moving around to the other side of the couch so I can take a seat. "Which seems like the perfect opportunity to reevaluate feelings."

"Honestly, I don't know. He's just so . . ." She trails

off, leaving me guessing what Liam is. "Nice? Funny? Supportive?" Each word sounds like a question.

"Don't look at me to validate my brother's attractive qualities," I say, trying for a joke.

She finishes tucking her phone in the outside pocket of her strappy purse. "He gets me and what I'm into, and there's chemistry there." She takes a shuddering breath, one I'm afraid might break my brother's fragile heart. "But after what happened with Jason, how completely and utterly wrong I was about him, I want to be cautious, especially since Liam is practically family."

Jason is Sage's ex, who, despite them having grown up together and practically dating their entire lives, remained an adolescent on the inside. When they ended things, it shattered Sage's confidence. I can see signs of healing, but it still scares me to see her so fierce in her work and yet so shaky in love.

"I respect that." I dip my chin, setting my now-empty wineglass on the end table. "Just so you know, it would be okay with me if you two wanted to give it a go."

She sinks into the couch next to me. "Things are so up in the air with everything, I don't want to change too much at once."

I get the feeling Sage is referring to more than her relationship status.

"I have an interview next week," she says, crinkling her nose.

I nudge her foot with my toe. "And why am I just now hearing about this, missy?"

"Because I don't want to jinx it."

"You must want it bad."

"It's exactly what I'm interested in. A public defender. Helping out those who can't afford an attorney."

She fiddles with the strap of her purse. "Don't take this the wrong way, but it's been good helping Reid out, like a trial run or something."

"I'm glad there's some silver lining to this mess." I cover my face with my hands. "Is there anything else I can be doing to help Reid?"

"No," she says. "It's tough, but you need to let the justice system do its job."

"What if the system is broken?"

"Hey, that's my livelihood you're talking about," Sage says, faux chastised. "But I can see how you might feel that way."

"What about DNA evidence?" I ask, grasping at straws.

Her voice is quiet when she speaks next, her eyes flitting to mine. "I wouldn't count on DNA evidence in this case."

"Why not?"

"It's going to take a couple days for anything to surface, and it's only happening that fast because the law enforcement agency is making it a priority."

My hunch was right, then; they want to put the perpetrator behind bars ASAP. Or at least *someone* behind bars, to make the public think all is right and rosy in the world.

Sage continues, "Besides, the murder weapon was Reid's knife. His DNA is bound to be all over it."

A lump forms in my throat and I rub my temples. "And you still won't tell me where he was that night?"

In answer, she pointedly changes the subject. "How's the harvest?"

While her wine knowledge has steadily been improving, I know she's asking to get my mind off Reid. It doesn't work.

"About as good as Reid's case," I say with a snort. "I failed to come up with a new blend this morning, and any day now, a new truckload of grapes is going to turn up at my winery and completely bury me." I sink back into the couch, my lower lip trembling.

"Then I'll come dig you out. Anytime." There's a knock on the door and Sage stands up quickly, patting my knee. "Except not tonight, because that's Arthur."

"Have fun," I say, putting a cork in my self-pity. "Call if you need anything."

Sage and I have each other's backs. The dating world can be intimidating for a woman, and it's important that someone knows whom you're with and where you'll be. She used to be that person for me, and now I'm gladly reciprocating the gesture.

"And remember," I add, "he's the lucky one in this scenario."

She gives me a nervous smile and pads to the front door. From where I'm hidden behind a beam, I eavesdrop on their greeting. Arthur is smooth, complimenting her skirt and asking if she likes Italian food (she does).

Even as I'm mentally wishing my friend a successful first date, I text my brother: *Get a move on asking Sage out.*

I watch the ". . ." that tells me he's responding. He stops, starts back up, and then stops again.

He never does respond.

I roll my eyes. No wonder Liam and Reid are friends.

Chapter Thirteen

If I thought having one cat was like sleeping with a hot-water bottle, two is like sleeping with a wood-fire oven. After a night spent constantly vying for space in my queen bed, consumed with thoughts about the owner of the extra kitty snuggled in the folds of my comforter, the morning comes none too soon.

I desperately gulp my coffee, not even caring how it singes my throat as it goes down, gripping my ceramic mug with both hands.

Zin greedily scarfs down her bowl of kibble, per usual, but William sniffs at his, takes a small nibble, and shoots me a baleful look as if his breakfast is underseasoned.

"I know, buddy," I say, kneeling beside him. "It may not be up to snuff, but I'm doing the best I can."

He twitches his tail before leaning his furry cheek

into my offered hand, purring into my palm. Tears prickle at the corners of my eyes at the vulnerable gesture, at how badly we both miss Reid.

I place William's squishy guitar toy and catnip ball near the French doors overlooking the balcony, giving Zin an extra directive to watch out for him today. Am I asking a cat for help? Yes. Is there a chance she has no idea what I'm communicating? Indubitably. Am I ashamed for resorting to such measures? Absolutely not.

And if I'm not mistaken, Zin winks at me in the affirmative.

Before I shut the door to my apartment, I catch the two cats sitting side by side, watching a rambunctious squirrel squaring off against a blue jay as if it were their own private Netflix documentary.

Saturday mornings in Boulder are arguably the best. Especially in the fall. Interspersed with evergreens, leafy trees turn brilliant shades of burnt orange, golden yellow, and deep red. And there's this scent in the air— crisp, clean, and almost sweet, like maple syrup.

If only I could fully appreciate it.

Faced with such natural beauty, I can't help but imagine Reid in his cinder-block cell, devoid of colors except for gray and harsh orange, the stale stench of bleach in the air.

With the heat of summer behind us and snow still a month out, this is the optimal season to enjoy the great outdoors our state has to offer. If you have the freedom to do so, that is.

Thus far, I've operated under the assumption that the real killer will be apprehended and Reid's name will be cleared. But with the police having written him off and only me advocating for him, the harsh truth is, Reid could very well be convicted. And if he is, he'll miss out on way more than a season. Like, his entire life—our entire life.

Bile coats my throat and my vision blurs. I force myself to focus on my surroundings. On the fabric of the seat beneath me, of Pearl Street passing by outside the window of the mostly empty bus.

Early risers beating the brunch rush, bikers and runners enjoying a relaxing workout along Boulder Creek Trail, and vendors setting up for the weekend farmers market, their produce spilling across tables in a rainbow of colors and shapes.

Selling at the Boulder Farmers Market is a big deal. It involves getting permits, renting a booth, having an eye-catching display, and carting goods to and from the park where it's held.

I signed up early in the summer, time-sharing a weekend booth with Olive You, a local store specializing in infused olive oils. Tomorrow is my day. And, yes, it's an opportunity to reach a new customer base, increase market share, yada, yada, yada, but right now, it just sounds like a pain. I have enough on my proverbial plate, and besides, as far as commodities go, wine is about as heavy as it gets.

Then I see something that makes me forget about my misery and endless to-do list: Spoons, dark with a CLOSED UNTIL FURTHER NOTICE sign stuck to the window, and Britt Hartmann unlocking the front door.

I frown, unable to fathom what she's doing there. Nor why she went through the front when she usually favors the more private entrance in the back alley. With the arraignment hearing, this is the second time she's unexpectedly popped up.

My curiosity too strong to deny, I pull the cord above my head, signaling the bus driver to stop.

I disembark in a cloud of exhaust. Waving it away, I dash down the sidewalk, grateful I went with my leather boots, jeans, and ruffled top, comfortable enough for the hours of work ahead—and this unexpected run—but dressy enough to appeal to patrons. Pulling on the ladle-handle, I open the door to Spoons.

"Hello," I shout as I walk through the quiet restaurant.

This place has Reid written all over it, and I feel his absence keenly. The navy leathers, classy musical decor, and dark wooden tables. I run my hand along the stage, where Reid's alternative band Spatula played to celebrate his opening. He'd beamed that night last month, a light sheen of sweat mixed with pure joy on his face for having accomplished his dream. And now he's not even allowed to step foot in here. My, how quickly things can change.

There's no answer from Britt, so I look for her in the kitchen.

She glances up at me from where she's layering a round sheet cake on top of a larger base. The cake doesn't look like much, a basic yellow, but from the aromas wafting from it, I can tell there's more to it. Vanilla, cinnamon, and nutmeg.

"You should be more careful who you sneak up on," she says, her focus entirely on the task at hand.

"I tried to holler so I wouldn't spook you."

"It'll take more than that to catch me off guard." There's a twinkle in her gray eyes.

"By golly, did you just make a joke?"

"Alert the media."

I slow-clap. "Two in one morning."

She smiles, the briefest flicker across her lips. "What are you doing here?" she asks, not harshly, just curious. "Is there news on Reid?"

"Not since the arraignment." I set my purse on the counter and marvel at her meticulous cake-handling.

Britt gathers a large metal bowl and whisks the contents—what looks like cream, sugar, and vanilla extract—until they're perfect standing peaks. "How's Operation *Shawshank* going?"

"It could be better," I say. "Did you know Oscar and Katy were involved?"

Her forehead creases. "I always thought she was seeing Tony."

"What makes you think that?" I ask.

"He asked her out once, guess I figured it progressed from there."

Could this have been what he and Katy were talking about that night? Maybe Oscar and Katy had an ulterior motive for keeping their relationship secret. Tony doesn't strike me as the jealous type, but if he did somehow find out, could it have spurred him to take action?

I drum my fingers on the stainless-steel island. "Did Tony seem weird at all when you told him about Oscar and Reid?"

"Weird how?"

"I dunno, just . . . off."

"Not that I noticed," she says. "But clearly I wasn't paying that close attention."

"Huh," I say, eyebrows furrowed. "Any chance I could get his number?"

"It's on the board."

Britt's referring to a bulletin board hanging outside of

Reid's office, where weekly shift schedules are posted. There's a sheet of paper tacked to the upper-right-hand corner with all of Spoons's employees' names and contact information. I find Tony's and add it to my phone, making a mental note to call him later.

"So, who's the cake for?" I ask, returning to the island. "Are you having a party or something?" If she is, I'll be tempted to beg an invite just to watch her attempt to schmooze and small-talk.

"Hang out for a few more minutes and I'll show you." She dollops a large spoonful of the whipped cream onto the outside of the layers of cake and proceeds to smooth it over with the edge of a knife.

In another bowl, sliced and sugared plums glisten under the fluorescent lights. Barely pausing in her icing, she pushes the bowl toward me. "Place these around the outside."

I wash my hands in the farmhouse sink, honored she trusts me with this task. I press the plums into the luscious frosting on the cake, moving around while Britt shapes the remainder of the whipped cream on top.

The finished product is stunning, like something from a magazine or *The Great British Bake Off.* And I only snuck one bite of plum, which I count as a major win.

Britt carefully packs the decadent dessert into a large box and starts for the door. "Okay, let's go."

I wonder what it says about me that I'll willingly follow cake to an unknown destination with a killer at large.

Britt carries the heavy cake box like it's filled with feathers instead of a decadent dessert, her eyes and platinum hair barely peeking over the top. She leads me down a familiar street off the east end of Pearl.

Leaves crunch deliciously beneath my feet, the wind from yesterday having knocked them loose. There's a kiosk covered in posters advertising local happenings like concerts and protests. This street plays host to a mixture of quaint homes—likely student rentals—and lesser-known shops selling art supplies, musical instruments, or incense.

I've been down here a number of times, and yet I can't begin to fathom where she might be taking me. A posh art gallery, an equally intimidating friend's house, a competing restaurant?

She slows to a stop outside a nondescript brick building, readjusting the box.

Eyebrows furrowed, I move to her side, reading what's written on a placard beside the door. Boulder Food Bank.

I'm momentarily dumbfounded. I look at Britt again— her hard gray eyes, Rocky Balboa tattoo, and buff arms. Beneath the hard exterior, she's as soft as her whipped-cream icing.

"Mind getting the door?" she asks, widening her stance.

"Oh, right," I say, leaping to action.

I hold the door open for Britt and follow behind her.

Even though Boulder is affluent, we're not without our share of homeless. People who are down on their luck, or maybe never had a whole lot to begin with.

Honestly, it's hard sometimes, going about your day and seeing someone you wish you could help but not knowing how, the guilt gnawing at you. Because there's always more we could be doing.

A place like this is actually helping people, and I'm in awe.

We enter into an open community area with crowded circular tables and a kitchen along the back wall. There's a counter lined with steaming platters of food, aromas of bacon, charred toast, and coffee wafting from them. People occupy each table, talking and eating, both a form of sustenance.

Britt walks into the kitchen with a purposeful, unbroken stride that leads me to believe she's done this many a time.

"Is Susie here?" she asks one of the men piling a plate high with food.

My head snaps up at the name. Because something just clicked.

The name on the piece of paper I found on Reid's apartment, the number I tried dialing, and the bubbly voice of the outgoing message on the other end. It was Susie.

I trail behind Britt like a curious finch collecting bread crumbs. She's chatting with a round-faced lady with rosy cheeks and curly black hair pinned back. I'm guessing this is the mysterious Susie.

"Thanks, Britt," Susie says. "This will be a treat later."

She turns to me while Britt places the cake in a commercial refrigerator in the corner. "Did you bring a volunteer?"

"I—uh—just wanted to tag along," I say, smiling awkwardly. "Parker Valentine, nice to meet you." I extend my hand and give her a firm handshake.

Her wrist and fingers are like limp noodles. She's all

softness and smiles, even as she's waiting for more of an explanation.

"Reid's girlfriend," Britt answers. She pours herself a cup of coffee and then meanders out of the kitchen to the main area, where I see her, without pause, take a seat at a table with a gruff-looking middle-aged man and a woman in heavy layers. She must come here often.

I'm left alone with Susie, whose face lights up at Reid's name.

"We are *so* appreciative of *everything* Reid does," she says, emphasizing with her eyes as much as her words.

"R-really?" I ask.

"Absolutely," she gushes. "His food is always everyone's favorite, and it's so nice he personally delivers everything."

She emanates a glow of admiration I'm all too familiar with. The downside to having such an attractive boyfriend is that other women fawn over him. I've gotten used to it. Mostly.

On a hunch, I ask, "Was he here Wednesday night?"

She nods. "Yep, he came by late, like usual."

"What time would you say?" I ask mildly.

She puffs out her cheeks and exhales her answer. "Oh, probably ten, maybe later."

Every cell in my body seems to melt into a pile of mushy relief. So Reid was here. Delivering food for the homeless. That's what was in the reusable bag Katy mentioned seeing him with.

But why didn't he just tell me?

Susie must see the concern etched in my face because her smile falters. She checks for eavesdroppers at the window counter that opens to the cafeteria. After confirming the coast is clear, she lowers her voice and whispers, "Honestly, we're not supposed to accept donations outside normal hours. But I gave him my number, told him I'd meet him here whenever."

Then I see it. Reid didn't want to cause Susie or the food bank trouble. He only told those who needed to know, not wanting word to spread. Which I guess makes sense, given the nature of social media and society's current proclivity toward outrage.

He's protecting her and the food bank in the same way he's protecting me.

Damn him for being so valiant. I don't know if, given the chance, I'd rather throttle or kiss him. The latter. Definitely the latter.

And suddenly, I feel so sad I'm afraid I might coalesce into a pitiful puddle of Parker on the linoleum floor. Because even if Reid didn't trust the general public with his secret after-hour deliveries, he should have trusted me.

My throat is hoarse when I ask my next question. "Do you recall if he had a cut on his hand?"

Susie shakes her head, flabbergasted. "I can't remember, sorry."

"It's okay," I say quietly. "Thank you for telling me."

"We missed him last night." She leans against the counter. "Even when he was working at The Pantry, he usually stopped by Fridays after the rush."

The ease with which she references the restaurant Reid worked at prior to opening Spoons makes my chest clench. He's been coming here for a while. Probably years.

Still, none of this is Susie's fault. She's been nothing but helpful.

"I'll see if I can scrounge something up," I say. "I don't suppose you accept wine as a donation?"

"No." She laughs, a sound that now fills me with unexpected warmth.

"Figured." I shoulder my purse, rocking back and forth on my boots.

Noticing my hesitation, Susie says, "You're welcome to stay, if you'd like. Some of our regulars come for the company as much as for the food."

I check the time; the pinot punch downs can wait a few extra minutes. "I'd love to. Honestly, I could use the company, too."

Chapter Fourteen

Even with my impromptu stop by Spoons and the food bank, I make it to Vino Valentine an hour before opening.

I check on my fermenting wine. You may not always be able to hear or see proof, but there are intense chemical reactions taking place. Yeast feeding on sugar, churning out carbon dioxide and alcohol, the skins and stems of grapes breaking down. It's like a microcosmic mosh pit, or maybe a battlefield, depending on where your head is at.

I complete the morning punch downs and, wielding my new pH tester, check the acidity levels of the red varietals before moving to the chardonnay racked in oak barrels. Pleased with the results, I make my way into the tasting room to make a phone call.

With the promise of a free meal, I convince Tony

Robson to meet me for lunch. Then I kill time until we're supposed to meet—not hard to do as a business owner.

I go about routine tasks—lighting pillar candles, filling baskets with palate-cleansing crackers, putting soft folksy music on in the background, taking stock of the bottles beneath the hard maple countertop.

The morning goes as expected, since weekends are typically busier than other days, and by the time Felix arrives, there's a decent crowd.

Thanks to a positive review by an adrenaline-seeker foodie, one of the first who braved Vino Valentine after the poisoning, my clientele is varied. Leather-clad motorcyclists sit at the bar happily imbibing the Campy Cab. College students, still high on their legality to drink (and maybe something else), occupy a large table by the window. And a swooning couple work their way through mirrored wine flights, comfortable enough with each other to make the telltale gurgle as they taste each varietal.

"Man, am I glad to see you," I say to Felix.

Dealing with so much ambiguity, I appreciate one of Felix's best traits: what you see is what you get. He doesn't hide behind a veil pretending to be something he's not. And what you get is an eclectic mishmash of generations, lifestyles, and genders.

Today he's wearing a blouse, its V-neck revealing his tanned chest, jeans so skinny they threaten to cut off the circulation to his ankles, and moccasins.

"Wish I were always greeted with such enthusiasm," he says.

"I've never been a rah-rah gal," I say, snagging a bottle of Ralphie's Riesling to wrap up the swooning couple's tasting.

"There's always time to change your tune."

The conversation is a slice of normal in a world that no longer makes sense. And gets even weirder as a group waltzes through my door, the bell overhead jingling merrily in contrast to the sour expression on Camilla's face.

That's right, the Wallaces are in my winery.

In response to their unexpected presence, I immediately fumble the bottle of Riesling, almost sending it crashing to the floor.

"Need some help there, boss?" Felix asks.

"Bring this to table four," I say, passing him the bottle. "And in case you're wondering, that shift in the atmospheric pressure was hell freezing over."

Felix does as he's told, eyeing the Wallaces curiously.

Camilla and Gary look as stiff as the drink I'm going to need after this. Camilla's arms are crossed over her chest like she's afraid to touch anything, and Gary is clearly there solely to oblige his wife. Tristan, however, takes in the decor and jammy aromas of my winery, nodding in approval. Ben is pacing back and forth on the sidewalk out front, his phone glued to his ear.

I have no idea why they deigned to visit this lowly winemaker, but I plaster a smile on my face and grab tasting menus from the stash at the end of the counter.

"To what do I owe the pleasure?" I ask in greeting.

"We're here for a tasting," Camilla says, as if this should be obvious.

My eyebrows shoot up into my bangs. "Of course. Right this way."

I navigate the bustling space, leading them to a long table that's really three oak barrels smooshed together.

"Reid said it was worth a visit to your winery," Camilla says, looping the strap of her purse around the back of her chair.

She's wearing a rose cardigan with jeweled buttons that I would normally compliment up one side and down the other. Instead, I look up sharply. "You talked to Reid?"

"This morning," she says. "He called *collect*." This last word is uttered with a disproportionate level of disgust and horror.

"Who knew that was still a thing, right?" Tristan asks, tongue sticking out in distaste.

"Cool." I try to keep my tone flat so as not to betray the emotions churning through me—the astonishment, hopefulness and, okay, I'll admit it, jealousy. "Have you thought any more about bailing him out? It's a shame you came all this way to see your son and, you know, haven't actually gotten to spend any time with him."

While Gary's gaze is fixed annoyingly on my chest, his displeasure is directed at my entire person. "I'm afraid that's out of the question."

"Why?"

"You're barking up the wrong tree," Tristan says with a snort. "Even if they wanted to, Reid wouldn't accept."

Both Camilla and Gary turn their attention to their middle son, aghast.

"What?" Tristan asks. "It's true. Besides, Parker's practically part of the family." He plucks one of the tasting menus from my hand and starts perusing it.

My cheeks flush, unsure how Reid would feel about that statement. I mean, he can't even trust me with his secrets, or be troubled to say *I love you.* But there's no need to open that can of worms right now.

"Have you heard any more from the detective working the case?" I ask. Although, honestly, I don't know why I bother. Reid's parents are about as interested in his current predicament as they are in volunteering to help with punch downs. Still, Eli might have told them something he neglected to mention to me, given his general iciness toward all things Valentine.

"No," Gary answers gruffly. The collar of his shirt is upturned and he missed a spot shaving, silvery whiskers growing in a patch on his chin. "Why would we have?"

"To share that he's reconsidering the evidence. As he should be."

Felix busies himself at the neighboring table, pouring samplers of the Mile High Merlot for the group of college students. Ever the charmer, he pleasantly laughs at their boozy jokes, even as his ear is turned toward me. Probably assessing whether I need help.

Gary's indignation is palpable. "We are upstanding citizens who believe the brave officers of the esteemed law enforcement agency."

Spoken as someone who's never had cause to question authority, I want to retort.

Instead, I go with a milder: "I never said you weren't."

Fortunately for everyone, Ben saunters up and sets his phone on the table, screen up. Because God forbid he misses a call. If he notices the tension, he doesn't let on. Perhaps he's used to this level of crazy.

"Good to see you, Parker." Ben admires my tasting room, seemingly surprised at its level of cleanliness.

"Yeah, you, too," I say glumly, toeing the floor with my boot.

He pulls at the knees of his slacks as he sits down. "We weren't sure we'd be able to make it before our flight."

"Wait, you're leaving?"

"First thing Monday morning," Camilla says. "We tried to catch an earlier flight, but none were available."

"I've gotta get back to work," Ben says, as if he hasn't been working this entire time.

"And my conference is wrapping up," Tristan adds. "There's no real reason to stay on."

My jaw drops. I knew this was an inevitability, and one I was very much looking forward to earlier in the week, but now the timing just feels . . . wrong.

"What about Reid?" I ask, turning from Camilla to Gary. At their placid faces, I swivel on Tristan and Ben. "Isn't your brother reason enough to stay?"

Tristan and Ben bow their heads sheepishly. The same can't be said for Camilla and Gary, who turn to ice. Upper-class ice.

My blood boils and I snap. "Shame on you for leaving now. Reid needs you." If I were a cartoon character, tiny flames would be dancing in my eyes. "Why did you really come into town?"

The silence that follows is so complete it enhances the sounds around us, the tinkling of glasses and shuffling of chairs.

Gary and Camilla glance at each other before Gary grumbles, "We had miles to use."

"The sad thing is I believe you," I say. "Because it was obviously not to spend time with your son."

Camilla straightens her back. "It's not as if we can see him now."

My voice rises to a decibel I didn't know I was capable of, but I'm beyond caring if I make a scene. I own this establishment, after all. "And you think he's going to want to see you if—when—he gets out? You're about to lose your son for good unless you step up."

The iciness in Camilla's gaze shifts to shock and, if I'm not mistaken, uncertainty. She looks as if she's been slapped. I doubt there are many people who have challenged her.

Before she has a chance to respond, Felix appears at my side. He carefully passes out the remaining tasting menus and smooths everything over. "Why don't you take a look at the menus and let us know when you're ready to taste something?"

I'm so frustrated and angry on Reid's behalf that I'm visibly shaking. It takes every ounce of effort to compose myself enough to muster a nod and follow Felix into the back.

Surrounded by stainless steel and bins full of bubbling must, Felix talks me down.

"They're trying to get a rise out of you," he says.

I bite my bottom lip, resting my back against the cool cellar door. "Why would they do that?"

He runs a hand through his short black hair and leans against the giant vat opposite me. "Because they don't have anything better going on in their lives."

My rage abates, like bubbles fizzling down in a glass of champagne. I heave a sigh. "They just . . ."

"Completely suck."

"Exactly." Our eyes meet in a moment of mutual understanding.

"I've dealt with my share of people who would rather

tear you down than ignore you. Who choose not to like someone just because they're different." He gestures to himself with a pained expression on his face.

I cock my head to the side, considering my assistant afresh. I'm tempted to ask Felix who these people are, and if they're the reason for his nomadic lifestyle.

He continues, "The best revenge is to not let it show that they got to you."

"How am I supposed to do that?" I ask. "If you hadn't interfered, things would have gotten messy. And by messy, I mean bloody. Like, full-on *Kill Bill* style."

He bows his head, smiling ironically. "You don't have it in you."

"You're right," I say, clicking my tongue. "More's the pity."

"Here's what you're going to do." He pushes himself away from the vat and stalks toward me in a distinctly feline fashion. "You're going to march back in there and serve those assholes the best damn wine they've ever had."

"Okay," I murmur. Rolling my shoulders and bouncing on the balls of my feet, I say with more confidence, "Okay!"

"That's the attitude." Felix claps his hands together.

"You're just hankering for a raise, aren't you?"

"Obviously," he quips, holding the door to the tasting room open. "You've got this, Parker."

"Thanks." All jibing aside, I'm not sure what I'd do without Felix.

"Don't mention it."

Somehow, I manage to serve the Wallaces their requested flights of wine. We don't talk any more about Reid, or anything at all, really. I graciously acknowledge every uninvited bit of criticism on my craftsmanship (the Mount Sanitas White lacks depth of flavor, the Campy Cab is too tannic, the Mile High Merlot's not tannic enough). Until, finally, they pay their bill and leave.

I'm wiping down their table, covered with more cracker crumbs than I would have thought possible, when Tristan sneaks up behind me.

"They forgot me again," he says, shaking his head. "I hate it when that happens."

I fold the cleaning cloth and start piling glasses onto a tray. "They're just outside."

He makes no move toward the exit. "You held up well. Better than the others."

"Others? I thought I was the first girlfriend you've met."

"Of Reid's, yeah," he clarifies. "There was Ben's wife, Liza, who Mom put through the wringer, even with her distant ties to the Kennedys."

So, that's the caliber they'd hoped to have for Reid. No wonder they were disappointed when they met yours truly.

Tristan continues, leaning his forearms on the back of the chair. "Liza cried during her first family dinner. Locked herself in the bathroom and refused to come out. After Ben finally coaxed her out, we didn't see her again until they were engaged."

"Ouch," I say with a wince. "Must've been bad."

"Yeah, but the sizable rock Ben put on her finger made up for her long-suffering."

I snort despite myself. "What about you, no girls in the picture?"

"Why? You interested?" he asks, flashing me a flirtatious grin that reminds me so much of Reid it hurts.

I channel all my discomfort from the last hour into one withering glare, so intense it could level the foothills.

He throws his hands up in front of me. "Kidding, kidding."

I stand up straight, resting one hand on my hip. "Why were you so nervous to see Oscar?" I ask, for it hits me now he never answered when I'd asked in the courtyard of their hotel.

"Ah, don't make me say it." He puts his palms together, begging. His fingers are long and delicate—doctor's hands. "It's not something I'm proud of."

"I bet Reid would be interested in the fact you were hitting on me."

His eyes flash, more with amusement than irritation. "Oh, you're going to play that way, huh?"

"I'm not above blackmail." At least, not when it could potentially help someone I care about.

In his long-sleeved tee, khakis, and a leather bracelet around his wrist, Tristan has the muted fashion of an undercover celebrity. And an ego not accustomed to being bested.

"Fine," he says, squirming on his feet. "Oscar was a frequent guest at my parents' house when he and Reid were in culinary school. Once, he caught me in—er—illicit circumstances."

Tristan glances around my winery, at the patrons engrossed in their own conversations, and then out the storefront window, where his family is waiting, craning their necks impatiently.

"What I said about Liza was true. What I neglected to mention was that their engagement was a disaster, too." He stuffs his hands in his pockets and swallows nervously. "We'd all come to stay for Reid's graduation. My parents threw a little party—this was back before they gave up on him entirely, still assuming the chef thing was a phase. Well, anyway, my mom made some offhand comment to Liza, and later, I found her upstairs."

He rubs his chin, his eyes flitting to mine. "Ben is partially to blame because he should have gone looking for her. But as fate would have it, it was me. She needed comfort and there I was. One thing led to another and, well . . ." He trails off, clearing his throat.

I blink rapidly, pushing my bangs away from my forehead. "Make a habit of going after your brothers' girlfriends?"

"Like I said, it's not something I'm proud of."

"Oscar saw, didn't he?" I ask, so many pieces falling into place. I can't help but wonder if this is why Ben's family—Liza and his son, Linus—didn't tag along for this little reunion.

Tristan nods reluctantly, his shoulders slumped. "We came out of the spare bedroom where I was staying as he was walking by. Oscar promised not to say anything, claimed he didn't want to make trouble for our family after all Reid had done for him."

"Did he?"

"As far as I know, Ben never found out." He gauges my reaction, his demeanor guarded. "It never happened again. And things are good for Ben and Liza now. When I saw Oscar the other night, I panicked and worried he might forget his promise."

I cross my arms over my chest, keenly aware of my phone in my pocket and Eli's number in the contact list. "How far would you go to protect your secret?"

"Are you asking if I would stoop to murder?"

"Yes."

"Of course not," he says, shifting on his feet. "I know I'm not an ethical role model, but I'm not *that* bad."

I raise one eyebrow at him.

"If Oscar had let something slip, I would have accepted the consequences for my actions."

"If you say so," I say, my curiosity satisfied, if not my inner sleuth.

"You're really investigating on your own then?" Tristan asks. "To get Reid out of jail?"

"So it would seem." I give him a small smile and collect the tray of glasses. "I'd better get back to work, and you'd better get back to your family before your mom sics the hounds on me."

Pearl Street is a hop, skip, and jump away from Vino Valentine. Well, technically just a skip. A ride on the Skip RTD line, that is. And after the dumpster-fire morning I've had, wherein I learned my boyfriend doesn't trust me enough to share the basic goings-on in his life and confronted his family, who already hated me, I'm eager for a change of scenery.

Tony Robson looks like a guy who thoroughly enjoys a good meatball sub, which is coincidentally exactly what he orders at our prearranged lunch. With so many toppings I'm envious of Katy's memory as I make a mental note of his order.

We're dining at my favorite dive, a local treasure called Snarf's, famous for their oven-roasted sandwiches and homemade spicy pickles and peppers.

The restaurant is warm and inviting with scents of butter and fresh-baked bread wafting through the air. Bright-colored murals surround photographs of their original location, a dinky pink shack on the Hill. Their square footage is still modest, which is why it's pure luck we managed to snag a private table in the corner.

With broad shoulders and a middle-aged doughnut around his midsection, Tony is snug on his side of the booth. His wild curly hair, easy smile, and goofy mannerisms have always given him a childlike quality. Is it possible this man could have killed Oscar in a fit of passion?

"Sorry to hear about Oscar, and the whole dealio with Reid." He unwraps his sub, licking a stray bit of tomato sauce off his finger. "Can't believe he'd do a thing like that, to be honest."

"That's because he didn't." I unwrap my own sandwich—portobello and swiss on wheat—and take a dainty bite.

"What a relief," Tony says around a substantial mouthful. "So, when'll Spoons be open for business?"

"Soon, if you can answer a couple questions for me." I smile innocuously at him and take a sip of iced tea.

"Shoot."

I wring my napkin in my lap. "I heard through the grapevine you asked Katy Gonzales out."

He guffaws, wiping crumbs from his unkempt beard. "That the question?"

"I guess so," I say, slightly apprehensive.

"I never asked Katy out."

"Really?"

"Not sure who told you that, but they oughta get their

story straight before spreading rumors." He slurps from his soda while I wait patiently for him to elaborate. He doesn't.

"Did you ask her something?"

Tony squirms, taking another bite of his quickly diminishing sandwich. At this rate, he'll be done before I get any actual answers.

He turns as red as the tomato sauce dripping onto his wrapper. "I asked her to read my novel."

I lean back on the bench, momentarily stunned. "You're a writer?"

Tony shrugs and leans forward, lowering his voice. "Katy and I got to talking one day about books during one of our shifts, and I asked if she wanted to read mine."

"What did she say?"

"Said it wasn't really her cup of tea—see, it's a political thriller set in space. Of course, Katy being Katy, she said to send it to her anyway." He pops a chip in his mouth and chews.

"Is that what you two were talking about during your last shift?"

"Yeah, she'd just finished it and had some pointed criticism that I—er—didn't take very well."

"That's why you two looked like you were arguing."

"I just had to let her feedback sink in, that's usually how it goes." The bag of chips crinkles as he reaches for another one. "We talked again later, made amends, and joked about the odds we'd get any tips."

I drum my fingers on the table. "So there was never anything romantic between the two of you?"

"Nah, I always got the feeling she was into Oscar."

He scratches at his stomach, the soft cotton of his T-shirt stretched to its limits. "The way she hung around him and stuff."

Tony is more perceptive than I gave him credit for. I wonder what else he may have noticed on the job.

"Do you know what happened to the food the night Oscar was killed? Did you see anyone tamper with it?"

He shakes his head, flummoxed. "Waste of good scallops, if you ask me."

"I couldn't agree more."

We munch in silence for a minute, the earthy mushrooms and salty melted cheese a dream for my senses.

Then Tony adds, almost as an afterthought, "It's funny, though."

"What's funny?"

"Nick," he answers, crushing his now-empty sandwich wrapper into a ball. "Every time I saw him that night he was distracted."

The bread turns to a lump of cement in my mouth. I force myself to swallow and ask, "What do you mean *distracted*?"

"Like he was in zombie mode or somethin'." He guffaws again, a sound that reverberates through the entire restaurant, earning stares from our fellow diners. "Eh, I'm probably reading too much into things."

I highly doubt that.

I recall Nick's vehement frustration, the frequent arguments he'd had with Oscar about cooking philosophy. How Katy said he was jealous of the preferential treatment Reid bestowed upon Oscar. And now they're both out of the picture—Oscar deceased and Reid behind bars.

Tony pulls me from my spiraling thoughts. "Hey, do you like spy thrillers?"

My iced tea goes down the wrong pipe and I cough, patting my chest. "Um, sure, but I'm pretty busy with the harvest right now." I glance at the screen of my phone. "Speaking of, I should be getting back."

"Me too." He gets to his feet with a sigh. "The blank page waits for no man. See ya around, Parker."

As Tony lumbers through the door, a wave of relief washes over me. At least I've crossed one suspect off my list.

I spend the rest of the afternoon in the back of my winery, furiously combining varietals in slightly different concentrations. Testing the results. Trying again. And again, and again.

Waves of laughter and chatter float through the door to the tasting room, and the aroma of jam is rife in the air from the bin of recently punched-down pinot. I ignore it all.

Because the only way I'm going to create a new blend is if I actually try. As Tony so wisely articulated, a blank page waits for no man. Or, in this case, woman.

I embrace my emotions—pouring my sadness, fear, and frustration over Oscar's death and Reid's implication into my work.

Because I finally know which varietals to try. Ones that symbolize the best and worst qualities about Reid and me, in hopes that they can meld together into something delicious.

For Reid's passion, unpredictability, and kindness,

the temperamental cabernet franc mixed with the silky pinot noir.

As for me, I select merlot for loyalty, cabernet sauvignon for unwavering idealism, and Malbec for spiciness.

We both have a stubborn streak, which is Viognier to the core. These grapes can grow in limestone and need to be harvested within a short window to achieve the perfect level of acidity. While not typically found in red blends, I have a hunch it might make all the difference.

I stir my most recent concoction with a metal stick, the *clinking* echoing through the cavernous space. I pour the resulting mixture into a wineglass and hold it up to the light. The color is a deep ruby, and the legs dribbling down the side of the bowl indicate an appropriate alcohol content. Sticking my nose in the glass, I breathe in aromas of peaches, cherries, and a hint of smoke. I'm eager to take a sip when my phone buzzes.

I glance at the caller ID before answering. "Mom?"

"I was just on my way home and wondered if you'd like any company at your shop."

I pull the phone away from my ear and double-check that this is indeed my mother. "You're making me nervous. Is something going on I don't know about? Like a life-threatening disease of some sort?"

"Of course not," she says over the steady thrum of NPR in the background. "I just thought we could spend some quality time together. You can teach me more about the chemistry of wine."

I smile, sniffing at my wineglass again. Then I check the time. The Squeeze Keys perform in just over an hour, and I still need to get to Union Station if I have any hope of talking to the witness. "Rain check?" I ask. "I'm kinda swamped."

"Oh, okay," she answers, disappointment practically dripping from her voice.

I feel a stab of guilt. This is how it's always been with us. Like we're ships passing in the night instead of mother and daughter. And I'm not sure how to fix it.

Maybe by accepting her offer. Maybe by appreciating the fact that she's not nearly as horrible as Camilla.

Before I can tell her I've changed my mind, she continues, "I have some work I can finish up anyway. I'll see you, well, when I see you. Love you."

"Love you, too."

I hang up with an ache in my chest and an annoying buzzing in my brain. I clench my teeth at the self-doubt coursing through me. I hate feeling like I've let people down. And that's all I seem to be doing lately.

Aunt Laura and I were always on the same wavelength. We got each other. There were no hidden meanings or expectations. There was just acceptance and love.

She used to be the go-between for my mom—her older sister—and me, a master interpreter and ambassador. My dad has tried to fill in that role now that Laura is gone, but there's only so much he can do.

I let out a long sigh.

At least wine is readily available.

Finally partaking in a sip from my glass, a warmth spreads to my fingertips as flavors dance on my tongue. Tannins on the front that give way to earthy undertones—cocoa and currants—and a refreshing citrusy finish.

Doth my palate deceive me, or is this blend hitting all the right notes?

Normally I would call Reid in a frenzy, wanting to

gush to the only person even nerdier than I am about flavor. Unfortunately, that isn't an option.

I put a cork in the beaker and leave a note for Felix to taste the blend before he heads home for the night.

Then, intoxicated with my success, I grab my purse and hit the road. I have a bus downtown to catch, an accordion performance to attend, and, if all goes well, a witness to interview.

Chapter Fifteen

Union Station is a refurbished train station located at the gateway to LoDo—Lower Downtown—in Denver. Adjacent to the central public transit hub of the city, it plays host to eclectic shops, restaurants, and even a fancy hotel in the upper levels.

Red neon lights glow on the side of the building, welcoming one and all to this hot destination. Inside, the aesthetic hints at its previous life as a train depot, with benches in addition to tables at the Terminal Bar, impressively high arched ceilings, and indoor lampposts. The bustling throng even feels like a train station crowd.

Tucking my hands into the pockets of my coat, I stroll past the vendors selling bright-colored bouquets of flowers, ice cream shops, and newsstands. My target is on the other side of Union Station, where it opens into a courtyard with fountains, hip restaurants, and, as it so happens, a stage for outdoor performances.

Down the street is the 16th Street Mall, and, in the opposite direction, the historic Tattered Cover Book Store, one of my favorite haunts when I'm on more leisurely errands.

At a restaurant called Thirsty Fox I snag a small bistro-style table with a clear view of the stage. The sun catches the water spouting from the fountain, making it sparkle, and children laugh as they play a game of tag over the cobblestones. Adults lounge at tables around me, professionals just off the clock, hipsters, and tourists.

A server approaches my table and I put in an order for a frothy Belgian beer by a local microbrewery, a caprese salad, and a side of fries (I'm only human).

"When will the Squeeze Keys be coming on?" I ask the server as I hand him my menu.

He looks toward the stage, giving me a view of his impressively wide-gauge earrings. "Should be any minute now."

I thank him and turn my attention to the three musicians milling about behind the stage. They're twenty-something and dressed in old-timey getups—slacks, vests, neckerchiefs, and bowler hats. Not all matching but close enough you can tell they're together. Handling each of their accordions with care, they play a few keys and compress the boxes to warm up. I wonder which one of them is my guy, and how on earth I'll be able to tell.

My food and drink arrive. I nibble on a French fry and chase it with a sip of beer, the warming spices and light flavors pairing perfectly with my salty snack.

The musicians step on stage and begin performing, starting slow and building to a crescendo of surprising depth, given the quirky instrument. They play covers of upbeat pop songs like "Somebody That I Used To Know," "We Are Never Ever Getting Back Together," and "Since U Been Gone." The themes of which, all told, leave me feeling acutely aware of my aloneness.

I shake off my gloom and study each of the musicians' faces in turn. I have this theory. When you've seen true darkness—like the death of a fellow human, or a glimpse of your own mortality—it leaves a trace on you. Something in your eyes that's forever altered, a haunting figment of what befell you. Only recognizable by others who have experienced similar sadnesses.

In other words, it takes one to know one.

And I know death. I saw it earlier this year.

I search the eyes of the men while they're playing. Their focus alternates between their instruments, one another, and the audience. All except for one. Whose gaze continues to linger on something unseen on the horizon.

Goose bumps rise on my arms and somehow I know he's the witness. He saw the fight with Oscar—maybe even saw the moment life left his body. My concentration is fixed on him throughout the whole performance, so intensely I'm sure he can sense it.

When they're done, I approach him.

I'm not sure how to introduce myself. Miss Manners never gave instructions on talking to the witness in a murder investigation, but flattery will get you everywhere.

"I enjoyed your music," I say.

He has curly ginger hair peeking from underneath his bowler hat, lightly freckled skin, and blue eyes that pierce me. "Thanks," he says softly.

I guess flattery *won't* get you everywhere. I decide to play it straight with him. "This is going to sound weird, but did you happen to see something on Pearl Street the other night—a fight outside a restaurant?"

He freezes, fear entering his eyes as he takes me in. Wide-leg jeans, ruffled top, embellished blazer. What he sees must not come across as threatening. Maybe it's the look of utter desperation on my face.

"What did you say your name was?" he asks.

"I didn't." I thrust my hand out to him. "Parker Valentine."

"Magnus." He takes my hand, his fingers calloused from all the hours catering to his instrument. "We'd better go somewhere to talk."

"How did you know it was me?" Magnus asks.

After telling his bandmates he needed to chat with me—followed by a couple *nudge nudge, wink winks* on their part—we parked ourselves back at my table. I pulled my coat tight around me, the autumnal air chilled without the glare of the sun.

"I put two and two together," I say. I offer him a fry, but he politely refuses. "Don't worry, I doubt anyone else will be able to track you down."

"That's probably good." He rubs his forearm, chuckling nervously.

"Yeah, especially since I'm pretty sure the killer is still out there."

Blood drains from his face as he registers my meaning, his freckles standing out even more. He undoes the kerchief tied at his neck and dabs his face, the performance coupled with the threat of a murderer making him perspire.

"That's not possible," Magnus finally says.

Is he really that confident in what he saw, or is his denial that deeply rooted?

I cock my head to the side. "Can you tell me what you saw that night?"

Magnus shudders and finally takes one of my fries, twirling it in his fingers. "Why? Who are you, anyway?"

"Someone who wants to see justice served," I answer vaguely.

"A true-crime enthusiast?" He tosses the French fry back on the plate and gets to his feet. "Find a new hobby."

"Wait," I say, and then lower my voice so the neighboring tables can't hear. "Look, my boyfriend is behind bars, on your word alone. I'd like to hear why you're so sure it was him you saw."

For a split second, I'm afraid he might bolt. He looks at the cars driving past on the busy street parallel to us, at the people waiting for their rides.

"I know what you're going through," I say quietly.

His gaze cuts sharply to mine. "How could you?"

I lick my lips and grip my beaded necklace for strength. "You keep picturing it," I start, the words heavy on my tongue. "When you least expect it, an image will flash through your mind, and momentarily, a weight rests on your chest and shoulders. A pressure that almost feels like you're underwater." I look at him sadly. "It gets better over time, but I can't say for sure if it will ever go away entirely. It hasn't yet for me."

Magnus sinks back into the chair.

"I really am sorry to make you relive everything." I sniff. The air in Denver isn't as crisp as it is closer to the mountains. It smells of exhaust, exotic foods, and whatever is being smoked nearby.

Magnus starts talking, his voice smaller than it was a minute ago. "I was walking to where I parked my car and I heard this scuffle. Two voices arguing, getting louder and louder."

"Could you tell what they were arguing about?"

He wrings his kerchief on the table, twisting it together and then letting the checkered material unfurl. "There was something one of the guys wanted from the other one. Help of some sort. *I know you can get it*, one of them said."

I frown, my eyebrows furrowed.

Help with what? What could one of them get?

"Did it seem like they knew each other?"

"I have no idea." He casts his gaze toward where his bandmates are chatting up the manager of Thirsty Fox, drinks now in their hands. "Do you want to hear the rest or not?"

I mime zipping my lips and wave for him to continue.

"I was at the opening to the alley, ready to check and see if everything was okay. The two guys were really going at it. Wrestling hard-core, almost to the ground. One of them pulled at the other's shirt and then stumbled, lost their balance. That's when I saw the flash of metal." He hesitates, his breath catching. "A knife. I saw the stabbing motion. Then the shorter guy grunted and fell to the ground. After that, I bolted."

My blood runs cold at the end of his story. His seems to as well.

"And you got a good look at them?"

He opens and closes his mouth. "Enough."

I pull up a picture on my phone, one of my favorites of Reid. It was from a day we'd gone hiking in Nederland over the summer. We'd started up the trail exchanging witty remarks—mainly challenges, both of us competitive by nature. Soon, though, we fell into the companionable silence of two people comfortable with each other.

He'd packed a picnic lunch, I'd brought the wine, and we backpacked together through miles of secluded wilderness, finally finding a spot near Lost Lake to enjoy our vittles. For Reid, a meal is never *just* a meal. It's an opportunity; a blank canvas. And that day, he'd made roasted summer vegetables, rustic oat crackers with walnut pesto and gooey burrata, and for dessert, truffles. White chocolate stuffed with homemade raspberry jam. Without discussing, I'd brought the perfect wine to pair with our feast. A rosé that was a touch sweet but with enough tartness to cut through the creamy cheese.

We'd made our hideaway in the shadow of a massive pine tree. Reid's hair had a darker tinge to it in the shade, and as he flashed me a broad smile, I'd snapped this picture. His teeth are stark white against tanned skin, and there's a spark of danger in his green eyes. Because the moment I lowered my phone, he'd cupped my chin in his palm and brushed his lips over mine.

Lying back in a bed of wildflowers, we'd kissed, limbs lazily intertwined, songbirds chirping around us. It was a long while before we made our way back down the trail.

I keep my face bland as I show Magnus the photo: "Is this the man you saw?"

"The detective already went through this with me."

He grows antsy, only briefly deigning to look at the screen. "He was wearing a chef's coat, but yeah, that's him."

My heart sinks, dragging my hopes and dreams with it. I stare across the courtyard, the dusk lighting obscuring the scene. The moon is barely a sliver overhead, and the twinkling stars are camouflaged by the glow of the city. I have to squint to see the children, still absorbed in their game of tag. That's when I realize something.

"How can you be so sure?" I ask, leaning forward. "There wasn't a full moon that night and you were at least a dozen feet away. That's not the best for a visual."

"Look, I know what I saw, okay?"

"I don't think you understand. A man's life is at stake." I throw my napkin on the table, the plates of food no longer the least bit appetizing.

Magnus stands, a finality in his motions. "Sorry I can't tell you what you want to hear." He readjusts his shiny vest, giving me another once-over. "You know, my bandmate is single if you want an introduction."

I grind my teeth. "Tempting, but I'll pass."

He shrugs. "Suit yourself."

Then Magnus walks away, leaving me confused and, if I'm being honest, completely terrified.

Chapter Sixteen

Buses are great for thinking.

There's something about sitting next to complete strangers, all observing the same segment of world passing by. It smells of upholstery and the mingled scents of perfume, cologne, and mint chewing gum. We leave the hubbub of Denver behind, steadily heading west toward Boulder.

My EarPods are in and I'm listening to a French electronic band Reid introduced me to. Upbeat enough to keep me awake but instrumental enough to provide room for other musings.

There's no way Magnus could have seen the level of detail required to identify Reid. It had been too dark that night. Or maybe I'm the one in denial.

Even though I'd rather ask for Camilla's opinion on my new wine blend, I force myself to consider the possibility that it was Reid. Could he and Oscar have gotten into a fight and that's how Reid really cut his hand? Is there any chance their tussle wasn't what killed Oscar? Could someone else have come along and finished the job?

Now I'm really stretching.

I shake my head, my hair brushing my shoulders. There's one tidbit the witness cited that I keep coming back to: the chef's coat. Reid never mentioned his chef's coat. Why would he? He would've taken it off, ostensibly, around ten o'clock, when he left the restaurant, without a second thought. And even if he circled back, he would've had no reason to put it back on. I wonder what Eli made of this detail, if he noticed the incongruity.

The bus pulls into my stop and I get off with a murmured *thank you* to the bus driver.

My street is dark, one lone streetlamp casting a feeble glow over the sidewalk. On my left, condos line perfectly manicured lawns, the centerpiece of which is an outdoor pool open from Memorial Day to Labor Day, and on my right is a residential neighborhood with funky architecture that looks like it was built in the seventies.

My mind plays tricks on me.

Trees sway in the breeze, their branches looking like skeletal limbs in the shadows, and the rustling of leaves sounds like the swishing of a jacket. A bunny darts across the street, sending my heart racing. My purse bounces with each stride, almost resembling footsteps.

Hair rises on the nape of my neck. I clutch my purse to my side, but the footsteps behind me don't stop.

My breathing uneven, I glance over my shoulder. That's when it happens.

I'm tackled, going down hard on my right side and

skidding across the lawn. Time seems to slow as I process what just happened.

I roll quickly, clambering to my feet, my gaze darting around for my assailant. From self-defense classes, I know my best bet is to run in a zigzag pattern. I start running, but I'm not fast enough.

Someone large grabs my legs and pulls me down.

I flail, scratching and kicking out hard with my feet. I hit what feels like a soft middle and there's a grunting sound.

My assailant lets go and I seize my opportunity to open my purse and sift through it for my pepper spray. I get my fingers around the canister, but it's knocked out of my hand. There's a weight on my chest and my hands are pinned in place over my head.

"Fire," I scream at the top of my lungs. "Fire!"

In that same self-defense class, I learned a depressing truth about humanity—there is a better response to the word *fire* than the word *help*. Unfortunately, no one hears my cries.

My heart pounds so fast in my chest, I'm afraid it might explode, and fear pulses behind my eyes.

A figure in dark clothing looms over me. Whoever is doing this is big, taller than I am by at least a foot, and they have some muscle. They tug at my purse so hard my shoulder threatens to pop out of its socket.

I let go of the strap quickly, practically shoving it toward them. "Take it."

I can always get another wallet, credit card, phone, but I can't get back my life.

Thinking I'm home free, that this is just a random mugging, I crab-walk backward, scrambling for purchase with my feet. That's when the attacker remembers I'm there.

He—I can only assume it's a he—grabs one foot and pulls me toward him. I dig my fingers into the grass, pulling up sod by the roots, the clay soil working its way under my fingernails.

He leans down until his breath is hot in my ear, his voice gruff. "Stop looking into Oscar Flores's murder."

My eyes open wide and a choke comes out, a pitiful sound like a cornered animal might make. I hate myself for it.

I'm shoved so hard against the ground, my head snaps back with whiplash. I reach around me blindly for something to help. Anything. Then I touch a smooth and cylindrical object. The canister of pepper spray.

My breath comes up short as I twist the nozzle and take aim.

Spray pours forth, hitting my attacker directly in the face.

He stumbles backward with a shout, wiping at his eyes with both hands.

I watch, my chest heaving, as he drops my purse, turns, and stumbles into the darkness, weaving between the condos and disappearing into the night.

Shakily, I retrieve my purse and hobble toward my apartment, my pepper spray at the ready.

I shut the door to my apartment behind me and lock the dead bolt.

Then I sink to the floor. That's when the sobs come, shock making my whole body convulse with tremors.

I hug my knees to my chest and try to take deep breaths—in through my nose, out through my mouth—but the tears streaming down my face make it impossible.

Zin comes over and rubs up against my legs. She goes back and forth, her little kitty cheek and torso alternately leaning against me, until I finally acknowledge her.

"Hi, Zin," I say with a sniffle.

She meow-purrs, looking at me with concern, although that could be more for her empty food dish than her distraught owner.

William trots over, too, sniffing at my flats, which are caked in dirt from my tumble. His whiskers twitch before he headbutts my hand.

These two might take up more than their fair share of the bed, but they're making up for it now. Together, they calm me down enough to consider my next step.

Hands still shaky, I reach for my cell phone. Even though I'd rather not call Eli, especially after our last confrontation, I know it's the right thing to do.

He answers on the third ring, sounding mildly annoyed. "Eli Fuller."

"It's me. Parker."

He must sense something is wrong because his voice turns serious. "What's up?"

I lick my lips and tell him everything, the words gushing out like a bottle of shaken prosecco.

When I finish, all he says is: "I'm on my way. Be there in twenty."

Knowing Eli will be here soon makes me feel better, soothing the part of myself that feels fractured after my scuffle. I go to the couch, pulling a pillow into my lap, completely dazed. My mind reels with how lucky I was to escape; how powerless I felt with the weight of my attacker on my chest.

It's as if almost no time passes when there's a knock on my door.

I peer through the peephole because, duh, and seeing the detective, I sigh in relief, hurriedly opening the door.

"Are you okay?" Eli asks, his dark hair falling over his eyes. He's in jeans and a white T-shirt, more casual than his usual attire. "Do you need a paramedic?"

"I'm fine," I say, although what I really am is a mess. Physically, mentally, and emotionally. My side and neck ache, my jeans are scuffed with grass stains, and the palms of my hands smart from scrapes.

Eli's gaze softens, and there's understanding in his caramel eyes. "No, you're not. But you will be."

I usher him into my apartment. He switches on more lights and, without asking for permission, goes into the kitchen. I hear him open a cabinet and turn on the faucet. He returns a moment later, carrying a tall glass of water.

"Drink this and tell me what happened."

So, I do. From my sofa, with a cat perched protectively on either side, I tell him about going to Denver and chatting with Magnus about what he witnessed, and how I was attacked on my way home from the bus stop.

"You mean to tell me you were interfering in the investigation?" he asks, his tone growing frigid. "How many times do I have to tell you to stay out of police affairs? It's dangerous. You could have been seriously hurt, or killed."

"I know."

"I don't think you do." He clenches his jaw, his nostrils flaring. "You were reckless, stupid. You could have botched the whole investigation."

Rage courses through my veins where moments before there had been fear. I snap, water sloshing out of my glass, to the dismay of Zin and William. The latter hops down and laps the offending drops from his fur. I set my glass on the coffee table more forcibly than necessary. "Maybe if you did your job, I wouldn't feel the need to do it for you."

Eli stills, staring at me without moving, a dare entering his eyes now. "What are you implying?"

"That your judgment is clouded. That you're not being fair to Reid because of"—my cheeks flush as I gesture between us—"whatever you may feel for me."

It feels like an impetuous accusation—egotistical, even—but I can't take it back now. And I don't want to. There's a part of me that's wondered since this all began if he was biased from the start against Reid.

"You think an awful lot of yourself, don't you?"

I rub my temples. This is not the conversation I want to be having now. The shock of the last hour is still catching up with me, making my teeth chatter.

I force myself to continue. "All I'm saying is you jumped to Reid awfully fast. Would you have come to that conclusion had it been anyone else?"

He rubs a hand through his hair, making his dark locks stand on end in a very uncharacteristic way. When he speaks next, it's as if the words are being squeezed out of him, like grape juice through a winepress. "I suppose not."

My heart leaps into my throat. "Does that mean you'll keep looking into Oscar's murder?"

"Yes," he says, but then continues quickly, "but I can't make any promises. The Flores case still seems open-and-shut to me."

"Thank you," I say, tempted to hug him.

"Does this mean you'll be more careful?"

"I can't make any promises," I retort, holding his gaze until he looks away with an aggravated sigh.

He sinks into the far side of the couch and leans back into the cushions. "I don't know whether to be annoyed or impressed."

"Probably both."

He chuckles. "Reid's a lucky guy."

"He is, at that," I say cheekily.

I study Eli, almost wishing for some flicker of emotion. It would be so much easier if I'd fallen for him instead. But my heart is steadfast with Reid, as it has been since the day we met.

I raise my glass to my mouth, my panic easing with each sip of water. I get to my feet, my motions still awkward and twitchy. "I have something for you."

"Right," Eli says. "The *evidence*." He utters the last word with skepticism.

I give him a pointed look. "It will come in extra handy now that you're reexamining everything."

"It would if it were admissible in court, which it isn't since you removed it from the crime scene."

"Oh," I say sheepishly.

"Still, I suppose it can't hurt to take a look."

I sift through the junk drawer and pull out the Ziploc bag containing the off-white button, the thread still attached. I hand it to Eli.

He does a cursory examination before tucking the Ziploc bag safely in his jean pocket. He crosses his arms over his chest, his biceps flexing. "I know this is the last thing you want to do right now, but you need to go down to the station and file a report."

"You're right," I say. "That is the last thing I want to do." Even the thought of reliving my experience makes my stomach roil.

"It could mean stopping someone else from getting hurt."

"We both know this is related to Oscar's case," I say. "Figure out who really murdered Oscar and you'll find whoever assaulted me."

That shuts Eli up. But I know it's only a momentary reprieve.

"Fine," I say, rolling my eyes. "Let's get this over with."

Eli drives me to the sheriff's office, an impressive building constructed in flagstone and sleek windows. Maple trees line the perimeter, the edges of their leaves tinged crimson. They sway in the breeze as we approach, almost sounding like the tinkling of tiny bells. There's a chill in the air as absolute as the darkness.

I hobble down the walkway toward the entrance. I cleaned myself up as best I could, wrapping my hands in gauze bandages and changing into leggings, a hoodie, and trainers. But I still feel grimy in a way that a shower won't fix.

I have more experience than I'd like with this building, having already been here twice this year under less than ideal circumstances. An officer prompts me with questions while I answer as best I can, thinking back on the details. There's not much I can be sure of.

My attacker was mannish, tallish, and strongish.

With a deep voice, although that could have been exaggerated.

"I got their face pretty good with pepper spray, which should leave a mark." My eyes are stinging from residual capsaicin. "Does that help?"

"Every detail helps," Eli answers at my side.

We wrap it up quickly, and I allow myself to be herded out of the station and back into Eli's warm car. There's a laptop on the center console and a siren mounted on the dashboard. Otherwise, it could pass for a civilian vehicle. The interior smells woodsy, like Eli's aftershave.

My phone buzzes in my lap, earning a heightened glance from Eli, the angles of his cheekbones enhanced by the shadows. "Expecting to hear from someone?"

"No." I check the screen and let out an expletive that makes Eli raise his eyebrows.

"What's wrong?" he asks.

"Nothing." I readjust the headband keeping my bangs out of my tired, puffy eyes. "It's just that this couldn't have come at a worse time."

Because I recognize the number; it's my grape supplier in Palisade. A friendly guy named Gus with a penchant for gardening and produce puns. He owns a forty-acre vineyard on the Western Slope, his fruit sought after for its extra sweetness, thanks to the neighboring grove of peach trees.

"Hey, Gus," I say.

Eli focuses on driving, his hands at precisely ten o'clock and two o'clock, and yet I can tell he's drinking in every word of my phone conversation, wary and perhaps a touch curious.

Gus begins our exchange as he usually does, with a joke. "What did the grape say when it got squished?"

"I don't know, what?"

"Nothing, it just let out a little wine." He chortles on his end of the line. "Get it? Whine? Wine?"

I force out a tiny laugh. "Nice one, Gus."

He gives one more chortle before getting down to business. "Good news, Parker," he starts. "We harvested the sauv blanc, and I think you'll be real pleased with the flavor. The truck just left. Should be there early to-morrow morning."

I wince, switching my phone to my other hand and shaking out my fingers. How am I supposed to handle unloading and processing grapes if I can barely grip my phone?

"Awesome," I say with faux cheeriness. "I'll be there."

After I hang up, I slump back in the passenger seat, chewing on my bottom lip. My brain is already churning through plans, coming up with a list of people I can beg to help me. When the last shipment came in, I had Reid and Oscar by my side. This time, well, I'll have to get creative.

Eli clears his throat. "I couldn't help but overhear . . ." He trails off, shifting awkwardly as he changes lanes.

"You mean you were desperately trying to glean every word."

"Touché." He side-eyes me as he slows to a stop at a traffic light. "Do you want some help with your harvest?"

"Are you offering?"

"Yes."

"Why would you volunteer for that?" I ask, silently chiding myself for debating. "It's going to be at the crack of dawn and involve an exorbitant amount of work, haul-ing crates of grapes into my winery and getting them ready to crush and de-stem."

He turns to me, resting his hand on the back of the passenger seat. For a minute, he just looks at me as if trying to find the words. "Because that's what friends do."

"I guess it is." I flash him a smile, heaving a sigh of relief at his offer. "And I would be grateful."

His shoulders relax and his lips twitch in amusement. "You see, there's this bossy girl who keeps ragging me about a case. It's what she'd do."

I chuckle, genuinely this time, which is a miracle, given the events of the night.

After parking at my apartment complex, Eli escorts me up the three flights of stairs to my unit. "I'll stay if you want, keep an eye out so you can get some rest."

It's a tempting offer, but would inevitably complicate the fragile threads of our friendship. "I'll be okay. I've got a couple of guard cats watching over me."

Eli shakes his head skeptically.

I continue, "At least their puffy tails will signal an alarm." I unlock my door, glancing once more at Eli before disappearing inside. "Thank you. For everything tonight."

He just nods. "Stay safe, Parker."

"I'll do my best."

Throughout my life, my best has proven to be good enough. To graduate college. To climb my first four-teener. To open my winery. But I wonder if this is one instance where my best won't be good enough. And what that would mean—not only for me, but for Reid.

Chapter

Seventeen

A ragtag team gathers outside Vino Valentine at six o'clock the next morning. Eli, who made good on his offer, which I'd actually started to think was a dream. Sage and Liam, who are constant in their support. And, as much to my surprise as hers, my mother.

I texted her last night on a whim while Zin and William batted a catnip ball back and forth across my kitchen floor. My mom has been showing interest in spending time together, so I figured I could do the same. Not to mention, another pair of hands is more than welcome. She responded enthusiastically in the affirmative, turning up bright-eyed and bushy-tailed.

Felix, as the only employee currently on my payroll, got out of helping with the grape shipment to prep our booth at the farmers market. When I said this was the worst possible time a grape shipment could come in, I meant it. I'm spread thinner than authentic Parma prosciutto. At least I live in a world where there's caffeine.

Stifling a yawn, I take a sip from my latte, stuffing my hands in the pockets of my puffy vest. I dressed in layers this morning—toothpick cords, scallop-trimmed tank, and a worn flannel shirt that belongs to Reid. Partly for the temperature swings Colorado is famous for, and partly to conceal my injuries. A dark bruise blossoms on my side, and scrapes cover both palms and one of my arms. Ibuprofen eased the pain in my sore neck and twisted ankle; if only my psyche were as easily assuaged.

We mingle together in the back of my winery, the roll-up dock door opened to the brisk predawn air. We sip on coffee and nibble assorted pastries, courtesy of the Laughing Rooster, making small talk about the weather and the one thing everyone has in common: me.

"To think you never liked raisins growing up," my mom says to the merriment of the group.

"Raisins are just grapes that missed their true calling," I respond, sticking out my tongue.

Then my brother shatters the effortless camaraderie by asking Eli, "How'd Parker rope you into helping?"

I'd sensed Liam's dismay at seeing the detective. He's tenser than usual, toying with the zipper of his fleece jacket and casting barbed glances at Eli. Guess Liam hasn't totally forgiven him for the small matter of suspecting him of murder earlier this year.

"I offered," Eli says, taking a sip of his coffee, his features relaxed and agreeable. "I figured Parker could use the help after her ordeal last night."

I wince as everyone's eyes turn to me. I'd secretly hoped my attack wouldn't come up.

"What ordeal?" Liam asks.

I wave one hand through the air, the one with fewer scrapes. "Oh, someone tried to mug me on my way home last night," I say, downplaying the truth of what happened. "Nothing to worry about."

It's clear no one buys my bland explanation. Luckily, at that moment, headlights breach the darkness, putting a halt to further conversation. A large white truck turns onto the lane that leads behind the shopping complex housing Vino Valentine.

I step outside to greet the driver with Sage hot on my heels. "Don't think you're getting out of telling me what really happened, missy," she hisses.

I counter, "And don't think you're getting out of telling me about your date."

She rolls her eyes. "There's not much to tell. Do you remember the scene in the last Avengers movie where everything goes to hell in a handbasket?"

"Yeah," I say cautiously. Even though I have a limited knowledge of Marvelverse, I'd accompanied Sage to the opening night of the climactic film. What I recall most are the chase scenes. And Thor, obviously.

She continues, "Picture that, except with no redeeming moment at the end."

"That bad, huh?"

"We weren't compatible at all." She shivers, rubbing the arms of her Golden Snitch hoodie. "At least I tried, right?"

"Absolutely." I twitch my lips to the side. Fueled by my friend's honesty, I say, almost under my breath, "I was attacked for my interference in Oscar's case."

I hate the concern that floods her face, the way her eyes go from prying to pitying. Her gaze lingers on the ankle I'm favoring.

I shift uncomfortably. "You should see the other guy."

"Parker—" Sage starts, but whatever she was going to say is cut off by the rumble of a diesel engine.

I wave at the driver, ushering him into a parking place. "All right, let's unload some grapes."

Not dissimilar from detectives working a homicide case, the first twenty-four hours following a harvest are pivotal. Which is why it's imperative we start processing ASAP.

These sauvignon blanc beauties are pale green and roughly the size of marbles. I pop one into my mouth, detecting traces of lime and white peach. Gus is right, I am pleased with the flavor.

We spend the next two hours completely absorbed in manual labor. Eli hops into the back of the truck with the driver, moving crates onto a forklift, which Liam maneuvers masterfully, thanks to his landscaping experience.

As for me, I'm the conductor of this symphony. The executive chef of this outdoor kitchen. The lead climber routing this rocky cliff. You get the picture.

I direct Liam to dump the fruit onto the grape-sorting table, where my mom and Sage, in matching latex gloves, remove bugs, sticks, and rocks.

Then it's time for the crusher de-stemmer. I rub my hand over its stainless-steel exterior, making cooing noises. If you're thinking I'm nuts, you're probably right. I'm just not quite over the honeymoon phase with my equipment.

I adjust the settings accordingly. For reds and rosés, grapes are only partially de-stemmed and crushed, the stems, skins, and seeds being what give those varietals their trademark hues and mouth-puckering tannins. But for whites, like this sauvignon blanc, I want to remove these so-called imperfections to make the wine crisp and clear.

By the time the sun pierces the sky with streaks of pink and orange, we're sweaty and exhausted. But for all our effort, the winepress is spouting fresh grape juice. Gloriously opaque and smelling sweet and citrusy.

I snag a wineglass and catch some of the juice before siphoning off the rest to one of the giant vats, where it will ferment.

While everyone takes a hard-earned water break, I wave my mom over. "My grower tested the Brix yesterday and deemed it ideal for harvest. I'm gonna check it again now."

My mom dons her cat-eye glasses and watches as I use a pipette to drop samples of the juice into my handheld refractometer. The digital display shows the sugar content. "Still good for early fermentation."

My mom looks at the vat. "How long will this one ferment?"

"Probably a few months, which is on the shorter side." I stash my measurement tools on the shelving unit. "In stainless steel, since oak would overpower the delicate flavors of this varietal."

"I look forward to tasting it." She smiles at me, her eyes oddly glassy. "What you do—this particular application of chemistry—it's really very . . ." She trails off with a sniff. "Neat."

Understanding washes over me, the kind that can only be found in retrospect. Maybe my mom invited me over for dinner with Sai Iyers not to convince me to switch careers but because she genuinely wanted to spend time with me. Maybe she really is proud of me.

I mirror her smile. "Organic chemistry at its finest."

"You've got a knack for it."

"Where do you think I got it from?" I ask with a wink.

I go into the wine cellar and grab a bottle of the Campy Cab, fully aware she'll likely make a spritzer out of it, as is her tendency. In the past, this has driven me crazy, the fizzy beverage masking the subtle flavors I work hard to imbue in my wine.

I hand her the bottle. "For all of your help. It's Dad's favorite, will pair great with leftover enchiladas, and"— I hesitate, hardly believing what I'm about to say—"it'll make a refreshing spritzer."

She hugs me, her lavender perfume enveloping me in nostalgia. Her embrace communicates more than words ever could: acceptance, respect, and a plea to stay safe.

After my mom leaves, I get to thinking about beginnings and endings.

How the end for a grapevine signals the beginning of the winemaking process. How the death of my aunt Laura was really the birth of her legacy. And how maybe this is just the start of many such special moments between my mom and me.

There are certain events that can't help but bond you with those around you. Apparently, unloading a shipment of grapes is one of them.

The tension melted away between Liam and Eli at some point during the hard labor. Now, they're finishing the last of the morning punch downs while chatting about the CU Buffs' chances at making the college football playoffs. Which has recently improved from pigs-flying to slim.

I dole out a bottle of wine to each of my helpers as a small token of my gratitude.

To Sage, the Pearl Street Pinot, her personal favorite.

"I'll be seeing Reid this afternoon," she says, tucking the bottle under one arm. Her ponytail is drooping, as if even her strawberry-blond hair is tired from the morning. "To prep him for his first appearance."

My chest clenches. I get the sense of time slipping away too quickly, like grains of infinitely fine sand rushing through a misshapen hourglass.

"Is there a message you want me to give him?"

A pit forms at the bottom of my stomach, one that instantly fills with acid. There are so many things I want to tell Reid—need to ask him. That I know about his after-hour deliveries to the food bank. How the witness is so certain it was Reid he saw. That his brother divulged the story about Tristan and the basement. If he knows of the old friend Oscar was supposed to meet. And, more than anything, that I wish he would confide in me. How there's more than a detention center between us.

I go with the simplest option. "No message."

Sage frowns but doesn't push it. She glances to where Liam is now taking candid photos of the wine-making process—the bins of bubbling must, remnants littering the grape-sorting table, giant wine vat chock-full of sauvignon blanc.

Sage clenches her jaw, seeming to be waiting for something. She exhales and turns on her heel, grumbling something under her breath that sounds faintly like *Valentines*.

"What was that?" I ask.

"Nothing," she says cheekily. "Chat with you later."

I fold my arms across my chest and then wince. I was able to ignore my injuries throughout the morning because I had to. But now the aches and pains are returning with a vengeance.

I pad to where Eli is reattaching the lid onto the bin of cabernet sauvignon and Liam is sorting through photos, and I hand them each a bottle. A Mile High Merlot for Eli (for old times' sake) and a bottle of the Farmers Market Cherry to Liam, the latter reminding me of where I'm supposed to be.

"You owe me big-time, sis," Liam says, arching his lower back. "I've gotta go sleep this off."

If only I had that luxury.

"You know Sage was waiting for you, right?" I ask, crinkling my nose.

The way he bows his head lets me know he did, in fact, pick up on her lingering. He avoids my gaze, carefully tucking his camera into his bag.

I'd smack him upside the head if it weren't for my chafed palms. "Why haven't you asked her out yet?"

"Did people rush Michelangelo?"

"Are you really comparing your wooing skills to the Sistine Chapel?"

"Help me out, man," Liam says, turning to Eli. "These things take patience and planning and—"

"A willingness to be shot down," Eli supplements.

I risk a glance at Eli but find his attention fully on my brother, his face devoid of emotion. He slips his hands in the pockets of his jeans. In his casual wear, he's more like my old climbing friend than an aloof homicide detective.

"Yeah, that," Liam says, readjusting the strap of his camera bag. "I like her too much to risk making it awkward."

"Funny," I say. "Sage tried to make the same argument."

"Because it's a good one," Liam says, sidestepping toward the door.

I shout after him, determined to get the last word. "Keep telling yourself that."

"I'd better be going, too," Eli says, grabbing a hoodie he folded neatly on the back table. "I'll let you know if there are any developments in the Flores case."

"Likewise."

He spins around, his eyes narrowed.

"Kidding." I throw my hands up in surrender. "There's no extraneous sleuthing on today's menu."

Dark hair falls over his eyes as he shakes his head, his lips twitching into a lopsided grin. "Why is it I don't believe you?"

"Because you're a dynamite detective?" I try.

"Sure, we'll go with that," he says, completely deadpan.

Felix outdid himself.

Not only does he have access to a truck, which makes the whole farmers market thing possible, he also has a keen eye for detail. Our booth features a gorgeous white and cerulean tablecloth with Vino Valentine's logo, bottles organized from light to heavy, and brochures with pairing suggestions for each varietal (Reid's idea). I give Felix two thumbs-up in approval.

"I owe you," I say, starting to lose track of all the people I'm currently indebted to.

Felix looks cool as a cucumber, which, ironically, is what the neighboring booth is selling. "I'll consider us even if I can get in on some grape-stomping action."

"Deal," I say. "Did you get a chance to taste my new blend?" I'm curious if it was actually good, or if I was deluding myself.

"Top-notch. What's it called?"

I sag in relief, tying my flannel shirt around my waist. "Still figuring that out."

His eyes open wide as he takes in the cuts lining my forearm. "The grapes get the best of you, boss?"

I quickly shrug my shirt back on, settling for rolling up the sleeves instead. "I had a tumble last night." I guzzle water from the bottle I brought. "The delivery was easy peasy. So smooth I was able to come here to help." *And to keep an eye out for a certain sous chef*, I think.

Because here's the thing I realized: whenever Reid couldn't make it to the farmers market, he'd send Nick. And I have a hunch Nick is the sort of rule-abiding sous chef who would stick to a routine, even with everything up in the air and Spoons closed. If I can catch Nick off guard, meandering the aisles, there's a chance he'll finally spill whatever he's been hiding.

I plop a large, floppy sun hat on my head and settle into the folding chair beside Felix. We usually stay at the farmers market until it's time to open Vino Valentine, which is still a couple of hours away.

"How are sales?" I ask.

"A few of the chard, one of the rosé," he says with a shrug. "I keep trying to push the reds, but with this weather, no one seems to believe it's autumn."

"Can't blame them." I glance at the blue sky, a dense wall of clouds barely visible over the mountain peaks. "The storm we're supposed to get this afternoon ought to change folks' minds."

Booths around us sell a rainbow of produce—purple heirloom tomatoes, pumpkins, corn on the cob, and kale. There are flowers everywhere—sunflowers, mums, even late-season cosmos. And across the way is Haystack Mountain's stall with their trademark goat cheese.

The market is swarming with people. I do my best to keep an eye out for Nick, but it's tough in the crowd. Felix and I alternate schmoozing with customers, describing the flavors of my wine, and talking up my tasting room. By the time the sun is directly overhead, my throat is hoarse and I'm afraid I've missed Nick.

Then I have a breakthrough.

I almost don't recognize him. His shirt is wrinkled. That's right, *wrinkled*. And he has a layer of peach fuzz on his chin. His eyes are bloodshot.

Momentarily, I'm stunned by the change in his appearance. You know what could do that to a person? Guilt.

In a hurried whisper, I tell Felix I'm taking a break, tossing my hat in my vacated chair. He furrows his eyebrows but doesn't ask any questions.

I hurry around the table just as Nick is walking past. "Hey there."

He starts when he sees me, his shoulders slumping forward. "I didn't know you sold wine here."

"Only on Sundays. I have a time-share with Olive You."

The look on Nick's face clearly states he'd rather they were here instead of me. He switches which hand is holding his reusable tote, the stem of a plump butternut squash sticking out.

"Got gourds?" I ask.

"What?"

"Just a little farmers market humor."

His smile looks more like a grimace. "Well, I'd better be . . ." He trails off, gesturing with his hand.

"Hold up," I say. "Mind if we chat for a minute?"

He gazes longingly down the aisle at all the gorgeous stalls seeming to call to him.

"It'll just take a few minutes."

"Fine."

"Come into my office," I say, waving him behind my booth.

The backside of the market opens to the rest of the park. Brick edging separates large oak trees from a sprawling green lawn interspersed with perennial flower beds. Boulder Creek babbles at the bottom of a gentle slope, with a paved trail running parallel to it.

I perch at one end of a wooden bench, gesturing for Nick to join me. He sits down hesitantly, setting his bag of produce at his side.

I give Nick a once-over, checking for a sign that he might have been involved in a knife fight or hit with pepper spray. His neck is blotchy, whether from stress or the sun, I don't know, but other than that he's clean.

"So, what do you want?" Nick asks haughtily.

Picture of politeness, this one.

"I'll cut to the chase," I say, crossing my arms over my chest. "Reid's still in jail for a crime we both know he didn't commit and I think you know something about it."

"Why would you think that?"

Is it just me or is there a touch of fear in his voice?

"Everyone has tells, little things they do when they're hiding something. Yours is that you flush, from your neck to the tips of your ears. Like they are right now."

He rubs a hand over his buzzed head, his fingers rubbing one ear anxiously. I watch the change in his demeanor, how he morphs from guarded to fearful in a matter of seconds.

"I was so stupid," he says, his face twisted in anguish.

"What did you do?"

And, with a backdrop of passersby shopping for local, organically-grown, sustainable produce, he tells me.

Nick wrings his hands in his lap, his bloodshot eyes fixed on mine as if imploring me to understand. Although he's barking up the wrong grapevine if he's looking for sympathy for killing Oscar and letting my boyfriend take the blame.

"Oscar had Reid in his back pocket," Nick starts, licking his lips. "Reid listened to him, gave him opportunities to try his hand at more complex dishes. It wasn't fair—" His voice breaks and he swallows. "I'm the better chef. I have better technique, better discipline."

"So you thought you would get revenge?"

He nods, wordlessly.

"How did you do it?" I ask. I sneakily pull my phone

from my pants pocket in case I need to call the authorities.

"Oscar was in charge of the sauces while I was cleaning the scallops. He had the audacity to tweak the recipe. Said it needed more acid, told me to trust his palate." His knees bob up and down, causing the whole bench to reverberate. "I knew how much Reid was counting on us that night, what it meant to have his family there."

A chill creeps up my spine and my mouth goes tannin dry.

"I bided my time, waited until the coast was clear. Then I made my move." Nick twitches, agitated. "I'd had enough of Oscar. Him telling me to relax and let the flavors guide me. What a load of bull."

He tries to laugh, but it turns into a hiccup. His eyes grow glassy with tears and he wipes at his nose.

I lean forward, scarcely daring to breathe for fear of interrupting his confession. At my side, my fingers hover over the screen of my phone.

"I watched Oscar leave and walked to the stovetop," Nick continues, the words coming out faster now. "I reached for the nearest canisters and started dumping spices in."

I snap to attention, sitting up straight. "Wait, what?"

He clenches his hands into fists. "I wanted Oscar to pay for all his experimenting."

It finally dawns on me exactly what Nick is admitting to. "You sabotaged the food."

"Not all of it," he says, as if that makes it any better. "Only the sauces, and the dishes that had just been plated."

"How could you do that to Reid?" I snap. "He trusted you."

I should be grateful he isn't a full-fledged murderer, but I see red, as if I'm peering at him through a glass of pinot.

"I didn't mean to hurt Reid. Honest," he says. "I realized immediately what I'd done, but it was too late. I couldn't take it back."

"That's why only some of the dishes were hit."

He nods glumly. "I'm pretty sure Oscar knew it was me, too, but for whatever reason, he didn't rat me out. Even though I'd done it to get him in trouble."

"Because Oscar was a decent human being." I think back to that night, the way Oscar stared determinedly at the floor when I'd asked him about the food. He knew. That's what he'd refused to say, figuring (correctly) that I would have told Reid.

"What I want to know is, when Reid chalked it up to a fluke, did you try to get back at Oscar another way?"

"No," he sputters. "It wasn't me that killed him, I swear."

Deceitful and an abysmal employee? Yes. Murderer? I think not. Nick doesn't have the backbone to do anything more sinister than add renegade spices to a sauce.

"I believe you," I say.

He exhales a deep breath, rubbing at the back of his neck, which is still splotchy from stress.

"But I wouldn't count on your job. I mean, Reid's pretty understanding, but he takes flavor very seriously, especially when his name is associated with it."

Nick's face floods with panic, his eyes darting about us as if the cyclists biking down the trail or people lazily roaming through the park can save him.

I leverage his desperation. "Do you want to keep your job?"

"Of course," he says.

"If you help me, I'll vouch for you to Reid."

He plays with the straps of his tote, his squash all but forgotten. "Help with what?"

"I want details about that night." When he doesn't object, I lean back, readjusting the clasp of my beaded necklace. "Let's start with Oscar. Was he acting strange at all?"

Nick chews on his thumbnail. "When he came back from your table, he seemed excited about something, almost slaphappy, and said he had to go make a call."

"That's weird," I mumble. From what I'd witnessed between Oscar and the Wallaces, there was no reason for him to feel the least bit encouraged. "Did he mention an old friend?"

"No," Nick says. "But after that, we were kinda busy making up for my, well, you know."

"For your astronomically poor judgment?"

"Yeah, that," he says with the ghost of a smile.

"What time did you and everyone else leave?"

"Britt and Katy left around ten o'clock, Reid shortly thereafter with the food he usually brought to the food bank."

I stifle a groan. Did everyone know about Reid's kind and giving spirit but me?

Nick continues, "Tony left around eleven o'clock, and Oscar a few minutes after that."

"Oscar left that early? You're sure?"

"Positive," he says. "It was my turn to close. By the time I wrapped up my side work and inventory, it must've been close to midnight. No one was around when I left."

That means Oscar lied to Katy when he said he'd be stuck at the restaurant late. Like some sort of investigative Hydra, there are more questions now than there were before. Where did Oscar go after he left work? How and why did he end up back at Spoons? And why wouldn't he tell his girlfriend about it?

Chapter Eighteen

While Felix loads up the unsold cases of wine, I sit in the cab of his roommate's truck, twirling my phone in my hand. All told, we sold a grand total of thirty bottles of wine and sparked interest in my tasting room, which I'm going to take as a much-needed win.

Now, though, I need answers. And there's one person who can help me get them.

I dial the number stored in my contacts. "Hi, Katy," I say. "It's Parker."

Her voice is guarded. "What's up?"

"Any chance you can introduce me to Oscar's family?"

"I guess," she says. "I haven't given them the painting yet. When are you hoping to go?"

Casting a furtive glance at Felix in the rearview mirror, I answer, "The sooner, the better."

We make plans to meet in twenty minutes at the house Oscar's parents are renting, and sign off.

I twist in my seat as Felix shuts the driver's-side door. "So, I promise I'll have a new batch of grapes to stomp soon . . ." I trail off, brainstorming other ideas to sweeten the pot. "Plus you can take extra vacation days this winter. And you can have a raise." The last bit slips out of my mouth before I realize I should run calculations first.

He raises one perfectly shaped eyebrow at me as he buckles his seat belt. "What do you need?"

"You to cover the shop this afternoon."

"Consider it done." He turns on the ignition and pulls out of his parking space, a car already waiting to snag the prime spot.

"I promise I'll be there as soon as I can," I say, more relieved than I care to admit. "I wouldn't ask if it wasn't an emergency."

"I know you wouldn't." He looks at me and then back at the road. "I don't know everything that's going on, but I've got your back."

It's as if a weight has been lifted from my shoulders. "You're seriously the best assistant. I know you've been working a ton this week."

"I don't mind." He shrugs, his arm casually dangling out his open window. "It's interesting work and, you know, my boss isn't *all* bad."

I snort, fiddling with a button on my (Reid's) shirt. "Gee, thanks."

"No prob," he says. "Where should I drop you?"

I rattle off an intersection close to the address Katy gave me.

Felix nods, and a few minutes later, he slows to a stop

on Balsam Street, just off Broadway. "Be careful and all that jazz."

"You, too," I say, a testament to my nerves.

I hoof it the final four blocks to a large gray house with at least six cars parked out front, including a delivery van of some kind. Kids are playing a rousing game of tag in the yard, which consists of more weeds than grass. The garage door is open, upbeat guitar music wafting from a speaker.

The wind whips my hair into my face. I tie it back with a spare rubber band, my bangs still awry. The clouds I'd noticed before are steadily drifting down the mountains.

"Hey," Katy says, walking up to me.

She looks more like herself than the last time I saw her. Sapphire eyeshadow sparkles around her eyes, and her braided hair is pinned into an extravagant knot on top of her head. She clutches her painting in both hands, the artwork wrapped in brown paper and bound with twine.

I gesture to all the cars. "Are there always this many people here?"

"Yeah," she says, snapping her gum. "Oscar's parents live here with his sister and their whole family, and I think a cousin who goes to CU."

"Gotcha." I hesitate, wondering if I should tell Katy that Oscar lied about his schedule, or if it's kinder to leave her memories alone—false as they may be.

I defer, instead prompting her to lead the way. "Ready?"

She holds up one hand. "First you've gotta tell me why we're really here."

"Because everything keeps coming back to who Oscar was supposedly going to meet the night he died. An old friend no one seems to know about." I dig the toe of my flat into the ground, dried leaves crunching beneath it. "I'm hoping Oscar's family might be able to enlighten us."

She chews her gum, staring at me. What she sees must appease her because she bows her head. "All right, then."

I follow Katy up the driveway, dodging a kid hoping to barricade himself from whoever is currently "it." I wipe my sweaty palms on my cords and grimace as my wounds protest the simple action.

She knocks on the front door, loud enough to be heard over the music, and a man answers. There's silver streaking his black hair and wrinkles etched in his brown skin. His dark eyes are wary as they take me in. I recognize his features, the same undeniably good looks as Oscar, only decades older. This must be his father.

"Hi, Mr. Flores," Katy says, color dotting her cheeks.

His gaze softens but only slightly.

Suddenly, he's nudged aside to make room in the doorway for a stunning older woman who can only be Oscar's mother. With cascading hair and a violet pashmina draped around her broad shoulders, she has a formidable presence.

"Katy, *buenos días*," she says. "Come in, come in." She waves us inside, shooting a disapproving look at her husband. "Would you like something? Tamales? Horchata?"

"Horchata would be great," Katy answers, and I nod enthusiastically beside her.

A milklike beverage imbued with vanilla and cinnamon, horchata sounds especially refreshing after my insanely long morning.

The first thing I notice upon crossing the threshold are the scents—heavenly aromas of roasted chilies, garlic, earthy spices, and fried dough. My mouth instantly starts watering.

I gaze around the space, astounded by the sheer amount of bright colors. The walls are a vivid burgundy, and paintings featuring beachscapes and tropical wild-life adorn the walls. A woven rug of sunshine-yellow and turquoise lines the floor, and everywhere I look are interesting pieces—clay bowls full of knickknacks, masks, and mosaic vases.

A table off to one side holds a picture of Oscar's smil-ing face surrounded by glowing tea-light candles, a bundle of herbs, and a folded serape blanket. Hesitantly, I step forward, wishing his image could speak. Could tell us what happened, whisper the identity of his mur-derer. But his likeness just smiles jovially, naive to the fact that his life would end too soon.

The kitchen is bustling with more kids, searching for snacks to fuel their play, and a woman behind the counter, her fingers covered in what I'm guessing is masa from the tamales. She's wearing a peasant blouse and colorful beaded earrings. She's basically a female version of Os-car, right down to the way her lips twitch into a grin.

She wipes her hands on a towel and embraces Katy.

She turns to me. "I'm Isabella, Oscar's sister."

"Parker," I say, shaking her hand. "A friend of Oscar's."

"And Reid's girlfriend," Katy adds.

I wince, nervous at how this revelation will go over. I'd been hoping to keep that tidbit on the down-low.

Isabella's eyes light up, but then she becomes distracted by her mother, who is carrying two cups of horchata and a steaming plate of tamales to the kitchen table.

"Mamá, let me help you," Isabella says, taking the glasses from her and leading us to spots at the table.

The older woman waves her off with a *phhht* sound. "Welcome," she says, cradling my hands in hers. "Call me Lucia."

Momentarily, I'm so overwhelmed by the friendly greeting that all I can do is blink. Maybe she missed the part about me dating the man accused of killing her son.

"Please sit or she'll just keep fussing over you," Isabella says, taking a seat herself.

I sink into a wooden chair and Katy does the same, passing her painting to Oscar's father, whose name I learn is Juan. He unwraps the paper and nods through his emotions at her masterpiece.

The painting is gorgeous. I can tell Katy added more layers of watercolors—and likely tears—since I saw it last. The colors and brushstrokes are so vibrant they might as well be alive. There's ample gushing and soon it's given a place of honor on Oscar's shrine.

I want to look away from the intimacy, growing more and more aware that I shouldn't be here, encroaching on their hospitality when they're in mourning.

"Drink, eat," Lucia says, seeing my untouched horchata.

Not wanting to be rude, I take a sip from my glass. The iced milk beverage is exquisite—spicy, sweet, and comforting.

"We're so grateful for everything Reid did for Oscar," Isabella says from across the table. "Back in culinary school and now, giving him a good job."

I shift awkwardly. "You mean, you don't think Reid is guilty?"

"Of course not," Isabella says. "None of us do, or you wouldn't be sitting here."

Even though she was the one bustling around the kitchen, I notice she hasn't eaten anything. There's a darkness about her features, a wanness in her frame, as if she's bearing the weight of too much grief.

What would it be like to be in Isabella's shoes? To be the one left behind to assemble the broken pieces? To comfort parents who should never have had to bury a child?

I remember how lost my mom felt after my aunt—her baby sister—passed away. A sibling is someone who, for better or worse, you should be stuck with forever. And vice versa. They know where you came from, how to drive you crazy, and what makes you laugh so hard milk comes out of your nose. I think of Liam; how gutted I would feel to lose him. My chest clenches.

"I'm going to find out who did this," I say, an impressive steeliness in my voice. "That's why I came here today. To see if you noticed anything different about Oscar that night."

The family exchanges looks—what's in them, I can't tell. Perhaps a question, of whether I can be trusted. Or perhaps communicating the quickest way to send me packing.

Lucia gazes at something over my shoulder and her eyes flutter shut. When she opens them, a fearful expression crosses her face like a shadow.

She says something in rapid Spanish to Isabella, who interprets for Katy and me. "We'll tell you what you want to know."

The Flores family practically force-feeds me lunch. Not that I put up much of a fight, mind you.

The tamales are out-of-this-world delicious. Earthy

and savory with a texture that tells me the masa was made from freshly ground hominy. The combination of spices is perfect, enough cumin and chilies to keep things interesting and the shredded pork full of umami. Apparently Oscar's affinity for flavor runs in the family. I tell Isabella as much.

She smiles demurely, a single curl of black hair falling over her forehead. "We learned together, cooking with Mamá in the kitchen."

"You're too modest, Isabella," Katy adds.

"Agreed," I say, and continue, with a nod toward Lucia. "And it sounds like you had a good teacher."

Isabella passes my compliment on to Lucia. My understanding of the language is limited to what I absorbed in high school Spanish, so I only understand a few words. But they must go over well, because Lucia and Juan beam at me.

Three kids tear into the kitchen, one of them blindfolded, their game of tag having escalated.

"Be quiet around your *abuelita*," Isabella says, shushing them with a gesture to Lucia. She peels back the blindfold and herds them back outside. "They've been extra antsy since school started. Guess it's good they're distracted. I'd rather them not hear this."

She returns to her seat, twisting the woven bracelets around her wrists. "I'm not sure where to begin."

Juan says something in Spanish to Isabella, who nods, exhaling a shaky breath. "Mamá gets migraines," Isabella says. "Auras start, like one is now. When this happens, it means pain follows within the hour."

I think back to the way Lucia's gaze fixed over my shoulder; it makes sense now. She was seeing the beginnings of an aura, a jagged rainbow of light dancing at the edges of her vision. I've experienced one such migraine and it was more than enough.

"I'm sorry," I say, wishing I could offer her more than empty words. For her pain, for their loss. I grip my ice-cold glass of horchata, the dew slippery beneath my fingers.

Lucia speaks in a rush, none of which I follow, concerned creases lining her forehead. Her eyes grow unfocused and her back stiffens as she trails off.

"She's reminding me that you're not here to hear about her pain," Isabella says, clearly accustomed to translating. "Although it's related."

"How so?" I ask.

I sense Katy leaning forward in anticipation. She'd been so adamant Oscar's family had nothing to do with his murder.

"Oscar called the night he . . ." Isabella trails off with a shudder. "He was excited, said he'd found a way to get Mamá relief."

At my frown, she explains. "You see, doctors won't give her the painkillers she needs. They think she's faking, seeking drugs."

"Or that it's psychosomatic, caused by stress," Katy interjects sadly, carrying her empty plate into the kitchen and depositing it in the sink. "It doesn't help they don't have health insurance."

"That, too," Isabella acquiesces. She glances at her parents, her shoulders tensing. "They tried to get health care, it's just too expensive."

"Double whammy," I say, giving her what I hope comes across as an encouraging smile. I'm certainly not one to judge. After pouring my life savings into opening Vino Valentine, I know what it's like to be broke. To not be able to afford much more than ramen, coffee, and cat food.

"Exactly," Isabella says, her gaze fixed on the flowering cactus centerpiece. "Well, on the phone, Oscar said he'd found someone who could help, that he'd tell us more the next morning, that he had to get back to the kitchen."

This must have been the phone call Nick mentioned. "Did Oscar tell you who?" I ask. "Or mention an old friend?"

Isabella shakes her head. "It was a short conversation and, honestly, I didn't prolong it. It was late, I'd just gotten the boys to bed."

An emotion I recognize clouds her features. It's in the way she purses her lips, furrows her eyebrows, and seems to seek something hidden to the rest of us. Regret.

I head it off as best I can. "You couldn't have stopped him."

She sniffles, crumpling her napkin into a tight ball. "I dismissed him, was impatient. If I'd known . . ." Her chest heaves as she swallows her sob.

Lucia squeezes her free hand, and beside her, Juan's lips form a thin line.

"Don't talk like that, Isabella," Katy says, going around the table to console her. "Oscar always said he was lucky to have you for a sister."

I bring the conversation back to the phone call, wanting to finish this so I can leave them in peace. "And that was the last you heard? There were no texts, nothing else?"

"That was it." She takes a shaky breath, bringing the napkin to her eyes.

I gnaw on my bottom lip, reeling through the information. There's a niggling at the back of my mind, an elusive thread that ties everything together.

Oscar's mother winces, lightly touching her temple.

"Please, tell her not to feel obligated on my account," I say with a worried glance toward Lucia.

Isabella interprets to her father, who stands and urges Lucia to her feet, whispering soothingly into her ear.

She concedes, tugging at the tassels of her pashmina. Even through her pain, she exudes a matriarchal poise, one that's accepting, loving, and strong. A far cry from Camilla's iciness, and infinitely classier.

Lucia kisses Katy on each cheek and says, "Visit again soon."

As Lucia passes me, she takes my hands in hers again, her wise eyes swimming with tears. "Thank you."

I can only nod, my vision blurring from how welcoming she's been. Despite being in physical and emotional pain from not getting the relief she needs—and deserves—on top of losing a son. I find myself wishing there was something I could do for her. For Oscar.

As she turns away, I catch a glimpse of Lucia's face in the mirror. The second her back is to me, the polite mask she's held in place fades away. She closes her eyes, leaning on her husband, her lips quivering in agony.

Lucia disappears into a dark room beside the kitchen, the windows covered with thick blankets, at the same time my phone rings.

My caller ID displays: *Boulder County Jail.*

My heart lodges itself in my throat as I answer. "Reid?"

"Parker, thank God you're okay," he says, taking a

ragged breath. "Sage told me what happened last night . . ."

Oh, right. Sage said she'd be seeing Reid today to prep for his court appearance. It'd been too much to hope that my friend would keep my assault to herself.

"Don't worry about me," I say, leaning against the exterior of the Flores house, having excused myself to take this call.

"But what were you thinking?" he asks, his tone unnecessarily harsh.

I cross my free arm over my chest, tucking it beneath my opposite elbow. "That since my boyfriend refuses to confide in me, I have to resort to searching for answers on my own."

"What do you mean I don't confide in you?"

I bark out a sarcastic laugh. "To start, why is it that everyone knew about your secret deliveries to the food bank except for me?"

"Because they didn't give me a choice. Britt, Nick, Oscar, they all pack up leftovers, even helped drop them off from time to time, after I warned them not to tell anyone about it."

"Fine," I say through a sigh. "Look, I get you're not used to sharing everything, and frankly, after meeting your family, I can see why. But I care about you. I want us to be there for each other, and, you know, it'd be nice to be able to go on a date with the guy I'm seeing."

"And I want my girlfriend to stay safe."

I smile in spite of the situation. "Wow, look at you, dropping the dreaded G-word like it's no big deal." Reid has come a long way since his bachelor days, from when he used to stumble over the word *girlfriend* during introductions.

"I have no problem admitting I'm in a committed relationship," he says, and I can practically picture him running a hand through his mussed hair. "That's not the point. You're deflecting."

"Look, I had to do something." I shove away from the gray siding and pace to the far side of the garage. The wind whips at my back and lively music still streams from the speaker, even though I'm the only one close enough to hear it. "At least it was good for something. Eli is reconsidering the evidence."

"Sage didn't mention that."

"Well, he is," I say. "So, you know, you're welcome."

Reid exhales deeply on his end of the line, so deeply I can almost feel his breath on my neck. I shiver.

"Confession time," he says. "While I don't like that you put yourself in danger, gotta admit, your bravery is one of the things I love most about you."

I stop short, gripping the back of a nearby rocking chair to steady me. His use of the L-word sends shock waves through my body, even as I remind myself he didn't say he loved *me*, just something *about* me. "Really?"

"When are you visiting me next?"

"Why?" I ask coyly. "Miss me?"

"You have no idea." His voice takes on a rough note. "I miss your face, your laugh, how you can tear me to pieces with one look. Your lower lip. Everything."

My insides melt into a pool that rivals my newly pressed sauv blanc.

"I miss you, too," I say, swallowing.

"Oh yeah?"

"Of course." I sink into a chair, rocking forward and backward in time to my pulse, which quickens as I say,

"Your smile, even that cocky one like I'm sure you have on your face now." He chuckles softly and I continue, "Being able to hug you, kiss you. The way you eat, weirdly. Your passion. I wanted to call you so badly the other day to share a new blend I'd made."

"I can't wait to taste it." There's noise on his end of the line. "Oh, hey, they're telling me to wrap up."

"Wait." I freeze. There are so many things I still have to tell Reid—about the witness, Nick's betrayal, Oscar's family—but I force myself to broach the topic I can't seem to forget, the burning question that's like acid on my tongue. "I have to ask you something."

"This sounds serious."

"It is." I lick my lips. If this is going to work between Reid and me, he has to trust me with his past, with the parts of himself he might rather keep hidden. Like how he once tormented his brother. "Ben told me about the time you locked Tristan in the basement when you were kids, even though Tristan was so scared he cried for help and was banging on the door." I grimace, trying not to sound accusatory. "It just took me by surprise."

"But that's not what happened."

"What do you mean?" A panicky feeling flutters in my chest.

"Ben got it wrong," he answers hurriedly. "What really happened was—"

But then there's nothing but silence. The line has gone dead.

Chapter Nineteen

Lazy grapes make for weak wine.

Fruit that's forced to struggle, thrive on less water, and cope in extreme climates tends to be more flavorful. Whereas grapes that are pampered and given everything they need may look plump and delicious, but they're usually watery.

Not dissimilar from people.

Maybe that's why the story from Reid's childhood matters so much to me. We never quite outgrow who we were as children. Every experience ultimately contributes to the person we become.

I have to know what Reid meant when he said Ben got it wrong, and I have to find out now. Not in twenty-four hours, when I can wrangle a visitation.

So, after bidding adieu to Katy and the Floreses, I

take the southbound Hop RTD line to Pearl Street. I've already skipped out on enough work to last me a life-time, and taken advantage of Felix's generosity, but at this point, what's one more hour?

The flags outside the St Julien flap in the wind, strong gusts teasing my hair out of its low ponytail. The sun is hidden behind storm clouds with a foreboding navy tint to them.

The bellhop opens the door to the lobby for me. "You just beat the rain," he says, gesturing to where large drops have started falling.

"Lucky me," I say. The hair at the nape of my neck rises at the change in atmospheric pressure.

There's less dread and more burning curiosity as I make my way up the elevator and down the meandering hallway to the Wallaces' suite.

I'm hoping to find Ben or Tristan but would even settle for Camilla or Gary if it means getting answers.

I knock on their door and wait, moving to the side to let a family pass, heading to the indoor pool, if their swimsuits and goggles are any indication. I knock again, louder this time.

There's a shuffling, a fumble with the dead bolt, and then Gary swings the door open.

One side of his face is crimson, as if he's been se-verely sunburned. The skin is blistered and peeling, and his eye is swollen shut.

I stumble backward, finding myself pressed against the opposite wall of the hallway. "It was you!"

I glance from side to side, my breathing loud in my ears.

"Parker, wait," Gary says, his voice unmistakably the

one I heard in my ear last night, demanding I stay out of Oscar's case.

My hand is around the pepper spray canister before I even comprehend that I've reached in my purse for it. "Come one step closer and I'll finish what I started."

Gary freezes, holding his hands up in front of him.

We have a standoff in the hallway, my arm raised in warning. My wounds hiss at me to stop, but I ignore them. Gary has a predatory glint in his eyes, cold and calculating.

We are making quite the spectacle. A bubble of laughter threatens to escape at the absurdity of this moment, but I swallow it down. There's nothing funny about this situation.

"Be civil," Gary says, as if I'm being ridiculous. He shifts his feet. "Come inside and let's talk about this."

I grip the canister tighter, my palm sweaty against the smooth metal. "There's no way in hell I'm shutting myself in closed quarters with you. You can't possibly think I'm that stupid."

He looks me up and down. "You don't want to know what I think of you."

His gaze makes me feel grimy, like there's a layer of sediment beneath my skin. "I can't believe I ever wanted to impress you." I think back to my naive self, how I'd pandered to their whims, took their criticisms silently. "Reid is going to go berserk when he finds out."

I mean, I know the Wallaces weren't *thrilled* with our relationship, but this is extreme. Seriously, how am I supposed to tell Reid? How can we possibly move forward after this?

"You don't understand," Gary growls. "Everything I did was to protect him."

"How does scaring the crap out of me help Reid? How does it fix anything?" My voice is growing louder and more frantic, my heart hammering in my chest.

That's when I realize what exactly he just said: *everything*. "You killed Oscar." Tears and sweat mingle on my cheeks, and my arm begins to shake. "For freeloading off your family? For leeching off of Reid? Because I've got news for you: that wasn't Oscar."

Gary considers me for a moment, his blistered lips twisting into a scowl. The armpits of his white shirt are yellowed from sweat. To think he always appeared so pristine in his cable-knit sweaters and fancy suits, when underneath, he was hiding this ugliness all along.

He bends at the waist, his body suddenly heaving.

I press myself farther into the wall, a picture frame digging into my shoulder blades. A knot of fear lodges itself in my throat.

Gary makes an animalistic guttural sound that chills me to my core and, all at once, I realize he's crying.

What a pitiful figure he strikes. But I'm too far gone with rage and fear to feel even an ounce of sympathy for the man who attacked me.

"My family is ruined," he says, standing, tears streaming down his grotesque face. He clamps his puffy eye with his hand, breathing in a sharp hiss of pain. "Dammit, how long is this going to sting?"

"Hopefully a really long time," I say. Then I turn on my heel and run.

My head is spinning and blood pounds in my ears as I race down the four flights of stairs to the lobby, not wanting to risk waiting for the elevator.

One hand still clutches the pepper spray, the other clings to the banister. My ankle twinges every other step and I grit my teeth through the pain. I glance over my shoulder, expecting to see Gary's figure, but he doesn't seem to be chasing me. At least, not yet.

Once I'm in the bustling lobby, with enough bystanders to rush to my aid if I shout *fire*, I hunch over my knees and take deep yoga breaths—in through my nose, out through my mouth—and try to get a handle on what I just learned.

My boyfriend's father assaulted me. And killed Oscar.

Gary must have been the *old friend* Oscar had planned to meet. Oscar had always been big on sarcasm; he must've used the phrase ironically. And the help he was supposedly getting for Lucia must have been cash. Cold, hard cash. But how could Gary let his own son take the fall for his crime? Even if he and Reid are estranged, that's low. Really low.

When I straighten back up, I have two simultaneous thoughts: one, that asshole is going to pay; and two, I really hope Camilla, Tristan, and Ben are okay.

The first thing I do is call Eli.

"No, I haven't found anything to help Reid yet," he starts with an aggrieved sigh, entirely oblivious to the real reason I'm calling. "And I won't be able to if you don't give me time."

"Listen," I blurt out, giving Eli a slightly frantic version of my run-in with Gary, finishing with a plea to hurry. "And bring backup, or whatever."

"You don't really understand how the police force operates, do you?" Eli asks.

"Does that matter right now?"

"Not a lick," Eli says. "On my way."

Next, I stop by the concierge's desk. The same helpful lady from the other day is working, pumpkins dazzling on her fingernails. Her blond hair is knotted in a low ponytail hanging down her back and she's in a posh pantsuit that gives her an air of authority.

"If you see Mr. Wallace, call security immediately," I say. "The police will be here soon."

She hesitates, her wide eyes blinking rapidly as she comprehends my warning. Maybe she's sensed some evil in Gary, maybe it's the dire look on my face or the pepper spray clutched in my hand, or maybe we live in an age where women have one another's backs, no questions asked. Regardless, I'm grateful when she nods and hurries to speak with the bellhop.

She returns a moment later, readjusting her blazer. "We've got the exits covered. Can I get you anything?"

"Not unless you have a time machine I could use." I lean against her desk, grateful to take the weight off my ankle.

Her lips twitch. "Sorry, not even for our premier guests."

"Figured."

My immediate panic has subsided, leaving in its place a numb disbelief. I turn toward the lobby, scanning the space for the rest of the Wallace clan. If Camilla and her older sons aren't aware of what a danger Gary is, I'll have to break the news to them. And if they *do* know . . . well, I really don't want to think about what that could mean.

I half expect to find them playing Parcheesi, or whatever it is the upper crust of society does on vacation, but don't see them.

It's pouring rain outside now, those few large drops I'd witnessed progressing into a full-fledged deluge. Colorado may resemble a desert, but when it does rain here, it's serious. Flash floods and mudslides are frequent occurrences, thanks to the heavy clay soil, and right now, the terrace is covered in puddles, and what I can see of the mountainside looks slick.

My teeth chatter at the rapidly cooling temperature and I rub my arms, finding them lined with goose bumps. I have flashbacks to the night before. Of the weight of Gary on my chest, his breath in my ear, the menace in his voice. I shudder, my throat constricting.

I can't stop fidgeting, can't bring myself to focus on the botanical upholstery of the cushy armchairs or stately wooden pillars. Rocking on my feet and wringing my hands, I cast furtive glances about, checking for Gary; Eli and his squad; or Camilla, Ben, or Tristan. But there are only relaxed hotel guests or passersby seeking shelter from the storm.

My phone buzzes.

I frown when I see it's the business line at Vino Valentine. "Hi, this is Parker."

I barely recognize Felix's voice. What's usually so deep and gravelly is now filled with panic. "Where the hell are you?"

"Pearl Street," I answer vaguely. "Why?"

"I'm drowning here."

"I don't doubt it," I say, eyeing the rivulets of water rushing down the street outside and into a storm drain.

"This isn't the time to be cute," Felix snaps. "I'm in way over my head. We've been slammed for hours. You've gotta get back here." As if to prove his point, there's a loud crash on his end of the line.

My heart flutters with nerves and guilt. I feel like I've been trying to juggle every aspect of my life and all the balls are dropping to the floor at once.

I chew on my bottom lip and run a hand through my limp hair, pondering the best way to handle everything. The hotel staff has things covered until Eli gets here, and perhaps it's time I heeded his and Reid's wishes and practice caution, take myself out of harm's way. In an instant, I've made up my mind.

"Be there in ten," I tell Felix. "Hang in there."

I end the call, send Eli a quick text, and jog to the concierge's desk for good measure. "Can you take a message for the detective?"

"Absolutely," she says, her hand poised over a pad of paper.

"Tell him Parker will meet him at the station." I've been involved in enough investigations to know I'll need to be questioned further after this ordeal, plus, this way I'll hear the second Reid is released from jail. "I need to make a quick stop first to take care of something and then I'll be there."

I don't wait for her response before dashing out into the storm, praying to Bacchus—god of the grape harvest and winemaking—that I can get a ride in this weather.

Chapter Twenty

Vino Valentine is completely packed when I get there.

Swirling, sniffing, and gurgling abound, and there's plenty of chatter about aromas and flavors, from strangely specific (eucalyptus) to the expected (cherry). Every oak-barrel table is occupied and it's standing-room-only at the tasting bar. The baskets of palate-cleansing crackers are severely depleted, and ambiguous glasses clutter every visible surface.

Romantic couples waiting out the storm, cyclists whose rides were cut short, students with nothing better to do on a Sunday afternoon. The rain, far from deterring people, seems to have driven them inside for the afternoon. No complaints here. The boom in business will ease the sting of closing early.

I flip the sign on the storefront door from OPEN to CLOSED to deter any new arrivals and hustle behind the tasting bar, where Felix looks extremely flustered, his hair sticking up at awkward angles, his tortoiseshell glasses slightly askew. He pulls two wineglasses from the nearly empty shelf above the dishwasher and fumbles. One of them slips, shattering on the floor.

He swears under his breath and, noticing me, swears again. "About time."

I ignore him, stashing my purse under the bar. I grab a wineglass and clink a metal aerator against it. "Can I have everyone's attention," I say loudly.

The chatter dims to a dull buzz.

"I want to thank you all for coming in today. Unfortunately, I have to close early for a family emergency." Whether Reid likes it or not, I consider him family. "Your tasting is on the house and I hope you'll come back another day. Thank you."

There are groans and muttering as chairs scratch against the floor and belongings are collected.

"What are you doing?" Felix hisses.

"Giving you the afternoon off," I say. "Now, you clean up this mess"—I gesture to the shards of glass on the floor, daintily stepping around them—"and I'll start clearing tables."

Felix nods, seemingly happy to have direct orders to follow.

I hop to, moving stray glasses to the counter beside the industrial dishwasher and tucking away baskets of palate-cleansing crackers. After gently urging some of my more sluggish customers to vacate the premises, my madhouse of a winery finally empties, just as the storm is dying down.

I get the sense Felix isn't accustomed to working under pressure. He held up well, all things considered. Sure, the storefront is a mess. There's wine splattered on the floor around the bar, making my flats stick as I walk by. Crumbs cover the tabletops yet to be cleaned, and I'm dreading checking the state of the bathroom. But it's still standing.

Angelic rays are shining through the clouds, already drying drops of water from the petals of the potted mums out front.

"Why don't you take off?" I suggest to Felix, shedding my flannel shirt. "It's the least I can do after leaving you in the lurch."

Felix rolls his neck back and forth, his cardigan as withered as he is. He narrows his eyes in concern. "What's the family emergency?"

"Trip to the police station, and then picking Reid up from jail." Just the thought of seeing Reid, of being able to throw my arms around him, makes me go all tingly.

Felix's eyebrows shoot up. "So, status quo for you?"

"Basically." I chuckle, arching my stiff back. "You'd better get out of here before I change my mind."

"You sure, boss?"

"Positive," I say with a smile. "I'll be heading out right after you, anyway." The majority of the cleaning and seeing to my harvest can wait until later.

With his customary salute, satchel slung crosswise over his body, Felix disappears through the back door, near where I know his roommate's truck is parked in the alley.

The bell over the door jingles, signaling a customer despite the CLOSED sign. My smile falters when I see who it is: Tristan.

*   *   *

Tristan is wearing a pair of black jeans and a button-up, cream-colored shirt with the sleeves rolled up to his elbows. He tucks his sunglasses into the V of his shirt, showcasing tanned skin beneath, and flashes me his pearly whites as he takes in my wasteland of a winery.

His hair is dewy, like he got caught outside in the storm, but it only adds to his devil-may-care vibe.

"I was looking for you earlier," I say, resting my palms against the hard maple countertop of the tasting bar, relieved to see he's okay. "Where have you been?"

"Had to check in at the conference," he answers. "I was on a panel."

"What about Camilla, Ben?" I ask, my voice pitchy and laced with concern.

He waves his hand through the air. "Ben had a call with some client and my mother wanted to go antiquing in Lyons."

"Oh. I thought Camilla might have sent you."

He snorts. "Not even the queen could convince my mom to be cordial to you." He sits on a stool and looks about the empty space. "I came here hoping to get a glass of your cab, but it seems like I'm too late."

"I'm getting ready to head to the police station . . ." I trail off, realizing he doesn't know about Gary. "Actually, we should go together."

Tristan stills, shifting his entire focus to me. "Why would I want to go there?"

"Because Reid is innocent. Your father . . ." I shake my head. "I'll explain the rest on the way."

"Why don't you tell me now?"

I hesitate and then pour him a glass of the Campy

Cab. "Here, drink this first. It'll lessen the blow." My eyes flit to his, dark like his father's, as I stopper bottles of wine. "Can I ask you something?"

"You just did." There's a bite to his words and an uncharacteristic guardedness in his stiff posture.

"Something else." I lick my lips. "Why did your family really come to see Reid?"

"To convince him to move back to Connecticut."

And there it is. The truth, finally. Their visit is nothing but a ploy to get Reid to give up on his dream. I grind my teeth, shoving a cork into a bottle with more force than necessary.

"Mom was worried Reid was laying down roots here, with you, and wanted to intervene before it was too late. For the record, I never thought it would work," he says. "I only came because the conference was going on at the same time."

Tristan shrugs, the sun hitting his damp hair. He takes a large swallow of wine, sloshing it around in his mouth. His attempt at nonchalance doesn't work; his knuckles are white as they grip the stem of his glass.

That's when I notice it: a button missing from his shirt.

I thought he'd tactfully left the top unbuttoned as a fashion statement, but it's really because there's a gap. The other buttons around the straggling thread are pearly white, the exact same color as the one I found in the alley outside Spoons.

Everything snaps into place and I realize—it wasn't Gary at all.

The reason the witness was positive he saw Reid was because Tristan and Reid are dead ringers for each other. They have the same build, the same hair, and, at least from a distance, the same features. Tristan's shirt even resembles a chef's coat.

And maybe the witness wasn't the only one to have gotten the brothers mixed up.

I take a chance, wiping my hair out of my eyes. "Ben told me the story about you and Reid and the basement."

Tristan scowls, shifting on the barstool. "He just won't let that go. It happened ages ago and, besides, Reid forgave me."

I knew it. Ben had misremembered. It wasn't Reid who locked Tristan in the basement, left to be tortured in the darkness for hours. It was Tristan. That's what Reid meant when he said Ben had gotten the story wrong.

Although Ben was right about one thing: the person behind that terrorizing act of their youth was capable of murder.

More thoughts rush through my mind, like wine through an aerator. When Gary said he attacked me *to protect him*, he'd meant Tristan, not Reid. Tristan, the son who was supposedly upholding the family honor, even if he, you know, *killed someone*.

And then there was the tension I'd sensed between Oscar and Tristan the night of the disastrous dinner. When I questioned him about it later, Tristan claimed it was due to Oscar having intel on the illicit affair between him and his older brother's new fiancé. Was that for real, or a fabrication?

Regardless, there's one thing I know: Tristan killed Oscar.

What I don't know is why. And how I'm going to get him out of my winery without arousing suspicion.

I realize I missed something Tristan said. He's staring at me, waiting for an answer, his glass hovering at his lips.

"Sorry, what did you say? I spaced out for a minute." I hesitate, trying to come up with an excuse. "It's been a long day, early grape shipment and all."

He nods and flashes me a smile so broad I can see his canines.

I turn toward the dishwasher, my heart pounding in my chest, my mouth completely dry. I sense rather than see him move around the bar.

"I should really be going soon," I say, backing into the cash register. "The detective is expecting me." I hope Tristan can't see through my fib.

"Just want a peek behind the curtain." He strolls lazily down the length of the counter, gazing around. "You really do have a nice thing going here."

"Thanks." Icy dread floods through my limbs.

I start to reach into my back pocket for my phone, but there's no way I'll be able to make a call without Tristan seeing and stopping me. And my phone won't be of much use in a fight. Blindly, my fingers pad across the counter, finally gripping the base of a stray wineglass. It's not much, but if I can break it in just the right place, maybe I can use the sharp edge as a knife.

Tristan runs his fingers over my wine bottles, organized from light- to heavy-bodied—the Mount Sanitas White, Chautauqua Chardonnay, Pearl Street Pinot—finally resting on the Campy Cab, like a mountain lion, all sleek stealth until the attack.

I must have acted too twitchy, or perhaps he saw the realization dawn on my face, because it's clear he knows that I know.

My breath catches in my throat, and I brace myself for his next move.

"Too bad it's all coming to an end," Tristan says, gripping the wine bottle by its neck and baring his teeth at me.

I strengthen my grip on the glass stem and try to reason with him. "Think about it. There's no one to pin a murder on this time."

"That only matters if someone finds you, which won't be an issue where we're going."

"You'll have to catch me first," I say.

I slam the wineglass against the counter, hearing the telltale shatter, and twirl around, raising the jagged edge to his neck. But I'm too slow. Much too slow.

With surprising speed he brings the bottle of cab down on my head.

My scalp erupts in pain as I crumple to the ground, the world going dark.

Chapter Twenty-One

My eyes flutter open.

My head aches and my mouth is dry, heightened by the cotton rag shoved in my mouth. Hair is plastered to my forehead. I tense my muscles, struggling to move them this way and that, but find my motions restricted. My wrists and ankles must be bound.

I feel the jostle of the road beneath me. I'm in a car.

My eyes adjust slowly and I take in my surroundings. I'm stretched across the backseat of some sort of SUV. It's dark outside. I can just make out Tristan's profile in the driver's seat against the crescent moon.

My eyes sting with tears I didn't realize I was shedding. How did I end up here? Is this what I get for trying to figure out what really happened to Oscar? For trying to protect Reid? For interfering with his crazy family?

I think of Zin, my feline extraordinaire, and William,

my houseguest who's already had his world rocked this
week. I picture them watching the door of my apartment, their tails twitching expectantly, as their kibble
dwindles. Will anyone think to feed them?

I think of my mom, who gifted me a pH tester, helped
me unload grapes this morning, and finally seems to
understand my passion. Understand me.

I think of my business. Of the harvest and new wines
currently fermenting in barrels, vats, and bins. The red
varietals will need punch downs soon, before the grape
skins dry out and effectively destroy all my hard word.

And, above all, I think of Reid. Of the time that has
been stolen from us, and the things unsaid between us.
Why didn't I tell him I loved him every chance I could?
Was our last kiss—our final embrace—really after we
stomped grapes together?

This can't be it. This can't be the end.

I try to speak, to say anything, but the gag is too
firmly in place. I scream into it instead, hoping maybe
we're driving in downtown Boulder and someone in a
neighboring car will hear.

"G'morning, sunshine," Tristan says cheerily. "Don't
worry, we're almost there."

His faux good humor is terrifying, a sign that he's
truly lost his marbles. I struggle against my bonds, wrig-
gling my wrists as hard as I can.

The car slows to a stop, gravel crunching beneath the
tires. I tilt my chin and look out the window but can
only see the moon and the tops of pine trees.

Tristan tucks the keys in his pocket, gets out of the
driver's side of the car, and, a second later, opens the
backseat door by my head. He drags me out of the car by
my shoulders, not seeming to care that I bump my elbow

along the way, that the bruise on my side makes me cry out in pain.

I squirm, fighting against him as hard as I can, but his hold is too strong, his fingers digging into my shoulders.

"Keep moving and I'll knock you out again," he says, slightly out of breath. "It would just take the right amount of pressure, right here." He adjusts his arms so they're around my neck, cutting off my windpipe.

I stop fighting. For now.

He drops me unceremoniously onto the ground, mud from the recent rain coating my cheek, and leaves to retrieve something else from the car.

I roll onto my side, the ground slick beneath me, and try to get my bearings.

I'm in a secluded clearing, the smell of pine needles, tree sap, and damp leaves in the air. Nearby are two benches and large rocks as a quasi-barricade to the steep cliff beyond that juts down. A post signaling a trailhead is to my left and, thanks to all the times I've hiked and climbed around here, I recognize it immediately.

We're on top of Flagstaff, a mountain that overlooks Boulder.

No one comes here at this time of night. Panic fully takes hold and my breathing quickens until I'm hyperventilating.

We're completely alone, the nearest sign of human life at least two miles down the steep mountainside. Even if I could scream for help, no one would come. I'm on my own.

Tristan returns with a black leather bag in tow. He kneels before me, his skin taking on a greenish hue in the scant moonlight. He unclasps the silver buckle and roots through his bag for something. A moment later his hand emerges, holding a syringe and a small vial of clear liquid.

My heart lodges itself in my throat and I try to scream again, thrashing my legs and pulling my wrists apart as hard as I can.

Tristan grins at me. "You're right to be scared, you know." He pulls the safety plastic covering the needle off with his teeth and pricks the tip into the vial, filling the syringe with mystery fluid. "OxyContin can have varying effects on people. Most respond with drowsiness, vomiting, respiratory compression. Don't worry, you won't be alive long enough to suffer through the worst of it."

Gee, thanks, I want to retort. Since I'm still gagged, I settle for staring daggers into him.

"Ah, don't be like that." Tristan removes the cloth from my mouth. "Any last words? Something you want me to tell Lover Boy?"

I refuse to let Tristan win. Not like this. I'm too stubborn and prideful to go down without a fight. Besides, I know two things that Tristan doesn't.

First, thanks to my climbing experience, I've learned a lot about knots. Which ones weaken over time (clove hitch), and which ones are nearly impossible to untie (constrictor knot). While I can't pinpoint the exact type he used, the fact that my wrists have a wider range of motion after just a few minutes of straining means it's only a matter of time before I can break free.

And second, this is my turf. I know this overlook, this trailhead. Sure, it's tough as nails and would be hell to navigate in the dark. Especially with the soil slippery from the storm and my ankle already smarting. But I could do it.

So, somewhere in the recesses of my mind, I realize

my best bet at surviving is to keep Tristan talking until I can get my hands free.

Lying on the ground with Tristan lording above me, it's as clear as a New Zealand pinot gris that he relishes being in control. I can use that against him. I roll farther onto my back to give him the impression of complete domination. And to hide my hands.

"You killed Oscar," I say, subtly working on prying my wrists apart.

"I'm disappointed, Parker," he says, the syringe dangling lazily from his fingers. "I'd hoped for something more . . . original from you."

"Untie me and I'll try to come up with something wittier."

"You know I can't do that."

"At least tell me why you did it."

Tristan doesn't answer, just dips his chin and stares at his boots. For a split second, I'm sure I've failed, that he's going to stick me with the needle and leave me to overdose on OxyContin.

But then he starts talking.

Tristan tells me his morbid tale with his gaze fixed on the ground. In the darkness, it's unfair how much he looks like Reid. The auburn undertones in his hair, his broad shoulders and chiseled jaw. It's just one more way fate has seen fit to torture me.

"I guess it all starts with this," he says, flicking the needle of the syringe. "I told you Oscar caught me doing something once at my parents' house."

"When you betrayed your other brother," I say, straining against my bonds. Whatever rope he used to restrain me digs into my skin until blood mixes with the mud beneath me. "Not a great track record."

"Nothing ever happened between me and Liza," he says, shaking his head. "That was a lie to throw you off my track."

"But Oscar still saw something, didn't he?" I prod.

"He walked in on me unpacking vials of painkillers. I'd smuggled them from work to sell under . . . we'll just say 'ethically questionable circumstances.'"

My eyebrows shoot up. That was unexpected.

I remember why Tristan tagged along for this family reunion in the first place: the dates aligned with an anesthesiologist conference he was already planning to attend. And now he's just admitted to selling drugs on the black market.

Real winner, this one.

I have to remind myself to keep working on loosening the knot. There's a hairbreadth between my hands now. Just a little longer and I'll be able to wriggle free.

"So?" I ask. "He must have kept your secret since you're still practicing medicine."

"I always knew you were smart." He taps his head, the needle point dangerously close to his temple. If only he'd accidentally stab himself with it. "Oscar promised not to say anything back then, not wanting to hurt Reid after everything he'd done for Oscar during culinary school. But when he saw me at Spoons the other night, he saw my presence as an opportunity."

I freeze, my mouth going dry, more pieces snapping into place.

"He asked me to meet him later that night after the restaurant closed. I didn't know why until I got there."

Now I understand why Oscar had been so excited when he'd returned to the kitchen after visiting our table. Because he'd seen Tristan, his supposed *old friend*. How desperate he must have been to resort to him for help.

"Oscar asked you for painkillers, didn't he?" I ask.

Tristan snorts, the whites of his eyes glowing madly. "He said it was for his mom, but you know his type . . ."

"What, you mean honest, decent?"

"Poor," he growls. "It was cute, really, he thought he could afford my price. He'd even gone to the ATM, said he could pay in cash, as if that would earn him a discount."

That's where Oscar went after leaving Spoons, why he'd lied to Katy about what time he'd be done working. He went to acquire the means for his seedy transaction and then circled back when he was sure no one would be there.

"Couldn't you have just said no?" I ask. "Let him go on his way?"

"I would have, if he hadn't threatened to turn me in to the medical board."

Oscar, you fool, I think to myself.

Tristan shifts on his feet, remaining on his haunches in front of me. "The restaurant was dark, just me and Oscar having it out in the kitchen. After his paltry attempt at blackmail, he left through the door into the alley." Tristan's lips twist into a cruel smile. "I grabbed Reid's knife and followed him. He didn't expect an attack. He tried to fight back. Even up until the end, he thought I might change my mind and help him. Pathetic, really." He chuckles to himself. "And the only person who saw us thought I was Reid."

Grinding my teeth, I tug once more, slackening the rope enough for me to squeeze one finger through. I shift my legs slightly, getting them into position for my maybe crazy, maybe brilliant plan.

"How could you let your own brother take the fall for your crime?" I ask.

"It served Reid right," he says, practically spitting. He gets to his feet and paces, his boots squelching in the mud. "He always got the attention, even when he was driving my parents crazy by *being true to himself*. Really, I killed two birds with his knife. I got Oscar and my idiotic brother out of the way."

While he's absorbed in his diatribe, I pull one hand free, subtly shaking the rope off my other wrist. I keep my hands tucked behind my back, pretending to still be struggling against the constraints. This is going to take precision, especially since my feet are still bound.

Tristan freezes, turning to me, his eyes burning with hatred. "Now there's just you to contend with."

He stalks closer and I know this is it. This is the only chance I'm going to get. My breathing is ragged in my chest and I can hear the blood pounding in my ears. My entire body is pulsing with fear, with a primal need to run. But I force myself to wait. To bide my time until he's closer.

"How did you know it was me?" he asks, only a foot away now.

"Your button."

He glances down at his shirt, and that's when I make my move.

I kick out with both legs, tripping Tristan at just such an angle that he stumbles backward, between the two boulders, and careens down the mountainside.

* * *

I scramble to unknot the binding around my ankles. For someone so conniving, Tristan is exceptionally bad at restraining people. Not that I'm complaining, mind you.

I kick off the rope, which turns out to be the tie-down ratchet Felix and I use to move oak barrels in the back of Vino Valentine. The nerve of Tristan to sift through my things. Then I picture his grubby hands touching me while I was unconscious, tying my ankles and wrists together, carrying me to his rental car, and shiver. But I don't have time to dwell on that now.

I push myself to my feet, my palms scraping against the ground, gravel and muck sticking to my fingers. My head pounds at the change in position and I double over, my stomach roiling. No doubt I have a concussion. With one hand pressed to my temple where the wine bottle made contact and the other on my stomach, I force myself to take a few steps forward.

Even though Tristan is out of sight, I know he won't go far before he regains his balance. And I can't be here when he does. In hand-to-hand combat—a battle of strength—Tristan would overpower me, no problem.

The only thing on my side is my knowledge of this trailhead. It's a treacherous two-mile path, riddled with rocks, tree roots, and who knows what wildlife lurking in the bushes. But the car keys are snug in Tristan's pocket, and I'd rather take my chances with the animal kingdom than face the psycho killer behind me.

I limp down the trail, my feet clumsy and prickling from the rush of blood returning to my toes. My flats are still on, but they're not the best for hiking and I immediately slip, grabbing on to the rough bark of a pine tree.

I take a deep breath before continuing, moving slow enough to be able to stop myself from tripping, but not so slow that Tristan can catch me. At least, I hope.

I hear something behind me, a high-pitched sound that urges me to pick up my pace. I hear it again and hesitate. It doesn't sound like footsteps. It almost sounds like . . . I risk a glance over my shoulder and let out a cry of relief.

There are flashing lights accompanying the loud siren as emergency vehicles charge up the winding road to Flagstaff.

I run back the way I came, up the trail and into the clearing, waving my hands in the air frantically, tears streaming down my face. My throat is hoarse from shouting, but I don't stop until the vehicles slow and pull into the overlook parking lot.

Eli emerges from the first sedan and I race toward him, my words coming out in a jumble as I point to where Tristan fell. "He couldn't have gone far," I finish.

Eli reaches beneath his jacket for his gun, pulling it from the holster strapped there.

He gestures to two officers and together they move forward in formation.

I follow them to the ledge and peer through the darkness. Upon hearing the sirens, Tristan must have turned and booked it down the mountain in an attempt to get away. I can barely make out his silhouette in the distance, staggering on the steep slope, dragging one leg behind him.

Eli and the two officers catch up with him in no time. They surround Tristan, two flanking one side, Eli taking center stage. They navigate the muddy, rocky terrain with ease. I see the moment Tristan gives up—realizes he's done for. He falls to his knees and clasps his hands on top of his head.

I savor the warm feeling spreading through me and recognize it for what it is: safety.

I sink onto a nearby bench, resting my head in my hands, unable to stop the tears from streaking down my face. I don't know how long it is before Tristan is led by me toward the patrol car. His cream-colored shirt is caked in mud and his leather pendant necklace is pulled across his neck like a choker.

When he sees me, he snarls, struggling against the handcuffs, but Eli has him in such a firm grip, Tristan only ends up hurting himself.

"You'll pay for this," he hisses, his eyes full of venom.

"No, I won't," I say, smiling sweetly at him, even as my head threatens to split open.

"Reid will never love you," he says, somehow pinpointing the one way he can continue to torture me. "He can't—it's not in our DNA."

He continues muttering horrible things under his breath—about me, Reid, and Oscar. About all the people he feels are to blame for his current predicament. I block him out, my mind stuck on one particular thing he said: *our DNA*. No matter what happens, nothing will change the fact that Reid is related to Tristan. To his father.

Eli maneuvers Tristan into the patrol car and shuts the door, cutting off his crazed monologue.

I'm all too relieved for the silence, and even more relieved when an EMT leads me to a waiting ambulance. She proceeds to give me a once-over, spending an inordinate amount of time on my head, where I was struck with the wine bottle. It must be bad.

She gives me an ice pack and goes to talk to her partner, and then says something to Eli, who breaks away from the police officers in charge of Tristan.

He shrugs out of his coat as he approaches me and drapes it across my shoulders, the heat making me sigh.

He's every inch the suave detective as he leans against the ambulance, arms crossed over his chest and dark hair slicked back.

"You're going to need to go to the hospital. The EMT says you suffered a concussion and they want to monitor you overnight." His eyes meet mine, soft and smooth as caramel. "I've asked them to give us a minute before they whisk you away."

I nod but then wince, the simple gesture causing my head to ache. My voice is raw as I ask, "How'd you know where to find me?"

"Camilla Wallace."

"*Camilla?* Are you sure?" I ask, the ice pack slipping from my fingers.

He places the ice pack back into my hand and, with surprising tenderness, guides it once again to my temple. "She returned to the hotel as we were escorting Mr. Wallace out. From his ramblings, she pieced together what happened and we were able to track Tristan Wallace's cell phone signal to this approximate location."

"Thank goodness for technology."

"And thank goodness you were able to hold him off until we got here." He runs a hand through his hair, letting out a long exhale. "I owe you an apology."

"You saved my life," I quip. "I think we're even."

"Technically, you saved your own life, and if I had listened to you sooner, you wouldn't have needed to." He hangs his head. "Frankly, you have me questioning if I'm fit for duty."

"Hey, don't say that. From your stance it was an open-and-shut case."

Eli eyes me with such profound regret that I feel a pang of sadness in my chest.

"Really," I say, drops of condensation from the ice pack trickling down my fingers. "I feel much safer with you protecting the mean streets of Boulder."

He lifts his chin and looks at me. "Thanks, Parker."

I relax, easing back against some contraption in the ambulance. I don't know what it's meant for, but it makes a good backrest.

"I already alerted the jail to release Reid," Eli says. "He's being processed as we speak. You'll be reunited soon."

A wave of disbelief washes over me. "Really? That fast?"

"Yes, I've told the sergeant in charge to let Reid know which hospital you'll be taken to."

My eyes swim with tears and I can't help the smile that blooms on my face. "Thank you."

He pushes himself away from the ambulance, standing up straight. "Now, don't take this to mean that you're completely off the hook for interfering in the investigation."

My smile falters. Because obstruction of justice is a very real, and very serious, crime. Even if I helped out the Boulder PD, they could still find a way to get me in trouble for talking to suspects behind their back.

Then he continues, holding out his hand, "How about we talk it over next time we go climbing?"

"Sounds perfect," I say, shaking his hand.

Chapter Twenty-Two

The anticipation of a glass of wine enhances the experience. The decanting, swirling, sniffing—they're all part of a ritual to prepare the senses for something special.

The anticipation of seeing Reid is all that gets me through the next hour of poking and prodding at the hospital, and even then, my senses aren't ready for when he finally appears in the doorway of my room.

We drink each other in with our eyes before he strides across the room, taking my hand in his. He intertwines his fingers through mine. It's more contact than we've had in days and I feel everything, the calluses on his fingertips, the warmth of his skin.

Reid tucks a loose strand of hair behind my ear, the back of his hand grazing my cheek, and then leans in, gently brushing his lips over mine.

Now, that was a fine kiss—tender and sweet—but not the kiss I nearly died for.

I grab his shirt and pull him in for a deeper kiss. His lips are somehow both soft and firm against mine, and our mouths move together in pure ecstasy. The connection between us is electric, full of desire, hope, and a need to make up for lost time. I run my fingers through his hair and he trails kisses down my neck, tickling me with his beard.

With him perched on the edge of my hospital bed, the starched sheets crinkle every time either of us so much as twitches. "I didn't want to tell you with some guard listening, or through Sage," he explains, quick to add, "as much as I appreciate everything she did for me."

"Sage is pretty great."

"Not as great as you." He's still wearing the same clothes he was arrested in, worn jeans and plain black T-shirt, and his beard is scragglier now. He hasn't stopped touching me, rubbing my arm, squeezing my shoulder, fiddling with my hair. "Of course, there's no time like the here and now, so I'll say it now: I love you."

In that moment, gazing at him, I have a flashback to Tristan—they really do look so similar—and worry courses through me that I'll never be able to separate the two brothers in my mind. But then Reid looks at me, his grapevine-green eyes full of so much warmth, love, and, yes, a hint of mischief, and the thought is immediately banished.

"I love you, too," I say, unable to keep myself from smiling through another kiss.

He rests his forehead against mine. "How can I ever thank you for never doubting me? Or apologize for my family?"

I prop myself up with an extra pillow, throwing him a wink. "I can think of a place to start."

"Truffles," he says, unable to keep the smirk off his face. "A lifetime supply. At your beck and call."

I crinkle my nose. "Besides, it's thanks to your mom that Eli was able to track me down."

"I can't believe Tristan had it in him." Reid stares at his knees, his eyes taking on a vacant, haunted look. "Or my dad."

I give his hand a squeeze, turning it over and running my fingertips over the now-healed cut, one of the reasons for Reid's immediate arrest. It's innocuous now, merely another scar among the many nicks and burns lining his arms. "You really just accidentally cut yourself?"

He furrows his eyebrows. "You didn't believe me?"

"You weren't exactly forthcoming that night," I say slowly, not wanting to put a damper on our reunion. "I want you to know you can tell me stuff, like about the food bank."

He nods and then nestles in, stretching his legs on the hospital bed beside me. "Are you ready to start now? Because I'll tell you whatever you want to hear." He drapes an arm over my shoulder, twirling a lock of my hair with his finger. "There may be more *Braveheart* references than you'd like, and probably way too much strategic football talk."

I nudge him playfully as there's a knock on the door. "Come in," I say, figuring it's the doctor coming to check on me again.

Instead, Camilla appears, taking a hesitant step into the room. She's in a cardigan and pearls, her hair pulled back into a chignon. Even now, with her family on the brink of disaster, appearances are so important to her.

Reid tenses, his arm flexing around me protectively.

"Hi?" I ask.

Camilla sniffs, taking in the beeping of a machine monitoring my heart rate. "It seems I owe you an apology." She takes another step inside. "A few, actually."

"That won't be necessary," I say, nuzzling closer to Reid. "I've got everything I need right here."

Camilla nods, fiddling with her purse. She turns to leave, but pauses, her hand resting on the doorframe, her wedding ring glinting in the fluorescent lighting. "At least one of my sons has found a way to be happy, even if it is because he's far away from me."

"It's not *because* of that, Mom," Reid says. "But the distance doesn't sound half-bad right now."

Camilla bristles, gripping her pearls, and I can see how this is going to end. With another year gone in a family feud. Not that Reid is wrong about his family. It's just that we're only given one. We have to make of it what we will.

"We're going to have a party," I say.

"We are?" Reid asks, shooting me a questioning glance.

"Yes," I answer, the plans just starting to take shape in my mind. "And it would be great if you, and Ben, would come. It might mean postponing your trip home, but I figure your plans may have changed anyway."

Camilla nods curtly and leaves without giving us an answer.

Five days—and one grape shipment—later, Reid and I prepare Vino Valentine for a grape-stomping party.

Interspersed between the oak-barrel tables and espresso

folding chairs are tubs full of Malbec grapes for those interested in literally dipping their toe in the winemaking
process. Four feet wide and made of wooden planks held
together by steel hoops, these tubs encourage mingling
and provide the perfect icebreaker.

Plus, I owe it to Felix.

He not only put in a ridiculous amount of overtime
last week, he also saved my harvest. When I frantically
called him from the hospital, he dropped what he was
doing and went to my winery to complete the much-
needed punch downs. He even cleaned up the mess
Tristan made while taking me hostage, assuming (correctly) it was a task I wouldn't be ready to face anytime
soon.

And now here we are, with candles softly glowing on
tabletops, accordion remakes of pop songs playing on
the speakers (courtesy of the Squeeze Keys), and ban-
quet tables lined with delectable dishes to pair with my
wines.

To mark the occasion, Reid unveils new seasonal
dishes he plans to serve at Spoons—wild-mushroom
gnocchi with an arugula pesto, crispy tandoori chicken
wings, and milk chocolate truffles with warming spices
of cinnamon and cloves doused in a luscious caramel.

As for me, I share my newest wines, those crafted last
year, before I knew if my business would succeed or fail.
I have no idea where I'll be when the batches currently
fermenting in back are ready, but I can't wait to find out.

I set up each of the wines beside their respective
dish—the Royal Arch Sauv Blanc with the gnocchi, the
Folsom Field Franc with the wings, and my newest blend,
affectionally named Jailbreak Red, with the truffles. The
Mesa Trail Merlot and What Happens in Viognier flank

a large platter of charcuterie. They're mighty fine on their own, if I do say so myself, and even better paired with Reid's dishes.

Everyone shows up.

The whole crew from Spoons—Britt, Katy, Tony, and even a very sheepish-looking Nick. My friends and rival winery owners, Moira and Carrick, recently back from a romantic and inspiring trip to Provence. Gladys, my favorite velvet-clad broad, who brought four friends with her. Brennan Fourie, Reid's former boss and current investor. My mom and dad, who, to my surprise, roll up the legs of their pants and enthusiastically hop into a tub of grapes. And Liam and Sage, who are on their first official date.

I approach the lovebirds, nestled across from each other at an oak-barrel table. My brother is in dapper slacks and a pressed, collared shirt. Sage is dressed in a pencil skirt, polka-dot blouse, and, true to form, a *Star Trek: Enterprise* pin adorning her strawberry-blond hair.

"I'm happy to see you two finally took the plunge," I say.

"Well, if you and Reid can make it through a murder accusation, jail stint, and meet-the-parents story from hell, I figured we could at least have a drink together."

"And some spectacular food," Sage says, taking an appreciative nibble of a truffle. "Seriously, pass my compliments on to the chef."

"Gladly," I say. "Can I get you anything else?"

Liam looks at Sage with one eyebrow raised before answering, "I think we're good."

"Wow, no jokes?" If my brother is refraining from ribbing me, this must be serious.

"About my sister, the badass detective?" Liam holds a hand over his heart. "I would never."

I snort. There it is.

But beneath his confident facade, I see the signs of nerves, his knees bouncing and the slight rosiness to his cheeks. And the same goes for Sage; the way she's smiling shyly and fiddling with her napkin. Yep, I'd say they're good. And completely smitten.

I make to back away, but Sage clinks her spoon against her wineglass. "Actually, I have some news . . ."

Liam and I watch her expectantly.

"I got the job I interviewed for," she says, letting out an excited *squee*. "You're looking at Boulder County's newest public defender."

"I knew you'd get it," I say, giving her a side-hug. "Congratulations, friend."

Liam raises his glass to hers. "Cheers."

Strong arms wrap around me and Reid nuzzles into my neck. "You'll be great at it," he says to Sage. "Let me know if you need any testimonials."

"I hardly did anything," she replies modestly. "In your case, you were lucky to have someone on the outside fighting for you."

"Too true," Reid says, giving me a lingering kiss on the cheek.

I rub his forearm, the tiny scars lining the muscle smooth beneath my fingers. *God, I missed him.* The only one who may have missed him more, if possible, was William. Their reunion was full of purring, headbutts, and lots and lots of treats. It was so adorable it made me go all gooey inside. That is, until Zin let it be known, vocally, how much she misses her kitty companion.

The bell over the door jingles and I turn to welcome our new guests. When I see who it is, I tug Reid along with me.

"Camilla, Ben, I'm so happy you decided to come," I say, meaning every word.

When I texted Camilla the party details, I wasn't sure she'd take me up on the invite. But I'm glad she did.

Reid stops a pace behind me. He nods curtly at each of them.

Camilla shifts awkwardly in her pumps, tugging at her pearls. Ben gazes around my winery as if he hasn't seen it before, which probably isn't far from the truth, given he was glued to his phone during his prior visit.

I babble nervously to fill the silence. "There's plenty of food—all Reid's doing—and wine, so please help yourselves."

Reid isn't the type to beat around the bush. "What's the news with Tristan and"—he swallows, jaw clenched—"Dad?"

"Both waiting for their next court appearance," Camilla says, her tone clipped. "But I came here to talk to you."

Ben clears his throat meaningfully.

"*We* came here to talk to you," Camilla corrects. "I'm sorry." The words sound like they cost her more than her Louis Vuitton purse. "For putting so much pressure on you, for not being accepting of what you want." Camilla pauses, taking in the tubs of grapes and partygoers up to their knees in jam.

I brace myself for her criticism, especially as Felix lets out a loud whoop from across the room, but find that I no longer care what Camilla thinks. Reid and I have each other, and if she doesn't approve, that's on her. Not me.

I needn't have worried, anyway.

She continues, letting her arms fall to her sides, "It turns out there's more to life than status."

"I'm sorry, too," Ben says. His cell phone chirps, no doubt with an important client on the other end, but he silences it. "If I'd been a decent brother, I would've seen Tristan for what he was."

I give Reid's hand a squeeze, hoping to communicate that I'm here for him, that I support him.

Reid rubs his stubbly chin, his eyes flitting between his mother and brother, his face unreadable.

Then his lips twitch into the barest hint of a smile, hesitant and unsure, but present nonetheless. "Maybe I'll see you guys at Thanksgiving."

With Tristan firmly behind bars and Gary being charged with obstruction of justice and assault, the Wallaces have a lot to work through. But it seems like maybe, just maybe, they're willing to try.

With everyone busy stomping grapes or gushing over the flavor of my wines and their accompanying dishes, I pour myself a glass of the Royal Arch Sauv Blanc and settle in at the tasting bar.

I tuck in to a plate of al dente gnocchi. The citrus of the wine cuts through the richness of the potato dumplings, the earthiness of the mushrooms, and the peppery pesto, making it the perfect bite.

My eyes flutter shut as I savor the flavors dancing on my tongue. I may let out a tiny moan.

"Jeez, get a room," Felix says, gripping a glass of the Jailbreak Red in his hand.

I dab my lips with a napkin. "I didn't picture you as someone to be thrown by a little PDA."

Felix rests his forearms on the back of the neighboring stool, his feet still bare from stomping grapes earlier. "You know, you don't have to worry about that raise you promised me."

"Now that Reid's out of jail and Spoons has reopened, I'll be able to," I say. "Plus, you've more than earned your keep this week."

"Thanks." He stares at his hands and when he speaks next, there's an unexpected roughness in his deep voice. "But that's not what I meant."

Suddenly, I understand what he's trying to tell me. "Adventure calls?"

"Argentina." He looks at me sadly, shrugging. "You know me, never stay in a place for long."

"Right. Well, I'll be happy to give you a recommendation, whatever you need." I hold out my hand.

"Ah, don't be like that, boss," he says with a wince, pulling me in for a hug. "For the record, if there was somewhere I wanted to stay, work at long-term, it'd be here."

I bark out a laugh of disbelief. "What, with all the murder and general chaos?"

"Even with all that." He takes a sip of his wine, gesturing at me with his glass. "It never got boring, and you're a good boss. A good friend."

"You'd better stop by when you're in town, and I expect a postcard from every place you visit." I force myself to smile, even as my throat constricts. "When's your last day?"

"End of the month," he says. "I'll work up until then."

"That gives you ample time for more grape stomping. And punch downs, can't forget those." I tap my biceps and wink.

"Wouldn't miss it." Felix waltzes off to chat with other guests.

Well, that puts a damper on the celebration. I take a large swallow of wine to ease the emotions welling inside of me.

"I couldn't help but overhear," my mom says, sidling to my side.

"It's a bummer." I retrieve my beaded necklace from where it's hiding behind the neckline of my little black dress. "Back where I started."

"You'll find someone else," my mom says. "In the meantime, I could always help you out."

I swivel in my stool until I'm facing her full on. She's holding her glass of wine—pure wine and not a spritzer, mind you—and her eyes, the same blue-gray as mine, don't waver.

"You're serious?"

"I am," she says with a smile. She waves her hands through the air, unable to keep still. "I've been enjoying learning about wine. And about you."

"But what about your job?"

My mom loves her work; there's no way she's going to quit unless she's forced out. And I would pay good money to see someone try.

"I could help you on weekends, just until you find someone else."

I think back to the last few days, her popping by unexpectedly, bringing me her favorite pH tester, and researching the chemistry behind fermentation. She even came to my aid when I needed help processing the un-expected grape delivery.

This could be a terrible idea, but it could also bring my mom and me closer, something I've desired my whole life, especially since my aunt died and left a hole in my heart.

"I'd like that." I wrap my arms around her, breathing in her lavender perfume. "Thanks, Mom."

The party is a huge success, continuing well past the time when the food and wine have all but disappeared. I sell case after case of wine, the proceeds of which are all going to Oscar's family. They refused my invitation, un-derstandably, but I still wanted to do something for them. For Lucia.

In addition to the sales from tonight, there are glass jars for monetary donations on each oak-barrel table, each one growing fuller as the hours tick by. I even catch Camilla sneakily add a check to one and wonder, fleet-ingly, what dollar amount she thought appropriate, given the crimes wrought by her son and husband. Hopefully enough to keep Lucia supplied with relief from her phys-ical pain, because, goodness knows, she'll never fully recover emotionally.

My feet are aching when everyone finally leaves. I flip my storefront sign from OPEN to CLOSED and go to find Reid.

He's carefully loading the commercial dishwasher with stemware.

I wrap my arms around him and he turns toward me, his green eyes flashing with mischief. "So, the Jailbreak Red? Very cute."

"Something to remind you of your time in the pokey."

He snorts, his fingers tracing tiny circles on my lower back. "You never told me how you came up with it."

I lean into his strong chest and play with the hair at the nape of his neck. "I made it in honor of us. Cab franc and pinot noir, which is you, by the way"—I wink at him—"and Malbec and cabernet sauvignon, which is me."

"Because of its spiciness and sheer beauty."

"Obviously," I say, fluttering my eyelashes. "And Viognier to bring them together."

He scoops me in his arms, and that cocky grin I love so much spreads across his face. "It's brilliant." He trails kisses along my cheek, sending a jolt of electricity through my body. "And delicious." Another kiss, another jolt. "Just like you." Finally, he takes my mouth with his, and it's without a doubt the best thing I've ever tasted.

Chapter Twenty-Three

Two weeks later, Reid, Liam, Sage, and I attend a CU Buffaloes home football game at Folsom Field.

One of the perks of Dad being a professor at CU are these seats, front row and right at midfield. There's a crisp edge to the air; fall had officially settled over Boulder and snow was in the forecast. We're in a sea of black and gold, proudly sporting our team's colors.

The esteemed buffalo mascot, Ralphie, runs the length of the field with her handlers, and we cheer in tandem. It feels good to let off some steam after the stress of the harvest, which has finally come to a close, not to mention the murder investigation.

Things have mostly returned to normal. Spoons reopened and is all the buzz again, especially since Reid's mistaken arrest made the news. He's somewhat of a local celebrity, which he's smartly leveraged to help promote his restaurant.

He hired a new sous chef to replace Oscar, as if Oscar could ever be replaced. But so far, despite having big shoes to fill, it sounds like she's working out.

And, after a firm talking-to, Reid decided to give Nick another chance. With the understanding that if he ever pulls another sabotaging stunt, he won't just be done at Spoons. He'll be done cooking anywhere. Because, as Reid reminded him, the restaurant world is small, especially in a town like Boulder.

Our joint business venture is going smoothly again, my new wines featured along with Reid's exquisite dishes. Almost as smooth as our romantic partnership.

Reid cuts a glance at me midcheer, a huge grin on his face. He still has his beard, which, I'm told, will remain through the entirety of football season. Or until the Buffs lose their next game, whichever comes first. His slate-green eyes flash in merriment and, with the sun hitting his face, I'm dazzled once again by his good looks.

"What?" he asks.

"Nothing," I say quickly. "Just happy to be here with you."

"Have I told you lately that I love you?"

"Not in the last five minutes," I respond, my insides melting like butter. "I love you, too."

I grab his hand. The fact that I can reach for him whenever I want is still a novelty. Maybe that's the secret to keeping a relationship fresh—sporadic arrests. Kidding!

Reid pulls me toward him, leans down, and kisses me, his fingers tangled in my hair and his beard rough against my cheek. We may be in front of a stadium of fans, but for all I'm aware, it's just the two of us in our own private bubble.

Oh, right. And my brother, who loudly clears his throat. "We're never doing another double date if you two don't cut that out."

Reid punches Liam lightly on the shoulder. "Dude, there's plenty else to look at."

Sage and I catch each other's eyes, unable to keep our laughter from spilling out.

"This was your idea," I remind Liam.

"Yeah, just don't make me regret it." He murmurs something else I can't hear, shoving his hands in his pockets.

Things have been going well between him and Sage. They're in the honeymoon phase, eating every meal they can together, watching all of Sage's favorite movies, which it turns out, are Liam's as well. I already know from Sage that they bought tickets to Comic-Con together. I couldn't be happier for my brother and best friend, and for this little community I've built for myself.

"Hey, what do you guys think about a ski trip this winter?" I ask. "Get out of town for a couple of days."

"After what you two have been through, that's a fabulous idea," Sage says.

She starts her new job as a public defender Monday morning. She'll miss her old job, even with its piles of work and the insane expectations of The Manual, but there's a nervous energy emanating from her. An excitement I haven't seen since she first started clerking.

"What, so I can watch you two make out on a ski lift?" Liam asks, blanching. But when Sage turns to him, a hopeful sheen on her face, all the fight leaves him. "I'm in."

Reid drapes one arm around me, and with his other hand, cheers for a touchdown our tight end just scored. I lean into him, breathing in his comforting scent—peppermint, citrus, and rosemary.

When pairing food and wine, there are limitless possibilities. As long as you follow certain rules to balance acidity, bitterness, and sweetness, you're likely to end up with something delicious. In life, however, things aren't so simple. Which means, when you find someone who truly complements you, who brings out new sides of yourself you didn't know existed, well, that just might be a pairing worth dying for.

Recipes and Wine Pairings

Pumpkin Ravioli in Sage and Butter Sauce

(Serves 4 to 6)

Pasta Ingredients

2 cups flour (plus extra for countertop)
3 eggs
1 tablespoon olive oil
½ cup water
Pinch of salt

Filling

1 tablespoon olive oil
2 medium shallots, chopped
3 garlic cloves, crushed
1 teaspoon fresh thyme, chopped
15 ounces canned pumpkin
½ teaspoon balsamic vinegar
Salt and pepper (to taste)

Sauce

½ cup (1 stick) unsalted butter
8 sage leaves, chopped
¼ cup grated Parmesan

For the pasta, mix flour, eggs, olive oil, water, and salt in food processor until combined and dough has a sticky texture. Knead the dough on floured surface for 2 to 3 minutes. Place in bowl, cover, and refrigerate for 30 minutes. Divide dough into 4 sections. For each, roll with rolling pin on floured surface, fold dough over, rotate, and roll out again. Repeat 7 to 8 times until dough becomes thin (approximately ⅛ inch) and pliable.

For the filling, sauté shallots in olive oil for 3 to 4 minutes, or until translucent. Add garlic and thyme and cook for 1 minute. Add pumpkin, vinegar, and salt and pepper to taste. Stir together and cook for an additional minute.

Dollop spoonfuls of filling onto pasta dough, roughly 1 inch apart. Carefully lay another sheet of pasta dough on top and press around edges of each dollop. Cut out ravioli with cookie cutter, or use rim of a cup, creating pillows of deliciousness. Repeat for the other 2 sheets of pasta dough.

Bring pot of salted water to a boil and place ravioli in, being careful not to overcrowd. The ravioli will float to the top when they're done, which should only take 1 to 2 minutes.

For the sauce, melt butter in pan and add sage leaves, bringing to a simmer. Cook for 2 minutes, or until fragrant.

To serve, place ravioli on plate with a healthy spoonful of sauce and sprinkle with Parmesan.

Suggested wine pairing: an oaky chardonnay that smells of vanilla and peaches and tastes like butter and citrus.

Salsa Verde Carne Asada

(Serves 4 to 6)

2 pounds flank steak
1 cup good red wine
4 garlic cloves (2 crushed, 2 whole)
5 tablespoons canola oil
Black pepper, crushed (to taste)
6 green chiles (such as Anaheim)
8 tomatillos, peeled and rinsed
⅛ cup lime juice
¼ cup fresh cilantro
Salt and pepper (to taste)
Tortilla, rice, and beans, for serving

For the marinade, place meat in long baking dish. Add red wine (preferably what will be paired with the meal), 2 crushed garlic cloves, 4 tablespoons of canola oil, and crushed black pepper and massage into meat. Let marinate for 1 to 2 hours.

Preheat oven to 425 degrees F. Coat green chiles in remaining 1 tablespoon canola oil and line on sheet pan. Roast in oven for 20 minutes, turning halfway. Place roasted chiles in bowl, cover with aluminum foil, and let sweat for 20 minutes. Then peel, destem, and deseed peppers.

Boil tomatillos in water for 10 minutes. Remove from heat and let cool.

In food processor, combine roasted chiles, tomatillos, lime juice, cilantro, remaining 2 garlic cloves, and ½ teaspoon of salt. Pulse until it's a smooth texture.

Preheat grill to medium heat.

Grill flank steak 3 minutes per side (it's a thin cut of meat so really doesn't take long!). Let rest for 10 minutes. Slice into strips against the grain and drizzle with salsa verde.

Serve with tortilla, rice, and beans.

Suggested wine pairing: a spicy Malbec with flavors of pepper and dried cherries on the tongue, and smoky aromas.

Cinnamon Apple Tart

(Serves 6 to 8)

2 cups all-purpose flour
½ cup granulated sugar
½ teaspoon salt
2 sticks (1 cup) unsalted butter, diced
½ cup ice-cold water
1 teaspoon cinnamon
3 Granny Smith apples, peeled and thinly sliced
French vanilla ice cream, for serving

In a food processor, combine flour, 1 tablespoon of sugar, and salt. Pulse a few times to mix. Next, add 12 tablespoons (1½ sticks) of butter. Pulse again a few times until butter is roughly pea-sized and then, with processor running, add water just until the dough comes together. Knead dough into a ball, wrap in plastic, and refrigerate for 1 hour.

Preheat oven to 375 degrees F.

On floured surface, roll pastry dough into a rectangular shape until it's roughly ¼ inch thick, trimming the sides if needed. Move dough to prepared baking sheet.

In small bowl, combine remaining sugar and cinnamon. Line pastry dough with rows of overlapping slices of apples. Sprinkle sugar-and-cinnamon mixture on top and add remaining cubes of butter uniformly.

Bake for 45 minutes, rotating pan halfway through, until pastry and apples are a beautiful golden brown.

Let cool and serve with a scoop of French vanilla ice cream.

Suggested wine pairing: an effervescent moscato d'Asti with floral aromas and sweet flavors of orange and honey.

Acknowledgments

This book wouldn't have been possible without the help of so many people.

Thank you to my editor, Miranda Hill, for all the insightful feedback and encouragement, and for astutely positing: Can we ever have enough cats? No, we cannot, and the scenes with Zin and William were some of my favorite to write.

A huge thanks to the rest of my team at Berkley: Elisha Katz, Jessica Mangicaro, Stephanie Felty, Liz Gluck, and Randie Lipkin. You've all been an absolute dream to work with.

I'm so appreciative of my agent, Pamela Harty, whose wisdom and support have been invaluable.

This story involved a great deal of research. I owe a debt of gratitude to Bookcliff Vineyards for giving me a peek behind the proverbial curtain during fall harvest, and to the kind deputy who gave me a tour of the Boulder County Jail.

Thank you to my beta reader and friend, Abby Reed, for reading an early draft and generously offering her thoughts.

I wouldn't be where I am without the pillars of support that are my parents. Thank you for being my constant cheerleaders and always encouraging me to pursue my passions.

To my husband, John, words can't convey my love for you. Thank you for everything you've done—and continue to do—to help make my dream a reality. Without a doubt, you are my pairing to die for.

My sweet and silly daughter, Sophie, thanks for making me smile, even in the midst of chaos, and for always reminding me that no matter where I am in the process, you're somehow one chapter ahead.

Lastly, thank you, dear readers, for taking the time to read my story. It really means the world to me.

Ready to find
your next great read?

Let us help.

Visit prh.com/nextread

Penguin
Random
House